Murder
in
Second
Position

Murder in Second Position

An On Pointe Mystery

Lori Robbins

LeVel
BEST BOOKS

Author Photo Credit: Alice Kivlon

First edition

ISBN: 978-1-68512-021-4

Cover art by Level Best Designs

This book was professionally typeset on Reedsy.
Find out more at reedsy.com

To Glenn

Praise for the On Pointe Mystery Series

"Hold on to your tutus. Once again, Lori Robbins delivers front row seats to a mystery complete with backstage intrigues, a Russian ballet mistress and the incomparable setting of bustling Manhattan. Prima Ballerina Leah Siderova executes the performance of a lifetime as she races to uncover the killer stalking her company. *Murder in Second Position* transports the reader to the glamorous world of dance with delightful diversions of humor, romance and deception." — Tina deBellegarde, Agatha-nominated author of *Winter Witness*, a Batavia-on-Hudson Mystery

"Drawing on her vast knowledge of the world of ballet, Lori Robbins weaves together an unputdownable mystery of outsized egos, family secrets, and deadly competition. This twisty suspense will keep you turning pages from the first pirouette to the final curtain call." — D.A. Bartley, author of the Abish Taylor Mysteries

"Lori Robbins's inside knowledge of ballet and agility at plotting perfect crimes are an ideal marriage for those of us who love our mysteries set in the world of arts. Like ballet itself, *Murder in Second Position* is beautiful, rugged, and elegantly paced." — Elizabeth Mannion, Edgar-nominated editor of *Guilt Rules All: Irish Mystery, Detective, and Crime Fiction*

"Lori Robbins jetés right onto center stage in her latest suspenseful murder mystery. With ballerina Leah Siderova once again in a spotlight of accusation and innuendo, she has to pirouette as fast as she can to solve the case and keep from becoming the next victim." — Cathi Stoler, author of *Straight Up* (A Murder On The Rocks Mystery).

i

"*Murder in Second Position* is a fast-paced romp through the high-stakes world of professional ballet, where almost every colleague is a frenemy ready to step over a body or two if it means a shot at becoming a principal dancer. This second book in the On Pointe mystery series features the welcome return of principal dancer Leah Siderova. As New York City prepares for a massive snowstorm, Leah becomes the primary suspect in the murder of ballet company director Pavel Baron. To find the real killer, Leah weaves her way through satisfying plot twists, confrontations with engaging characters (including her dysfunctional, loving family) and romantic complications involving NYPD Detective Jonah Sobol. The star of this show, though, is the dry, sly New York humor that permeates this mystery and makes it such a delight to read. If former ballerina and author Lori Robbins danced with as much heart and wit as her new book contains, she must have been a sight to behold." — Mally Becker, author of *The Turncoat's Widow*

"A compelling and superb murder mystery, this story captures the reader's attention at chapter 1. Robbins has a grand writing style, and a high knowledge of dance, particularly ballet. Masterfully written, *Murder in Second Position* is a showstopper. I look forward to reading many more stories by this author." — Amy Shannon of Amy's Bookshelf Reviews [5 star review]

Chapter One

And hand in hand, at the edge of the sand / They danced by the light of the moon.
—Edward Lear

I belong onstage. Not in an interrogation room at Manhattan's Twentieth Precinct. And yet, for the second time in less than a year, that's where I had a starring role. As part of my official statement, I'd like to go on the record to confirm this simple fact: When dancers say, "ballet can be murder," they're speaking metaphorically. Most of the time. More to the point, if I were going to kill someone, it would have been Savannah Collier.

Earlier, on that snowy day in February, I was at a routine rehearsal for *Swan Lake*. As I stretched my legs and ignored the growling noises from my stomach, I observed my fellow dancers jockey for position. They were trying to make a good impression on Pavel Baron, the new director of the company. He stalked several women, telegraphing his predatory sexual interest with a series of unappetizing grunts.

After a large group of dancers exited and gave way to a lovely waltz for two swans, Olivia Blackwell plopped down next to me. As we watched the dancers jump and pirouette, I readied myself for the last scene, the Swan Queen's dramatic suicidal plunge. It suited my dark mood.

I took a few deep breaths, wishing my practice tutu wasn't quite so tight. Tragic swan queens had no business gaining weight, and I was self-conscious about recent dietary indiscretions regarding salted caramel chocolates. The music deepened, foreshadowing the coming tragedy.

I said, half to Olivia and half to myself, "Have you ever thought about how many ballets deal with death?"

Olivia, still breathing heavily from her recent exertions, mopped her face and neck. "I hadn't thought about it, but yeah. Murder, suicide, and the ever-popular death via a broken heart. Those are the best dramatic roles."

I nodded. "If you're lucky, some emotional audience member will heave a loud sigh or groan. That's always gratifying. There's nothing like a corpse in a tiara to bring them to their feet."

She turned down the corners of her mouth. "That's true for you, Leah. But at this point in my career, the only way I'm going to get to die onstage is if it's a mass slaughter of errant swans, or peasant girls, or village maidens."

I gave her a consoling pat on the back. "I know it's hard. But be patient. Very soon, you'll be the one getting those curtain calls. You're a terrific dancer, and your time will come."

I waited for a response, but she just sat there and watched the swans. I tried again to cheer her up. "You're understudying lots of big roles now, which is a good sign."

Her glum expression remained unchanged. Time for drastic action.

I grabbed her shoulders. "Maybe you'll have a *42nd Street* moment. You know, like, 'you're going out a youngster, but you've gotta come back a star!'"

She finally smiled, then left me to join the rest of the corps de ballet. They took their places for the last scene, and as the music rose to a dramatic crescendo I fluttered in, exactly on cue, and pretended to die. My partner yawned twice before Pavel's sharp look jolted him back into his role as a heartbroken prince. Five minutes later we were done. Pavel pointedly tapped his watch. It was a rather raggedy run-through, and the rehearsal mistress probably had a pile of corrections, but no one except Pavel dared flout the strict rehearsal schedule.

I pulled off my pointe shoes to give my feet a brief moment of freedom and eyed the youngest dancers. "Tell me about the new kids on the block. Are the girls still catty and ruthless? Or has the corps de ballet become a kinder and gentler place?"

Olivia frowned. "I don't know about kinder or gentler, because I don't have much to compare it to. Some dancers are straight up awful. But nearly everyone pretends to be nice, although I'm sure most of my so-called friends would stick a knife in my back if they thought it would help them."

I suppressed a shiver when she mentioned a knife in the back. The memory of last season's murder still gave me nightmares. "I guess some things never change."

Olivia took out a protein bar. I longed to do the same, but I was saving my calories for the evening. Over the heavenly smell of peanut butter she said, "We're kinder in our language, if not always in our private sentiments." She laughed. "I'm not putting myself on a pedestal, by the way. I'm like all the rest. I wouldn't hesitate to do the same to them."

As we walked down the hallway to the next rehearsal we spoke softly, despite the hum of many voices. Gossip was the breath of life in our hothouse world, and scheming rivals with friendly faces were all around. After Gabi Acevedo retired I found myself without a trusted confidante, until Olivia came along to fill that void.

Bobbie York, our costume mistress, was not nearly as circumspect. As we ambled toward Studio D, she militantly pushed past us. Her angry threats included several graphic images that paired Pavel's face and an ice pick.

I let her pass without comment. To put it diplomatically, she and I were no longer friendly. A few months ago, she accused me of seducing her husband and committing murder, which can put some serious strain on a relationship. The fact that I was exonerated on both counts did nothing to quench her anger. Paradoxically, it infuriated her even more. The safest way to handle her volcanic temper was to ignore her, although that too had its perils.

Olivia, who was young in the ways of our world, walked more quickly to keep up with her. "What has Pavel done now?"

Bobbie stopped short to face us, and, with some effort, unclenched her teeth. "That miserable excuse for a ballet master has installed a corporate stuffed shirt in my costume department. As if any of those frat boys from Artistic Solutions knows a single wretched thing about costumes or props." Bobbie put air quotes around the word "Artistic" to indicate her disdain for the pretentions, and the name, of our new commercial and multinational overlord.

Olivia put her hand on Bobbie's arm. "Pavel said there was going to be a period of adjustment. I'm sure it will all work out. He's only been here a few months. Give him some time."

Bobbie removed Olivia's delicate hand with a thumb and forefinger, looking at it with the same antipathy one might feel upon finding an invasive, gelatinous, alien life form taking root.

"Wise up, Sunshine. You and all your clueless ballerina friends are not what I would call rocket science material. Go back to your pink and sparkly dream world. I'm too old to kid myself. These people are ruthless."

This was too much for me. "Get real, Bobbie. No one is more coldblooded than you, unless it's Pavel. He's hired and fired a dozen people in the last few months. Sit tight, be patient, and suck it up like the rest of us. And speaking of Pavel, how do you know he's the one who hired your stuffed shirt? Maybe it was Darius Kemble. He didn't get to be the head of Artistic Solutions by giving out lollipops and rosebuds."

She could barely contain her scorn. "I don't care if Moses himself handed me commandments about ordering fabric. Kemble may know how to run a business, but we are not a business."

She brushed a few specks of lint from her sleeve, as if flicking me away with it. "It will be a cold day in hell before I take advice from you, Leah. You haven't learned a thing in the last ten years. Or has it been fifteen or twenty? Hard to keep track after so long."

Bobbie emphasized my age to be mean, but she spoke the simple, if painful, truth. I am a thirty-something ballerina, with a surgically reconstructed knee and a limited professional future. After she marched down the hallway, I turned back to Olivia. "I see Bobbie has lost none of her charm and *joie de vivre*. But as much as I hate to admit it, maybe she's got the right idea. We're all trying to make nice with the new management company, and they're walking all over us. We probably should push back. Maybe if we did, Darius Kemble and his loathsome Artistic Solutions gang would already be a distant memory. Like those self-help gurus who gave us exercises to help us love ourselves." I couldn't help laughing, remembering how one of them, in an

4

attempt to ingratiate himself with Pavel, told our ballet director he was exceptionally gifted at loving himself. He didn't last long.

Olivia didn't answer me. She wordlessly pointed to the daily rehearsal schedule, which was posted on a bulletin board. Those printouts, with their handwritten notes, were the sole holdovers of life in American Ballet Company before Artistic Solutions digitized us. In the square marked Dworkin/New Ballet, Olivia's name was crossed off the cast list. She had been demoted to understudy, her name in parentheses.

I was still on the schedule as one of the lead dancers, but I too had been downgraded. Our guest artist from London was still in the first cast. She would dance on opening night, at the gala, and on weekends. I expected no less. But I was now third in line to dance in the new ballet, behind a lower-ranked dancer. This was a very deliberate humiliation. I'd be lucky to get a few matinees and, perhaps, a single weeknight performance.

Like the other principal dancers in the company, I was used to being shoved aside for a glitzier, more high-profile international star. What really stung, though, was seeing a dancer from the corps de ballet placed ahead of me. Kerry Blair was talented; that was undeniable. I preferred to remain silent regarding her conniving, spiteful, mean, and selfish nature.

My demotion was humiliating, as well as disappointing. Pavel might as well have installed a flashing sign proclaiming his intention to push me out of the company. From a public relations perspective, which was the only one that mattered, it was easier to downgrade and embarrass a dancer until she voluntarily left than it was to fire her outright. My modest but devoted fan club would spring to my defense if Pavel refused to renew my contract.

Olivia was bitter. "What was it that Bobbie said about Pavel? I'm beginning to understand how she feels. If I had the chance, I too would beat him about the face and neck."

I checked the rest of the schedule before answering. "Don't forget about stabbing him where his heart should be. That was my favorite part." Forgetting discretion, I added, "Pavel Baron has to go. One way or another. The man is pure poison."

5

Chapter Two

When you dance, you can enjoy the luxury of being you.
—Paul Coelho

The second shock of that fateful day in February occurred at our last rehearsal, which was for a new ballet choreographed by the dance world's latest overrated whiz kid, Austin Dworkin. I was a trifle unnerved to see two representatives from Artistic Solutions in attendance. Our new corporate managers had infiltrated the costume department, the office staff, and our public relations division. Despite the company's name, their reach wasn't supposed to extend to artistic or creative decisions, but the presence of two guys with AS nametags indicated otherwise.

I nudged Olivia. "Check out the AS initials on the nametags. I'm going to tell them they left off an 'S' at the end."

She didn't laugh. Looking enviously at a group of chattering ballerinas, she said, "I've always been one of the smallest dancers in the company, but this is ridiculous."

She had a point. Even before the new administration, American Ballet Company had begun to favor very tall, long-legged dancers, an aesthetic preference Pavel had wholeheartedly embraced. Olivia looked like a doll next to Kerry and the others. I'm as small as Olivia, but as a principal dancer it was less critical I fit in with a group. I wondered what my future would be like after ABC retired their shorter male dancers. I couldn't perform a pas de deux with any of the new men without inviting comparisons to King Kong and a dark-haired Fay Wray. Or the Jolly Green Giant and a single frozen pea.

We were interrupted by the arrival of yet another visitor, also wearing the Artistic Solutions badge. As she crossed the room I sank to the floor and hid my face. "Don't look now, but I think Pavel's unpredictability has reached a new high. Or low."

Before I could explain further, Pavel himself marched into the room and clapped three times. The last two claps were unnecessary. When the artistic director of a ballet company wants your attention, he gets it.

He announced, with his clipped Slavic accent, "I make known to you now Ann Rothman. She is specialist in health and wellness and a member of the Artistic Solutions team. We will make appointment for you to see her if you do not make appointment yourself. Everyone in company will get assessment from Ann." After that terse introduction, he spun around with the precision of a KGB agent and exited the room.

The intruder looked around and said, in measured tones, "Well. I certainly am extremely excited to be here. I guess I'll be meeting all of you soon."

Olivia, in response to my horrified expression, mouthed, "What's the problem?"

I whispered back, "Ann Rothman's married name is Feldbaum. As in, my father's second wife. And my stepmother."

She looked puzzled. "And you didn't know she was going to be working here? That's kind of weird, even for your family."

"Of course, I didn't know," I hissed. "I would have been less surprised to see the ghost of Anna Pavlova waft in."

Understandably, she was still confused. "You should be happy. Won't your stepmother automatically give you a good review?"

A full discussion of my relationship with Ann would take days. Possibly years. I limited myself to a simple *no*.

My fellow dancers, more concerned with their aching muscles, or how beautiful they were, or whom they secretly desired, barely flicked an eyelash in Ann's direction. She looked about uncertainly until she spotted me.

She walked over and reached out to hug me, something she rarely does. I stood up, and we bumped noses as we aimed for the same side of an air kiss.

I drew back first. "This is quite the surprise. Why on earth didn't you say anything to me? And how did you come to meet Pavel?"

Ann avoided my gaze. "I, uh, it was all rather sudden. As for Pavel, I met him at the gala. You, um, I think you were the one who introduced us. We, well, to tell you the truth, we started chatting, and then, after I was hired by Artistic Solutions…"

As I waited for Ann to explain herself, our nervous novice choreographer decided he was tired of being upstaged. Austin paraded to the front of the room and loudly announced that the rehearsal was starting. The young dancers sprang to attention, and those with more experience politely left off talking. Austin did not command the same deferential response Pavel inspired, but the unwritten rules of ballet afforded him the appearance of respect.

Ann didn't immediately get the message. I helpfully tilted my head to point her to the door. She nodded and turned but did not exit the room. Instead, she joined her two corporate buddies, who were seated at a table in a corner of the studio. I was not pleased to see her further invade my professional life, but there was nothing, as yet, I could do to stop her.

The rehearsal could have gone worse than it did, but not by much. The trio of AS representatives lost interest after about ten minutes. Ignoring the dancers, they chatted, yawned, and stared at their phones. I couldn't blame them. The ballet was deadly dull.

More interesting was Austin's unexpected gift for meanness, which his talent for choreography did not come close to matching. He was still a member of the corps de ballet, and, in an apparent effort to showcase his new power, was bitingly critical.

Perhaps I lacked the appropriate post-modern artistic sensibility, but I found little charm in the flatfooted choreography, which depended upon the relative distance of our right and left thumbs to carry the emotional weight of the work. Austin appeared unaware that this tiny detail would not register with anyone sitting farther back than the first row of seats.

He made us repeat the most physically taxing section of the ballet over and over, until all the principal dancers, by silent and mutual consent, walked off and told him we were taking a break. Austin, as if it were his idea, told the rest of the group, "Take five."

He approached us with a conciliatory look on his face, but my partner forestalled the young choreographer before he could get a single word out.

Daniel closed the distance between him and Austin until they were nearly chest to chest. "I'm a peaceful man, but one more word out of you and I'm going to rearrange the nose on your face. I don't know who you think you are, but if you don't get an attitude adjustment you will find yourself holding up the scenery in the back of the stage and choreographing for the kindergarten division. If you're lucky."

Austin adjusted his glasses and nervously pushed back his long blonde hair. His face and neck turned brick red. "You—you can't talk to me like that. I'll tell Pavel, and he'll tell Mr. Kemble, and you'll be the one sitting in the back of the corps de ballet."

Daniel smiled. "But at a principal dancer's salary. I doubt Kemble's analysts from Artistic Solutions would think that was a prudent use of funds."

Oh, how I envied him his freedom to speak his mind! Daniel had little to lose by alienating Austin, since this was my partner's last season with the company. He had landed the perfect post-retirement job, as artistic director of a dance division at one of the city colleges. I dreaded his departure, for he was far more than the prince to my Swan Queen. He was a good friend and steadfast ally.

Austin turned a deeper shade of purple. For his sake, I hoped he didn't play poker. I'd never seen anyone with a more transparent face. He spluttered, "Who even cares about you? Everyone knows you're leaving after this season." He stared meanly at me. "And Daniel might not be the only one."

Unlike Austin, I was an excellent poker player and a skilled actress. With perfect equanimity, I pointed to the table in the corner. "See that woman from Artistic Solutions? Maybe you missed the memo, but she happens to be my stepmother. And we're very close. In fact, I'm meeting her and my father for dinner this weekend. You've given us plenty to talk about."

The blood that had rushed to Austin's face and neck drained away. "I'm just trying to do my job. Of course, I didn't mean to disrespect you."

I adopted a two-aces-in-the-hole expression. "Of *course*, you didn't. Now, why don't you go back to teaching us the steps of this delightful ballet for twenty dancers and forty thumbs?"

Thirty minutes later the rehearsal ended, to the audible relief of every person in the room. I looked for Olivia, who had suffered in silence, but she left without a backward glance.

Ann also left without saying goodbye. Despite my claims to Austin of intimacy with my stepmother, we'd always had a rather cool relationship. This did not excuse her behavior. We didn't have to be best buddies for her to have told me she was joining the staff at Artistic Solutions. Her secrecy baffled me.

As I passed the bulletin board, a fire-engine red notice caught my eye. The flyer bore the Artistic Solution logo and provided information about how to sign up for one of Ann's evaluations. It was phrased as a polite request. This fooled no one. We all knew it was an ultimatum.

I was afraid. But as two NYPD detectives pointed out later, I wasn't the one who was killed.

Chapter Three

Why walk when you can dance?
—Ellen van Dam

T he threat of an imminent snowstorm motivated the number crunchers at Artistic Solutions to send us home early. Presumably, the risks involved in making us travel during a blizzard outweighed the cost benefit of more practice hours. The building emptied out in record time, but I didn't rush. My whole body ached, and I needed to cool down to avoid having my muscles seize up in protest at the bitterly cold weather that held New York City in an icy grip.

I started with my thighs, which were shaky from repeated stress. Sliding back and forth on a wooden rolling stick, I breathed through the pain. Figuring I couldn't get much more uncomfortable I called Ann, but my stepmother didn't answer. I left her a neutral-sounding message and a text. Next, I called my father. His silence regarding Ann's employment was as surprising as hers. As usual, his phone went directly to voicemail. Jeremy Feldbaum had not quite made his peace with modern electronics, although he'd written several papers about the ethical ramifications of technology. Dad, a professor of philosophy, spent his days teaching in a rather rarefied academic cloud. My mother, on the other hand—stylish, hilariously snarky, and an expert analyst of tacky behavior—was never out of touch. Maybe she would have some insight into the situation.

She answered the phone before the end of the first ring and greeted me as she always did, with delighted surprise, as if we didn't talk nearly every day.

"Leah! How lovely to hear from you!"

I apprised her of the day's events. The whip-quick, hyper-verbal Barbara Siderova needed a full minute to digest the news.

"Where are you?" I raised my voice to compete with the background noise. "You sound like you're inside a washing machine."

Barbara said, over the clacking and whirring, "In the salon. Having things done to make me gorgeous. Give me a minute. I'll go outside, where I can have my conniption in peace."

My mother was already gorgeous. Even without the laser therapy, Botox, and hair treatments that left every strand on her head lovingly cared for, she was a beautiful woman. "Going outside" was her euphemism for having a cigarette, which she claimed helped her stay skinny. I'd tried and tried, but couldn't get her to break the habit.

The tapping of high heels and the roar of traffic replaced the high-tech hum of the salon. When Barbara finally responded, she bypassed the essential issue and demanded, "Why didn't Pavel ask me to consult with the company? What does Ann have that I don't?"

I sighed. Sometimes you had to remind my mother of the obvious. "You write crime fiction, and we had no immediate openings for an expert in killing people. Ann, on the other hand, is a health and wellness coach. I guess Pavel wants the dancers to be healthy and well. Not invent new ways to commit murder, which is your area of expertise."

I heard the click of Barbara's lighter. "I'm willing to bet I have more to offer the ballet company than—that"—she finished with a dramatic flourish—"that woman."

I stretched my calf muscles while we spoke. "Let's discuss the theoretical implications of Ann's employment at some future date. In the meantime, I thought you might be able to give me some advice about how to proceed. The situation is more than a little awkward. I practically fainted when she walked into the ballet studio."

Barbara glossed over the social implications and skipped to the scheming stage of the discussion. "It's possible you could leverage your relationship with her to your benefit. But there's no guarantee of that, given the sort of person she is. Not that I have anything against the totally unsuitable woman your father chose to marry after our divorce."

I tried to interrupt, but Barbara wasn't done.

"I will say nothing negative about your father's wife. One might as well complain about a glass of tap water. But you're right, my darling. Her sneakiness makes no sense. It's positively weird. Even for your father, who lives in an ivory tower inside an ivory tower, it's weird."

I put the phone on speaker while I got dressed. "If you think that's bad, then brace yourself. Ann is going to be evaluating all the dancers. This puts both of us in an untenable position, no matter what she does. When I asked her how she happened to get the job, she muttered something about meeting Pavel at last year's gala. But technically, she's employed by Artistic Solutions."

Barbara's tone sharpened. "If she made a pitch to him at *your* gala, to which she was an invited guest, then that was unforgivably tasteless." She paused. "Obviously, I don't know Pavel at all, except through what you've told me, but he didn't strike me as the kind of person likely to become best friends with Ann." Before I could respond, she abruptly changed the topic. "Is Pavel still treating you well? Or has he reverted to his usual hideous self?"

I started with the good news. There wasn't much of it. "He's given me back a few of the roles I want, like the Swan Queen. But I'm mostly in the second cast. Or the third." It hurt me to say it, but I forced myself to be brave. "You probably know this already, but it's the kind of treatment dancers get when the administration wants to force them out."

Barbara was so upset she clicked her lighter for another cigarette. "Is there no way to expel Pavel, short of killing him?"

I exited the dressing room and shivered at the change in temperature. The building was usually well heated, to protect our muscles, but the hallway was frigid. I was sure I could feel the chill of winter air blowing through, although I didn't see any open windows.

I trembled, though not from the cold. "Can we not talk about murder? I don't think I'm completely recovered from"—I sought the right euphemism—"from what happened last year."

13

Barbara, while not unsympathetic, was her usual pragmatic self. "I said poison, not stabbing. Less messy."

I checked the clock that loomed over the door. "It's getting late. The weather people are predicting a blizzard. I'm going home, and you should do the same."

She cut me off before I could end the call. "I'm supposed to meet my agent for drinks. But if you're free, I'll put her off and pick you up. You're so busy these days. I never get to see you. You'd never know you live a few blocks from me."

I couldn't help smiling. "Nice attempt at making me feel guilty, but you're as busy as I am. Which reminds me, you'll have to tell me about your latest boyfriend and your field trip to the wilds of Brooklyn."

Barbara, who for the last two weeks had regaled me with stories of the handsome and charming new man she'd been dating, was uncharacteristically subdued. "I'm not sure he's my type."

That was an understatement to end all understatements. I'd met Philip Simone only briefly, but, even for my mother, her latest lover was an odd choice. He was so different from my professorial father, but perhaps that was his appeal. She met him through one of the Personals ads on the back pages of *The New York Review of Books*, which, for the uninitiated, is like Tinder for hyper-intellectuals aged sixty and over.

Barbara didn't wait for me to answer, which was good, because the silence would have stretched to epic proportions. Sounding cheerier, she said, "The weather really is filthy. We should both go home, and I'll call you later. We can talk trash about Ann and Philip. There's something fishy about both of them."

I was bundled up and ready to leave when I reversed course and headed to Pavel's office. If his predatory eye had fixed upon a less-talented, more sexually compliant dancer to replace me, I'd fight back with whatever ammunition I possessed, short of bonking him myself. Pavel had only a one-year contract. I'd survived worse threats.

In his first speech to the company, Pavel bragged about his "open door policy," but he was as inaccessible as the most paranoid of despots. We had to email our requests for a conference to Savannah Collier, his personal assistant, but it was patently ridiculous to electronically contact her while I was sitting outside the glass-walled office. Filling out a Google form and emailing her would have been the grownup equivalent of two kids sitting on the same sofa and texting each other.

Savannah didn't immediately see me walk in, and when she did, she started violently. With a savage look, she said, "What do you want? If you don't have an appointment, you can turn right around and get the hell out of here."

Her melodramatic response was almost comical. "I work here, Savannah. Where'd all your Southern hospitality go?"

She looked up at me. Her eyes were red, and her expression of abject misery made me feel sorry for her in spite of myself. Yes, she was a phony, a fake, and an arrogant pain in the neck, but seeing her so unhappy made me more sympathetic than I ever thought possible.

I put both hands on her desk and leaned forward. "I'm sorry you're not, uh, not feeling well. Do you want to talk about it?"

She stiffened. "I most certainly do not."

"Fine. Feel free to be lonely, as well as miserable. I'm here to talk to Pavel, not you, so it's all good. Is he in?"

Savannah pressed her lips together in disapproval, but I could tell she enjoyed turning me down. It probably cheered her up more than any heart-to-heart conversation would have. "You know the rules. You have to contact me via email. I'll get back to you with an appointment."

I studied her face, which was very pretty, and her body, which was considerably heavier than when she danced with the company. "You used to be one of us, before you joined Artistic Solutions. We didn't know each other that well, but back then you weren't such a complete..." I stopped to reconsider my choice of words. The ones that came to mind were unlikely to convince her to let me see Pavel. "What I'm trying to say is that you were a lot nicer when you were a dancer."

Savannah sniffed. "You didn't know I existed. Not that I cared. I was never going to get out of the corps de ballet, so why waste my time making lousy money until they let me go?" Her expression hardened. "People like you have no idea what that feels like."

I knew very well what rejection felt like but had no desire to discuss the perils of a life in dance. Heartbreak goes with the territory. I stared out the window, trying to come up with a diplomatic response. Billowing drifts of snow confirmed the opinion of the most pessimistic of our local weather forecasters. The promised blizzard had arrived, and if I had a brain in my head, I would have left thirty minutes earlier.

I took a deep breath. "Let's start again. Is Pavel here? I need five minutes with him."

With smug satisfaction, Savannah admitted Pavel had left for the day.

I zipped my jacket and slung my dance bag over my shoulder. "In other words, we could have skipped that entire conversation, and I could have simply gone home?"

She ignored me, and with an officious air shuffled the papers on her desk. I wasn't worried about myself, because my commute home, on a worst-case basis, would consist of a fifteen-block walk. But if Savannah lived outside the borough of Manhattan, she was likely in for a hellacious trip.

I advised her to leave, but she didn't take the suggestion in the spirit in which it was offered. Without looking up, she told me to mind my own business and quit bothering her.

I couldn't go without attempting to pry at least one bit of information from her. Ann's story of how she came to meet Pavel and begin working at Artistic Solutions didn't ring true to me. Savannah was a notorious gossip and eavesdropper. If anyone besides Pavel knew what was going on, it was she.

Trying to sound as if I didn't care much about the answer, I asked, "Was it your idea to hire Ann Feldbaum—er, Rothman? Because I think it was a brilliant move to bring in a health and wellness coach."

The non sequitur put her off-balance, and for the first time since I entered the office, she answered a direct question with a direct answer. "Wrong again, Leah. That was Pavel. And he is brilliant, which we all know. But even he got hoodwinked by that nasty old woman. They talk all the time. I don't know what-all he sees in her."

I was dumbfounded. How could my stepmother have formed such a close relationship with my boss without mentioning it to me?

A gust of wind rattled the panes of the window. On the street below few people, and fewer cars, were on the road. Broadway was nearly blotted out by drifts of heavy snow. I tried one last time to talk some sense into her. "Please listen to me. You must go home. We may not be best friends, but that doesn't mean I want to leave you here by yourself."

She pressed her lips together and looked at me as if I were the one who'd broken her heart. "I told you to leave me alone. What do I have to do to get respect from you people?"

I gave up. If Savannah wanted to wallow in misery in the middle of an epic snowstorm, who was I to stop her?

A grimy placard taped to the elevator door announced it was out of service. It was a biennial miracle that our antiquated piece of machinery ever passed city inspections. Half the time it was broken, and the rest of the time it was slow and unreliable. Adjacent to the elevator, the door to a display case hung halfway open, blocking the exit. I slammed it shut before heading to the stairway. Savannah, despite her protestations, reconsidered her plan to remain in the deserted building and followed me into the stairwell. The air grew icier with every step we took.

Despite her avowed interest in seeing me in hell, she trailed me so closely she nearly tripped on my heels as we walked downstairs. I stepped aside. "You go first. Since my knee operation, walking downstairs is more painful than walking up."

Savannah huffed but did not accept my offer and continued to tail me. She probably thought her emotional pain was more important than my physical pain, but she could have pretended she cared. I thought Southern women were supposed to be sympathetic and kind. Or was it the other way around, and people were supposed to be sympathetic and kind to them?

The bottom flight of stairs was shrouded in near darkness. As we made our halting way down, she finally spoke, in a high, artificial voice. "I do believe that dratted light is out again."

The wooden banister was tacky and wet, but it was too dark to see what turned my fingers so sticky. I figured one of the kids who attended our pre-professional program had spilled a protein drink. They were all the rage with the fifteen-and-under set.

I flicked the flashlight on my phone, and we inched toward the exit. We were nearly at the shadowy ground floor landing when I discovered Savannah and I weren't the only ones left in the building. Covered in a thin layer of snow and ice, the lifeless body of Pavel Baron had been with us the whole time.

Chapter Four

The one thing that can solve most of our problems is dancing.
—James Brown

Pavel was on his back, his eyes wide open. His face was a frozen mask of pain, horrific evidence of the violent attack that had taken his life. My breath emerged in bursts of frosty mist, but the air in front him was still. I didn't check his pulse. Those staring eyes had all the finality of a death certificate. In the dim light I realized my hand was stained, not with a spilled drink, but with blood. In my rush to wipe my hand, I dropped my dance bag and smashed my elbow into the hard plaster wall.

Trembling with fear and horror, my first instinct was to bolt. But my body didn't let me down. The disciplined habits of a lifetime supported me. With shaking fingers, I turned the phone's flashlight to the flight of stairs behind me. The banister was smeared with blood, but there wasn't nearly as much on and around the stairs as there was behind Pavel's head, where a large pool of bright red liquid formed a sickening backdrop to his motionless figure. His legs splayed out at an odd angle, and although he was face up, his torso was twisted to one side. The contents of his pockets—a ring of keys, bits of paper, and some coins—were scattered next to him. His cell phone was smashed. A scrolled, silver sculpture was wedged in the door. Bitter gusts of wind blew sleet and snow through the opening.

I told Savannah to call nine-one-one. She screamed wildly at the operator, making up in volume what she lacked in coherence. I fought a rising tide of nausea and flicked through my contacts until I got to Detective Jonah Sobol's number.

His tone was breezy. "How's my favorite ballerina? I hope you're calling me to rescue you from a lonely evening watching the snow fall."

I choked, looking for the right words to explain that once again I'd been the first person at the scene of a murder. Savannah redoubled her hysterics.

Jonah's voice quickened. "Leah. Talk to me, darling. Where are you? What's happening?"

I swallowed hard and said, "Need you. I'm at the studio. With Pavel."

His voice was calm. "What happened to Pavel?"

"He's dead."

"On my way."

If Jonah said anything further before hanging up, I didn't hear him. As the dreadful words left my lips, Savannah pitched her screams an octave higher. In the movies, tough guys slap out-of-control people across the face, but it's not easy to do that when the hysteric in question is rocking back and forth so violently she appeared to need an exorcism more than a sedative. And Savannah, like most people, was much bigger and heavier than I am. I certainly didn't want her to slap me back.

I grabbed her arm and pulled the phone from her hand. The emergency operator was still on the line.

"Hello? Miss? Are you there? Did you understand what I told you to do?"

I said, with more composure than I felt, "This is Leah Siderova. I'm here with Savannah Collier. I've contacted Detective Jonah Sobol of the Twentieth Precinct. We are at the studio of American Ballet Company with the dead body of Pavel Baron. We are in the ground floor stairwell."

The man on the other end of the line spoke slowly and distinctly. "Thank you. An ambulance will be there shortly. Please stay on the line."

I agreed, but Savannah lunged at me and took her phone back. I instructed her, in a voice loud enough to penetrate her wails, "It's very important you stay on the phone. Don't touch anything. Help is on the way."

Her eyes darted nervously from the door to the stairs. She babbled into the phone. "You don't understand. I-I can't stay here. What if she turns on me next?"

I pried the phone from her fingers and assured the operator one of us was *compos mentis.*

Savannah edged her way around the body. "I'm leaving. You handle this. You know what to do when someone's been killed."

Holding her phone with one hand, I pulled her back with the other. "You just found a murder victim and reported a crime, which means you're not going anywhere. You're staying here with me until the police say you can go."

She began crying, which was marginally preferable to the screaming. "I can't. I simply can't. I don't feel well. I have to go home."

Neither patience nor sympathy works with the truly selfish. "This isn't about you, Savannah. Yes, we were unlucky enough to find Pavel. But for heaven's sake, the poor man is dead. Show some respect."

She crossed her arms and stared at me with loathing. "What if he was murdered?"

I wondered how Pavel came to hire, and keep, a woman with the deductive capacity of a jellyfish. Exasperated, I explained the obvious. "Of course, he was murdered. People who commit suicide don't empty their pockets, shatter their phones, and then smash themselves in the back of the head."

"Maybe he fell and hit his head. Did you ever think of that?"

My nerves at the breaking point, I yelled, "Of course I didn't think of that. Look at how much blood has poured out of him." I pointed to the presumed murder weapon, a scrolled silver sculpture. "What's your theory? That he hit himself on the back of the head with a ballet prop, threw himself down the stairs, and then managed to wedge the weapon in the door?"

She shook with even greater intensity. "What if the killer is still in the building? And how do I know you didn't do it? Maybe you were giving yourself an alibi by hanging out with me. A lot of people still think you're guilty of last year's murder."

I glared at her. "If you really thought I was the killer, you would have long since run away. And you know I didn't do it for the same reason I know you didn't do it. We were together." Looking at her spiteful, swollen face, I added, "Maybe the police will arrest you."

Savannah snatched back her phone, where she found a sympathetic audience in the soothing tones of the nine-one-one operator.

I flashed my phone's light across Pavel's body. It was impossible to tell if his blood had begun to congeal, for the open door had allowed a thin layer of frost and ice to form across his body, including the pool of blood beneath him. The murder must have occurred within a narrow time frame since Pavel had been present at the last rehearsal of the day. Savannah had said many irrational things, but one statement was not as foolish as the rest. The murderer might very well be close by.

I was saved from further conversation with my emotionally unstable companion when the police arrived. Despite enormous temptation, I did not throw myself into the arms of Jonah Sobol. Even if I lacked my usual self-control, Savannah was there to save me from myself. The moment she saw the dark-haired, good-looking detective she hurled herself at him like a very blonde, heat-seeking missile.

He tried to break free of her embrace, but she responded by gripping him more tightly. Jonah's partner, Detective Farrow, gently unwound her arms from around Jonah's neck and was rewarded for his efforts by having her do the same to him.

"Detective!" she sobbed. "I simply cannot bear to be here another moment with the woman who killed Pavel! She threatened him. You have to take her away."

Jonah cut short my angry response with a quick shake of his head. He did not dispute Savannah's accusation, and instead, he took her hand and looked into her eyes. "You've been very brave. But I need you to be brave for a little while longer. Can you do that for me?"

She nodded, batting her long fake eyelashes at him. He looked back at her with unwarranted kindness and patience. I regretted not slapping her when I had the chance.

Detective Farrow cleared his throat. "Let's get you ladies someplace where you can sit down."

The ambulance medics pulled open the door, but Jonah didn't allow them in. He turned to Farrow. "This place is freezing. Let's have Diaz take them someplace warm until we're ready to interview them." He studiously avoided my eye and continued, "The Café Figaro is right around the corner. That okay with you, Leah? Um, I mean, Ms. Siderova?"

The Café Figaro was where we had our first date. Well, it wasn't exactly a date. I was under suspicion of murder and wanted to pump him for information. He wanted to do the same to me. Despite this unpromising beginning, we became friends.

I nodded gratefully, but Savannah had another round of hysterics. "Don't you understand? She's a murderer! I'm afraid to spend two minutes with her. What if she decides to kill me next?"

Neither detective answered her, but I could see we would not be going to the warm and fragrant Café Figaro, where the Pizzuto family made the best espresso and biscotti in New York City. Thanks to Savannah, we had to trudge back up the stairs and into the frigid studio, where the only available sustenance came from vending machines. I wished we still had the old ones, which were stocked with chocolate bars and chips, but thanks to our new healthy eating initiative the repurposed machines offered only sparkling water, still water, and vitamin water. I would have paid ten dollars for a package of neon-orange cheese crackers or a bag of salty pretzels. Or peanut M&Ms. Plenty of protein in peanuts.

In the well-lit foyer, my companion had another hysterical fit when she realized her pink coat was stained with Pavel's blood. That little episode required fifteen more minutes of everyone circling around Savannah, trying to make her feel better, while I watched from the side. She had a real talent for placing herself center stage, so she must have been a very mediocre dancer not to have lasted even one year with the company. By mediocre, of course, I mean unimpressive by American Ballet Company standards. You have to be exceptionally talented to get an offer from us. The dancers in our corps de ballet routinely perform starring roles with less-stellar companies.

Detective Farrow guided her into the office and took her statement there. I looked at Jonah. "I hope Farrow knows better than to believe a single word she says."

He peered into the office to make sure Farrow wasn't watching before pressing my hand and looking at me with an expression decidedly at odds with his usual cool, professional demeanor. Then he went back downstairs to supervise the crime scene, leaving one of the police officers to monitor my behavior and make sure I didn't make a run for it. I stared at the glass-walled office, at Farrow and Savannah, trying to read their lips. I was able to decipher exactly five words between the two of them: Pavel, Baron, Leah, Siderova, and murder.

I waited impatiently for Jonah to return. We'd gotten into the habit of meeting for coffee or a drink at least once a week, and I always looked forward to seeing him. He wasn't my boyfriend, although I harbored some very boyfriend-like feelings toward him. I never acted on these feelings, because I already had a boyfriend, whom my parents loved. They thought he was perfect.

After Jonah left, the delayed shock of finding Pavel's body kicked in. I couldn't stop shaking and I couldn't get warm, even after I sat on the radiator, wrapped in my winter jacket. Given how nauseated I felt, it was a good thing I'd eaten so little that day. But I also knew from experience that throwing up on an empty stomach was no more pleasant than throwing up a normal day's worth of food. I was on my way to the bathroom when Farrow emerged from the office and stopped me.

"Uh, Ms. Siderova? Can I ask you a few questions?" Farrow pointed to one of the narrow benches that lined the anteroom.

I pressed two hands against my stomach. "Give me a few minutes to be sick. I don't think I'll be long."

He laughed a bit uncertainly, as if unsure if I were joking. Savannah was still in the office, where she stared at me with a most unpleasant and triumphant look on her face. Her antipathy baffled me, and I wondered if I'd somehow insulted her without realizing it. But even if I had, accusing me of murder was too extreme a reaction for any perceived social slight.

Perhaps she had a pathological need for attention. That might explain her quick exit from American Ballet Company. We get many dancers who'd been the star of their neighborhood dance troupes and winners of their local dance competitions. Then they come to New York City and find themselves with dancers who are all that and a whole lot more. Some people can't hack the competition, and they're better off doing something less demanding, like brain surgery or quantum physics.

In ballet, only the strong survive.

Chapter Five

Dance, even if you have no place to do it but your living room.
—Kurt Vonnegut

I scrubbed my hands and brushed my hair. As Barbara often said, misfortune is no reason to let yourself go. I inspected my face in the cloudy bathroom mirror but couldn't do anything about the color of my skin, which was an unpleasant chalk-white with green undertones.

I rejoined Farrow, who looked extremely uncomfortable. The narrow bench was not kind to people of normal proportions. After a few minutes of fidgeting, he gave up and dragged a chair from the office to where I was sitting. I wondered why we didn't use the warm office and move Savannah to the frigid waiting room. Maybe Farrow was afraid of relocating his fragile flower of a witness closer to the exit.

Once settled, he said, "Ms. Collier tells me that you were the only one in the building when Mr. Baron was killed. She also said Mr. Baron deliberately humiliated you in front of the company and that he was going to fire you after this season."

I put my cold hands on my face to quell the sudden heat in my cheeks. "Savannah Collier is a loser and a liar. You shouldn't believe a word she says, especially about me."

Farrow didn't visibly react. "Is everything she said untrue?"

I took a deep breath. "What Savannah said is worse than untrue. It's a deliberate and unprovoked attempt to implicate me. How could she know the building was empty when Pavel was killed, unless she surveyed the entire place and then did the deed herself? And why would I have insisted she leave with me if I knew we'd find the body? Any self-respecting murderer would have sneaked out of the building, not alerted the sole remaining person."

Farrow said, "I can think of many reasons why a murderer would want an innocent person as a witness. But aside from that, Ms. Collier also said you were going to get fired. Was that a lie?"

I stood up to ease the cramps in my legs. "American Ballet Company is going through some major changes. Pavel reorganized his staff on a weekly, if not a daily, basis. There's no guarantee any of us will be here next season. And that includes Savannah." I thought for a minute. "Even Pavel had only a one-year contract, and he wasn't winning any popularity contests."

I stopped abruptly and clapped a hand against my mouth, aghast at the unkind words I'd used about the murder victim.

In a comforting voice, which was at odds with his words, Farrow said, "Ms. Collier also said you threatened to stab Mr. Baron in his—and I'm quoting here—nonexistent heart."

"No! That wasn't me. That was Bobbie York, our costume mistress. She's the one who said that." I felt guilty for throwing Bobbie under the bus, but I consoled myself with the thought that she'd rejoice in any opportunity to do the same to me.

Jonah joined us a few minutes later. Farrow said, "I think it might be best for the two ladies to come with us to the precinct."

Jonah stared at him. "You want them to come to the precinct in the middle of a blizzard? I think we can wait until New York City is no longer in a state of emergency."

Farrow grimaced. "Okay. They can wait until tomorrow." He jabbed his thumb in my direction but kept his gaze on Jonah. "In my opinion, that should be the last decision you make about the investigation into Pavel Baron's death. No disrespect to you, but tomorrow morning I'm going to request a different partner for this case. I'm sure you know the reason why."

Jonah's face was without expression. "If that's how it's going to be, let's get them to the precinct tonight."

Farrow shrugged. "Whatever you want. For now."

Officer Helen Diaz drove carefully. The snowplows, which had cleared both sides of Broadway earlier, hadn't yet returned, and the road was treacherous. A deep layer of icy snow and sleet was scored with wide, curved trenches where cars and trucks had slipped and swerved. Next to me, Savannah softly hiccupped with grating regularity.

With a sudden motion, she banged on the divider. "Let me out! I'm going to be sick!"

Diaz pulled up to the curb. Savannah tried to throw up but couldn't quite manage it. She reentered the police car, and through a tissue pressed to her lips said, "You won't get away with this. Justice will prevail."

I was feeling rather queasy myself. "If justice is done, it won't be by you. A piranha has a more finely-tuned sense of right and wrong."

She turned her back to me and didn't answer. With a furtive gesture, she withdrew a compact from her handbag, wiped her eyes, and applied a discreet amount of lipstick. It didn't help. She looked fully as awful as I did.

Savannah wiggled as far away from me as the seat belt allowed. I gazed at the back of her head. "Maybe you aren't as dumb as you look. Maybe you're blaming me because you did it. If that's the case, you're still not going to be a candidate for Mensa. You should have planned better than that."

We spent the rest of the ride in silence. Diaz escorted us inside the police station, which was exactly as I remembered it. Painted a hideous shade of green, it wasn't simply dirty. It looked as if the only way to clean it would be to dynamite the entire structure and start over again. Fluorescent lights cast a harsh glow over the grimy floor and scarred walls. The air was far less toxic smelling than the last time I'd visited, thanks to wide doors that police officers banged open every five minutes, sending blasts of freezing air in our direction.

I kept my coat on but couldn't get warm. The full-body tremors that shook me might have been a consequence of the temperature, or of the shock of seeing Pavel's dead body, but as bad as I felt, Savannah looked worse. Her face was a mottled red and white, and her pale blue eyes were swollen nearly shut. She fiercely picked at her manicured nails, sending little flakes of purple polish onto her lap.

As always, when I needed strength and discipline, I left the real world and turned to ballet. The discolored walls faded away. In their place, the Kingdom of the Shades appeared, and twenty-four ballerinas entered, one by one, for Act II of *La Bayadere*. After I mentally danced to the end of that enchanting scene, I returned from my daydream to find Savannah staring at me.

She shook her fist. "This is your fault. I'm getting a lawyer."

I assured her, "That's the smartest thing you've said since we met. When they charge you with murder, you'll need one."

Officer Diaz brought us to an inner room and invited us to sit on curved plastic chairs that once were orange. They were bolted to the ground and had Rorschach blots of undetermined provenance splattered over them. Savannah shuddered and declined to sit. I could not afford to be so picky, and I rested my aching legs and feet.

Diaz offered us some coffee. Savannah screeched, "I can't take any more of this! You should arrest her!"

Once again, my fingers itched to slap her. But Diaz did not appear to be vexed by Savannah's bad behavior.

The police officer said, in a gentle tone I found quite annoying, "Now, now. I understand how upset you must be. But don't you want to help us? Maybe you'd like a nice cup of tea to warm you up."

Savannah nodded like a five-year-old. She sat down and grudgingly drank from a murky brew that smelled as if it had been made with water from the Gowanus Canal. Without the pouting or the shouting, I accepted a cup of coffee that smelled only marginally more appealing, but at least it was hot.

The cold, the shock, and the exhausting hours I'd spent dancing continued to take their toll on my body. Against my will, I closed my eyes and didn't open them again until a gentle voice said, "Hey there, Sleeping Beauty. Time to wake up."

I looked into Jonah Sobol's dark eyes. He wasn't a prince. And he wasn't always charming. But I couldn't help feeling drawn to him.

The Prince Charming in my life was Zach Mitchell. Not this man, who had, not so very long ago, tried to arrest me for a murder I didn't commit. But Jonah was the one I was with. Again.

Chapter Six

To watch us dance is to hear our hearts speak.
—Hopi Indian Proverb

Jonah ushered me into one of the small rooms that lined the precinct's hallway. "What happened while I was gone?"

I was bitter. "Savannah Collier is what happened. She's pretending to think I killed Pavel, although even her pea-sized brain must realize I could make the same accusations against her, and with better reason. I was with other people for practically the whole day. You know what a dancer's life is like. We don't enjoy a lot of downtime or a lot of privacy. Nearly every minute of our day is scheduled."

He smiled and seemed to relax. "Tell me about the hour or so before you went to see Savannah. Where were you?"

After I gave him a thorough recap of my day, he asked, "How long was it, in between the time you left the rehearsal and the time you went to the office?"

"I honestly don't know. It wasn't long."

Jonah looked at me, his head to one side. "What was so important that you had to talk to Barbara and then Pavel? Why didn't you leave with the other dancers?"

I jerked my chair farther away from him. "Whose side are you on?"

He closed the gap between us. "Yours, of course. I'm asking you the same questions every other detective is going to want to know. Talk to me. What topic was so urgent you ignored a blizzard?"

I stretched my legs to relieve the tension in my joints. "It's going to sound trivial. So be patient."

Jonah smiled. "I am nothing if not patient when it comes to the trials and tribulations of my favorite ballerina."

I searched for a plausible reason, other than the real one, for going to see Pavel. I was too proud to admit to Jonah, or anyone except Barbara, how scared I was about the future of my dance career. Pavel's death magnified that fear. I had a powerful motive to kill him.

The truth, but not the whole truth, was the most prudent way forward. "Ann, my father's wife, showed up during Austin's rehearsal. That's when I found out Pavel hired her to be the company's health and wellness coach. I had no idea she was going to be working with the company. It's a very awkward situation since Ann is supposed to evaluate the fitness of all the dancers, including me. I wanted to discuss it with Pavel."

Jonah put his notebook aside. "I'm sorry, Leah, but I'm just not getting this. Why did you have to talk to Pavel about it tonight? Why not wait until tomorrow? For that matter, why not wait to discuss the situation with Ann?"

I stood up and started pacing. "Ever since Artistic Solutions took over, it's impossible to schedule a private meeting with Pavel. Since nearly everyone was gone, I figured if he was still in the building, he was probably alone, and I could get a few minutes with him. Pavel lived two blocks away, so it wasn't unreasonable to think he might still be there."

Jonah rubbed his temples. "But wouldn't it help you to have an inside track at Artistic Solutions? Wouldn't Ann automatically give you a pass?"

I stopped pacing and stood very still. "I wish I could say yes. But I honestly can't. The only thing I know about Ann is her position on various nutritional supplements."

Jonah, who had met Ann, choked back a laugh. "I'm not worried, of course, about Savannah's claims, but I do find it odd that she would so quickly, and with such anger, deliberately target you as the murderer. Does she have any particular animus against you?"

Tears pricked my eyes, but I forced them back. "It seems she does, although I don't know why. Savannah danced briefly with ABC, but turnover is high in the corps de ballet. I didn't take much notice of her when she arrived and didn't miss her when she left. She reappeared at the beginning of the season, as a new office worker and the most ardent member of the Artistic Solutions cult. After the way she acted tonight, I'd love to pin the murder on her, but she was so devoted to Pavel she would have smashed herself in the head before harming him."

"If she was obsessed with Mr. Baron, and he rejected her, she could have killed him in a fit of anger." Jonah leaned back in his chair. "How did she feel about moving from the stage to the back office? Seems like a lot of people might be bitter."

I opened my hands to indicate how empty of ideas I was. "She seemed happy to be working for Pavel. But since everything she said about me was a lie, maybe that was also untrue. Until tonight, I hadn't exchanged ten words with her."

"Maybe that's why she didn't like you. I've seen you in action. When you're concentrating on something, you barely notice oncoming traffic, let alone a discontented ex-dancer looking for attention and validation." He looked down at his notes. "What reason, if any, did she give for not leaving the building earlier?"

My heart raced. "She didn't give a reason. She was really upset, though. She'd been crying. I asked her what was wrong, but she blew me off." I shuddered again, this time from horror and not cold. "What if she wanted me to leave so I would be the one to find the body? There was a sign on the elevator that said it was out of service. Maybe she put it there. The elevator breaks down all the time. No one would think to question it."

Jonah stood up. "Dammit. We never checked. Wait here."

He left, presumably to have someone verify the elevator was broken. I hoped the long-suffering Diaz wouldn't have to go.

When Jonah returned, he said, "Let's go over this again. As best you can, word for word. Every detail. Don't leave anything out."

Reliving the moments before we found Pavel's dead body needed every ounce of strength I had left. "Obviously, we took the stairs. My knees hurt, and I told her to go ahead of me, but she refused, probably figuring if she tripped in the dark, she'd fall on top of me, instead of the other way around. She said something like "that darned light is out again." And then—then we saw Pavel."

He looked up sharply. "Was that a common occurrence? That the light was out?"

I shrugged. "I don't know. You can ask Ms. Crandall. She's the one who deals with the management company. Although her role may have changed since the reorganization of the office staff."

He jotted a few more notes. "I'll follow up with Ms. Crandall. What kind of a relationship did she have with the Artistic Solutions group?"

I had even less insight about our office manager than I did about Savannah. "Ms. C keeps herself to herself. She's worked with ABC for over twenty years, and it wouldn't surprise me if she resented having Artistic Solutions tell her what to do. I don't think Savannah was a threat to Crandall. The guy who appeared to possess the most power was Ron Wieder. He was Pavel's confidante. Or henchman, depending on your point of view. Savannah followed him and Pavel like an eager puppy."

Jonah scribbled without looking up. "What's Wieder's role?"

"He's the liaison between the business side and the ballet side of the company. Ron is always extremely nice and cheery and polite, but he's pretty cold. If Pavel told him to take someone down, he'd not only do it, he'd enjoy it."

He checked his phone for a silenced text before continuing. "Give me an example."

Episodes involving Ron's genial brand of cruelty weren't hard to come by. "About a month ago, Pavel hired a woman to teach us meditation. Two weeks later, Pavel lost interest in her and had Ron dismiss her. He could have done it privately, but he waited until she'd scheduled a group session. The poor woman was halfway through her first chant when he barged into the room and told her to collect her stuff and get out. He didn't have to humiliate her. Far from feeling bad for her, he seemed to enjoy shaming her. That's the kind of person Ron is."

Jonah was thoughtful. "Perhaps. But Ron was following orders, either from someone higher up at Artistic Solutions, or Pavel himself. When you work for one of these corporate outfits you have to be okay with doing all kinds of unpleasant things. If Darius Kemble thought he could save five cents by shoving his grandmother in front of a bus he wouldn't hesitate to do so. He'd expect the same behavior, and the same unflinching loyalty, from his employees."

I had no insights about Kemble, the fearsome owner of Artistic Solutions. "I suppose you're right. No one on the corporate side has made friends with anyone from the ballet side. Other than Pavel, Ron was the only link between the two."

He held up his phone to show me a picture of a twisted, bloodstained, piece of silvery metal. "Can you tell me anything about the murder weapon?"

I swallowed hard, to clear my closed throat. "Yes. It's a prop for a ballet called *Precious Metals*. It's rather famous. The sculptor Nakamura made it."

"Where was it kept? Have you seen it lately?"

I felt lightheaded, and the walls in the room slanted in odd directions. I forced air into my lungs, trying to stay focused.

Jonah kept me steady. "What's going on? Is it something about the murder weapon?"

"Yes. There are several copies of the prop, but the original was kept in a glass case next to the elevator. And no, I don't remember if it was in there when I left. The door to the case was open, so I closed it before leaving."

He was grim. "Leaving your fingerprints on the case."

I stood up straight but avoided his gaze. "Yes."

Jonah received several texts in quick succession, whistling softly as the last message came through. "The elevator may be unreliable, but right now, there's nothing wrong with it." He paused, and his tone became warmer. "Okay, Leah, I'm afraid I must leave, as much as I'd like to escort you home. Why don't I call you when I'm done, and you can fill me in on any details we might have missed?"

I wasn't sure what he was proposing. "Didn't Detective Farrow say he wanted someone else as his partner for the case?"

Jonah laughed, a deep and easy laugh that tended to make other people laugh, even when they didn't know what the joke was. "How did you guess what my nefarious plot was? I'm going to arrange for you to find a dead body every few months just so we can keep in touch. Because you are not so easy to pin down, Ms. Leah Siderova."

I trembled. "I feel as if some evil star is following me."

He shook his head. "Whatever is following you, it's not an evil star. But the whole setup is…interesting." He took my hand. His grasp warmed me, but his next words sent chills running down my spine.

"I'm worried about you. If Savannah is the killer, she will see you as a threat. Or as the perfect scapegoat. If she's innocent, it's possible the killer set her up as the fall guy, and you got in the way. Either way, one, or both of you, could be in danger. Be careful, and do not go off sleuthing on your own."

I grabbed my bag. "No problem. I only sleuth when it's my own life and liberty that's on the line." Which, of course, appeared to be the case.

Chapter Seven

Do it big; do it right; and do it with style.
—Fred Astaire

Prior to Pavel's murder, I'd given Savannah less thought than the ads that lined the subway cars of the A train. She was a woman of mediocre talent and limited brainpower, and her behavior in the hours after we found the body did nothing to change my estimation of her. In the days that followed, however, she proved herself a shrewd negotiator and self-promoter.

Savannah managed to get herself on every morning news show, and there were rumors she'd sold her story to a major publisher. In her interviews and posts, she was careful not to directly accuse me. But she picked out a few facts and wove them together in such a way that whoever heard her would inevitably assume I was guilty of murder. Every chance she got she dragged in last year's scandal, along with some truly hideous pictures of me. I could barely endure the humiliation of her endless insinuations. I wanted to retaliate but feared adding fuel to the stream of incendiary stories.

When I tried to approach her, she screamed and hid behind her desk. Her behavior would have been funny if it hadn't been so embarrassing and demoralizing. I simply couldn't find a rational way to fight her calculated nuttiness. Despite the seriousness of this public relations debacle, no one at Artistic Solutions tried to stop her.

I asked Gabi, who'd been my best friend since middle school, for advice. Before she retired from dancing to marry, have a kid, and "get a life" she'd handled the delicate politics of the ballet world more shrewdly than the most experienced diplomat.

While I fed Lucie bits of banana, Gabi considered the new parameters at American Ballet Company. For once, she was uncertain. "Things have changed so much since I left. Is Ms. Crandall still the office manager? Perhaps you should approach her first."

"She's still at ABC, but she doesn't handle personnel. Darius Kemble has restructured the whole company, and the people at Artistic Solutions have taken over a lot of the management."

Gabi moved restlessly about the tiny kitchen. Her long thin legs covered the space in three strides. "Tell me about Ron Wieder. He seems like the logical person to talk to, at least until they get someone new to take over as artistic director."

I paused, as Lucie became more interested in banana painting than banana eating. "I don't like him. He's the sort of bland, blonde, privileged guy who would spike your drink at a party. The kind of guy who would take pictures and brag to his friends that he bagged a ballerina."

Gabi picked up Lucie and hugged her tightly, bananas and all. "I hate those guys." She held Lucie at arm's length. "Never let one of those guys near you!"

Lucie gurgled agreement.

After some deliberation, on the following day, I did end up emailing Ron. He'd been Pavel's most trusted ally, which was a black mark against him, but he was still my best bet. He agreed to meet before the morning ballet class.

I got to the office before any of the other staff arrived. Even Savannah, who made a point of working longer hours than anyone else, wasn't there. I walked down the deserted hallway of interconnected offices and knocked on Ron's door.

He opened it slightly. "Hi, Leah, good to see you. I'm in the middle of an important phone conference. Would you mind taking a seat for a few minutes?"

I used the bench outside his office to stretch my calf muscles. Ron kept me waiting so long I had time to work on my hamstrings as well. He didn't open the door until a good fifteen minutes past our appointed time. I didn't complain about the delay, but I did make a mental note of it. That kind of cheap game playing, in combination with his condescending half-apology, told me all I needed to know about him. Nonetheless, he was all smiles as he ushered me into his office. "Nice to see you. What can I do for you?"

I ignored the noxious, faintly floral odor in the hot and humid room, which was filled with exotic plants. Ron had a space heater and humidifier turned to their highest settings. I was surprised his glasses hadn't fogged up. My dark hair responded to the moist heat by reverting to its pre-primp frizziness, but his fair hair and neatly pressed clothes were impervious.

"I know you dancers love the heat," he said. "You're all a bunch of hothouse flowers." He gently stroked the leaf of a plant I couldn't identify, but I wasn't exactly a font of horticultural knowledge. As for Ron, he lavished his green-leaved friends with more sympathy and attention than he did his human colleagues.

I sniffed one or two of the flowers but was unable to pinpoint the slightly funky, chemical scent that hung in the air. Perhaps Ron, like Pavel, was a germophobe. As if reading my mind, he genially pushed to my side of the desk a spray can of disinfectant and a silver-topped bottle filled with an oily liquid that looked like hand sanitizer.

Ron needn't have bothered decontaminating the place on my account. I never had the slightest desire to get close to him. Over my objections, he pressed the bottle of sanitizer into my hand. "You should try some. Several of the dancers recommended it."

I opened the bottle and sniffed. To be polite, I rubbed a few drops into my skin and then got down to business. "Savannah Collier is ruining my reputation. I don't want to get in a public fight with her, because that will simply keep the story going. You're her boss. Tell her to stop."

Ron looked only mildly interested. I searched for an argument that would be meaningful to him. "She's also ruining the reputation of the company. I'm surprised no one on your end has put a stop to her antics."

Ron gestured to a single-serve coffeepot. "Can I get you a cup? It might help you relax."

I rarely turn down coffee, even when the person offering it is a condescending pile of corporate dirt. "Fine. I take mine black, no sugar, please."

He laughed. "Oh, you dancers. Always watching your weight."

I didn't correct him. Although he was right about the weight part, I drank my coffee black because I liked it that way. I took a few sips from a surprisingly good brew before continuing. "You must know Savannah is implying I murdered Pavel. She never comes out and says it directly, but she's made enough damaging statements so that anyone watching, or listening, is going to think I'm the killer. If you don't care about the effect on me, don't you care that she's hurting the company?"

Ron spooned sugar into his cup. "Sorry to disappoint you, Leah, but we don't have the same ideas about what's good for the company. Or even what's good for you. Did you know her last three tweets went viral? Totally sick how all this publicity is driving ticket sales through the roof." He winked at me. "Mr. Kemble himself called this morning, so you don't have to worry about him. He couldn't be happier."

Sweat trickled down my back. "Kemble may be the president of Artistic Solutions, but Artistic Solutions works for American Ballet Company. Not the other way around."

Ron waved his hand as if swatting away a mosquito. "Of course. But he's a very powerful man. You want him on your side. And on that topic, you'll be happy to know you're now in the first cast of Austin's ballet. Above Mavis Ferris! It's going to be standing room only all season. And you have Savannah to thank for that." He looked as happy as if he'd been solely responsible for the uptick in sales.

My throat went dry. Ron did not appear to notice he'd provided me with the perfect motive to kill Pavel. Savannah herself couldn't have done better.

For many years, I thought there was nothing on earth, other than my family and a few friends, more important than ballet. I was wrong. Turned out, plenty of things meant more to me than dancing. My freedom, for one. My reputation, for another. When I left the police precinct on the night Pavel was murdered, I had no desire to involve myself in the investigation of that brutal act. Quite the opposite. I was an unwilling witness at a crime scene. That was all. And yet, forces beyond my control kept pushing me to act.

Perhaps a few graphic images could persuade Ron to intervene on my behalf. I pulled out my phone and tapped on a video of Savannah's latest bit of insanity, which she'd enacted in front of a live audience for a local news show. In it, she was sitting in a cozy twosome with Emilia Newsome, a woman whose skin was stretched to an impossible tightness across her cheekbones.

In the video, Emilia leaned confidentially toward Savannah, who wore a lime green dress of an unfortunately bright hue. "Savannah, please tell us what happened in those last fateful hours before you lost your beloved boss."

Savannah touched a tissue to her eyes, but it was clear she was enjoying herself too much to shed any tears. Her voice, however, quavered with a pale imitation of grief. "Well, Emilia, I thought everyone had gone home. If you recall, that was the day of the big blizzard. But Leah Siderova barged into the office, *claiming* she needed to talk to Pavel." She placed one hand on her chest and breathed deeply, as if overcome by emotion.

Emilia turned to look directly at the camera. "I should probably remind our audience that Ms. Siderova was the ballerina who was involved in the ghastly murder at American Ballet Company last year."

Even though I knew what was coming, her words still hit me with the force of a locomotive. Emilia omitted the fact that I'd been unjustly accused of the crime. How was I supposed to fight against these half-truths and innuendoes?

Emilia turned back to Savannah. "What about the time immediately before Ms. Siderova came to see you? Where was she then? Which was also, I understand, when the gruesome murder took place."

Savannah bore an expression of fake regret that shouldn't have fooled anyone old enough to question the existence of the tooth fairy. "Ms. Siderova *says* she was on the phone. And that she was packing up her dance gear. But what took her so long? And why was she the only dancer not to leave the building?" She shook her head. "Only one person can answer those questions, and as far as I know, she's not talking."

If that sorry excuse for a reporter had a brain in her head, she would have asked Savannah why she hadn't left the building either. But no such query was forthcoming. Instead, Emilia said, with all the charm of a used car salesman, "I understand you're writing a book about your career as a dancer with American Ballet Company and how it relates to your current position as a corporate executive with Artistic Solutions. I know I'm looking forward to reading it."

Ron, who had watched the video without editorial comment, put down the phone. He had a pleased look on his face that sickened me.

I tried to stay calm. "Pavel Baron was killed. And you think it's a good idea to use his death as a marketing ploy?"

He cocked his head to one side and didn't answer.

With more force, I said, "Can't you see the effect this is having on me? Even people who know me are avoiding me. If she doesn't stop I'm going to press charges."

This last statement moved him to respond. "Savannah at no point committed either slander or libel. I've already checked with our legal department. Did you really think everyone at Artistic Solutions hadn't already seen the interview?" He chuckled. "I haven't missed one. We've even had a few watch parties."

He took off his glasses and polished them. "C'mon, Leah. Face the facts. Savannah may have insinuated certain things about you that may not—or may—be true. But since neither she nor the people who interviewed her make direct accusations, everyone is completely in the clear." He looked at me with an air of smug satisfaction, as if his assurance of Savannah's legal right to trash me should make me feel better.

I'd accomplished nothing, other than to verify my low opinion of Ron. I stood up, but when I leaned over to pick up my dance bag my feet slipped out from underneath me. I grabbed the desk to steady myself.

Ron half rose from his chair. I examined my feet and the floor and waved him off. "I'm fine. But you need to talk to the cleaning staff. This floor is like ice."

He peered over his desk. "I've heard dancers are very clumsy when they're not on stage. I hope you're okay. Do you need any help?" He smiled slightly. "We have to keep you healthy, now that you're such a big part of the spring season."

My cheeks burned. His statement about dancers' klutziness was accurate, but it wasn't my fault I slipped. I lifted my shoe and showed him the powdery residue on the sole. "Is this a booby trap? What kind of game are you playing?"

He didn't miss a beat. "Relax, Leah. I fired half the cleaning staff, but I haven't had time to hire permanent replacements." He moved uncomfortably close. "I know you're upset about Savannah, but don't let that make you completely paranoid."

I took a few cautious steps and bent and stretched my legs. I was shaky, not only because I narrowly escaped injuring my knees again, but because I was furious over Ron's lack of concern. He stepped over my dance bag and opened the door to his office, not to be polite, but to indicate that our conversation was over. I didn't care how badly he wanted me to go. He'd kept me waiting, in a transparent act of one-upmanship, and I was pleased to do the same to him.

Ron looked pointedly at the clock. "I'd love to talk further about your problems, but don't you have someplace you need to be?"

That was the only thing he said that made sense to me. Worried I wouldn't have time to properly warm up before the daily company ballet class, I left without saying anything further. Every class begins with at least forty minutes of warming up, but most dancers over the age of twelve know they need to warm up before the warmup. And the older you get, the more important that preparation is. I was wearing a leotard and tights under my jeans, and so I bypassed the dressing room and headed straight for the studio, swapping my shoes for ballet slippers before stepping inside.

I grabbed my usual place at the barre. Daniel joined me, holding an imaginary phone to his ear. "Are you ghosting me?"

I searched my bag, and, realizing I'd left my phone on Ron's desk, rushed back into the office. Ms. Crandall, who was banging at the keys of her computer as if she had a longstanding grudge against them, ignored me as

I ran down the hall. Ron's door was closed. I knocked. Inside, I heard the faint sound of laughter.

Unwilling to wait any longer, I entered in time to see Savannah's hurried exit through the interior door.

Chapter Eight

The truest expression of a people is in its dance and its music. Bodies never lie.
—Agnes de Mille

Dashing back and forth between the studio and the office didn't make me breathless. It was seeing Savannah make her surreptitious exit from Ron's cubicle that sucked the oxygen out of me. I'd said nothing to Ron I wouldn't have told her to her face. Nonetheless, I was uneasy, not because Savannah might have eavesdropped on my conversation, but because Ron, perhaps, had deliberately deceived me. Maybe he was secretly helping Savannah trash me.

Daniel, seeing me rush back into the studio, once again strolled over. "Take your time. If you'd had the wit to keep your phone with you, you'd know I texted because class has been delayed. I know how obsessive you are about getting here early and wanted to save you the price of the therapy you so desperately need."

I loved Daniel. If he loved women, I'd be tempted to forget both the detective and the doctor and hook up with him. He understood, without explanations, my life and my work. Things being what they were, however, I was happy to have his friendship.

I did a few easy leg swings and then grabbed my heel and stretched my leg over my head. I had plenty of room, as the other dancers seemed to have mutually agreed to give me a wide berth. I ignored them and concentrated on Daniel. "Why the delay? Madame M isn't going to be happy about this. She's more obsessive than I am."

He very gently helped me stretch. "Madame Maksimova is the reason we're late. Well, not exactly Madame. It's the police who came early to interview her. That's screwed up everything. Ms. Crandall is beside herself, trying to reschedule rehearsals without stepping on the tender toes of our resident choreographic geniuses."

I peered through the window at the line of double-parked police cars below. "Are the detectives going to talk to us again?"

Daniel gave me a swift hug. "I hope not. All my interviews have been with the unattractive Detective Farrow. I wouldn't mind as much if for once I got to hang out with your boyfriend."

I didn't debate his teasing reference to Jonah. "I don't want to talk to either of them, although at this point, I should be happy to talk to anyone willing to spend time with me. Thanks to Savannah, people have been treating me like I'm some kind of ticking time bomb."

The expression in Daniel's blue eyes darkened. "You're telling me. But what can you expect? With so many new dancers, all they care about is keeping on the good side of whoever seems to be in charge. Even I don't know who to kiss up to." He patted me on the shoulder. "Chin up, old girl. You've been through worse."

This was true, although not a sentiment likely to make me feel better. I wanted life to go back to some semblance of normal, a life in which I was famous only to ardent balletomanes.

He wrinkled his nose. "Nothing personal, but something here really stinks." He grimaced and retreated to the other side of the studio.

I sniffed my hands, which still reeked of Ron's sanitizer. After a lifetime of sinus problems, I wasn't as annoyed by the scent as Daniel was. I also was cheered by the possibility that the smell was the reason people avoided me.

I'd forgotten to eat breakfast, so I took a small bite from a protein bar. I didn't risk more than one bite. No one wants to dance on a full stomach, and skipping a meal was preferable to public shame and disdain. In ballet, weight gain is the kiss of death. I hadn't yet been on the receiving end of the dreaded "fat talk," but those who had endured the mortification of one never forgot it. I studied the mirror to see where those extra pounds were lurking.

Olivia joined me at the barre with a load of damp paper towels and a sour look on her face. "Don't look now, but the British Invasion has stink-bombed our little corner of the studio." She pointed to a smeared section of the floor, next to an expensive, woven leather dance bag. A small, gold-topped bottle lay on its side. Next to it was a mound of powder that looked like rosin, but was slippery, rather than sticky. Mavis, the owner of the mess, was not around to assist. She was in the hallway, flirting with one of the company's wealthiest donors.

I grabbed a few of the paper towels and helped Olivia mop the floor. Some ballerinas deodorize the inside of their pointe shoes with sprays or powder, although I never had. If I did, it wouldn't have been with a product that smelled like Eau de Windex.

After we scoured the floor as best we could, I gave Olivia an abbreviated version of my conversation with Ron. She nodded, but I could see she wasn't really listening. I followed her gaze and saw Mavis reenter the room as if expecting a standing ovation. The British ballerina had made several cutting remarks about Olivia at a recent rehearsal, and my friend was still bitter. I cast about for something to say to make her feel better, which in the last few days had become increasingly difficult.

"You need to relax. Mavis is going back to London in a few more weeks. Ignore her."

Olivia sat back on her heels. "That would be like ignoring a runaway bus that could kill you. Or permanently scar you. I don't know what she has against me."

"She hates you for being so good. You're her understudy, but when she does double pirouettes, you do triples. When she marks the big jumps, you aim for the sky. My advice is to pretend she doesn't exist."

In a remarkably short span of time, Mavis inspired several ABC dancers with more loathing than any visiting ballerina since Zarina Devereaux. Like Zarina, Mavis's grace and beauty were exceeded only by her condescending nastiness. Both ballerinas carried themselves with the serene confidence of a modern-day Helen of Troy, an assessment most men heartily endorsed.

A majority of women, however, regarded them as female embodiments of Vlad the Impaler. The younger ones were less discerning and followed her every move with worshipful reverence. Mavis was kind to them, except for a few, like Olivia, who posed a threat to her dominance.

"Did I ever tell you about the time Zarina lost her temper and started throwing things at me and the guy she was seeing? I dropped by his apartment, and she thought he was cheating on her with me." Encouraged by Olivia's chuckle, I recounted a few more details, which were a lot funnier in retrospect than they were when they happened.

"I escaped unharmed, but the poor guy was left to literally pick up the pieces." I patted myself on the back, in mock self-congratulation. "Of course, I am too kind to discuss another ballerina's selfishness, jealousy, and cruelty." Pulling down the corners of my mouth, I said, "But that's just the kind of person I am. Generous to a fault."

Olivia smiled. "I'll be sure to let the powers that be know how selfless you are." She sniffed again and sneezed. "I think this stuff might be giving me an allergic reaction. Do you think it's deliberate? And that Mavis is trying to permanently eliminate the competition? Thanks to her, we're all in danger of literally breaking a leg."

I stuck a few extra bobby pins into my bun. "She's not the only one booby-trapping the place. I practically wiped out in Ron's office this morning."

Olivia looked puzzled. "Was Mavis there before you?"

Dammit. *I* should have thought of that. Maybe Mavis was part of Ron and Savannah's evil machinations. I didn't mention anything about it to Olivia. She had enough problems.

Two teenaged apprentice ballerinas, who were pretending not to eaves-drop, flinched when Olivia mentioned breaking a leg. Dancers can be rather superstitious, and they are wary of any transgression to the strict code of conduct we live by.

We know our superstitions are absurd, but dancers, like actors, are slaves to tradition. Before actors go onstage, they tell each other to break a leg, because wishing an actor good luck is bad luck. Dancers are understandably wary about telling each other to break a leg. Instead, we say *merde*. The two sentiments are not completely dissimilar. In both instances, performers say something bad to achieve something good. However silly it may seem to outsiders, no sane person would ever risk angering the dance gods, who lurk in the recesses of every theater and are not known for their sense of humor.

As soon as Olivia crossed the room to deposit the used paper towels, Mavis enacted a hostile takeover of her place at the barre, kicking my friend's dance bag out of the way. This was a serious breach of ballet etiquette. Mavis compounded her sin by refusing my polite request to move her skinny rear end, claiming she needed that exact spot because it reminded her of where she always stood when she was in her London studio. Cheered by her ability to disrupt our pre-class ritual, Mavis took out a long elastic strap and wrapped herself in it, stretching her hyper-flexible limbs into shapes a pretzel would envy.

I warmed up slowly, taking great care of my vulnerable knees, as we waited for Madame Maksimova to arrive. Madame M looked exactly as she did last year. And ten years ago. Except for a slightly slower gait and a tiny network of fine lines on her face, she looked much as she did thirty years ago. She still dressed in black and pink, her hair was still in a perfect French knot, and she still had those killer diamond earrings. She also still had Froufrou, her tiny poodle, who accompanied her wherever she went, and who knew the sequence of the ballet class as well as we did. Although Froufrou was capable of getting around on her own four paws, she preferred the view from her perch inside Madame's capacious dance bag.

To my surprise, Ron entered the studio ahead of Madame Maksimova, making a rather dramatic entrance and rudely leaving my beloved teacher to follow in his wake. Madame entered with small, careful steps. She looked more frail than usual, and I worried the cold weather had made her arthritis worse. Her posture was still graceful, if not quite as straight as it once was.

Ron reveled in this opportunity to address us in person, which, under normal circumstances, Pavel would have done. Unlike Pavel, who did not pretend to possess a sense of humor, Ron opened with a lame joke about a priest, a rabbi, and a dancer. He probably thought the joke made him more likable, since he got a big laugh. He did not appear to understand that all the dancers were anxious to curry favor with him. Every one of us hoped to get promoted or get a return contract. If we thought we could achieve our goal by laughing at his dumb jokes, we'd roar at anything he said, even if the punchline of the joke involved breaking a leg while getting booed off the stage.

When the fake hilarity died down, Ron said, "In all seriousness, I know how difficult the last few days have been. We all miss Pavel very much, and the manner of his passing makes the whole situation even worse." He lowered his head, and from over his glasses looked briefly at me. "Believe me, I understand what all of you are going through. I miss him too."

He must have had a much closer relationship with Pavel than the rest of us, for no one else evinced a trace of Ron's avowed sorrow. The manner of Pavel's death was horrifying and tragic, but only Savannah expressed grief over the absence of the man himself. Even the dancers who'd succumbed to his questionable charms were unresponsive. Pavel, unlike his predecessor, had the reputation of being rather boring in bed.

The people who'd been avoiding me didn't do so because they thought I was guilty of killing their beloved leader or lover. Their motivation was far more self-serving: they simply wanted to get on the good side of Savannah, who was now a media darling. Her comments about up-and-coming dancers had developed an ardent social media following.

We weren't an exceptionally insensitive group of people; we simply didn't know Pavel well enough to genuinely mourn him. He'd been the artistic director and ballet master in chief for only a few months. His most notable achievement was hiring Artistic Solutions, a move that had made him highly unpopular. When he was murdered, it was like an uninspiring public figure had died. Tragic, but not an event that touched us too deeply. On the other hand, it was quite possible someone in the room was hiding a more visceral reaction to the poor man's life. And his death.

As Ron changed the topic to discuss routine company business, I sat in a side split, stretching left and right, and doing my best to nod and smile with the rest. Despite ballet's strict rules of conduct, it's perfectly acceptable to warm up and listen at the same time. Mavis put her leg on the barre, and Olivia stretched her feet on a wooden roller.

Ron droned on. We were already thirty minutes behind schedule. I hoped Austin's rehearsal, the last of the day, would be cut. His choreography was dull, and the music was a clichéd echo of every atonal score written since Schoenberg first put pen to paper.

I jerked back to attention when I heard my name, but Ron wasn't looking at me. "I know some people are concerned about Leah Siderova's involvement with Pavel's murder. And some of you have come to me with your concerns. According to the police, this is still an open investigation." He pursed his lips. "I also want to emphasize that no one should jump to conclusions about recent changes in casting."

Ron's announcement spurred me to action. It was as if he wanted to cement Savannah's crazed indictment of me.

I jumped to my feet. "No one here could possibly think I had anything to do with Pavel's death." I turned to my fellow dancers. "The police are confident I'm innocent." I paused for a moment, to silently pray this was still true. "You should take your lead from them. Not from Savannah, who knows nothing."

In the sea of faces in front of me, most were work friends, people I didn't know well. If they left the company, I probably would never see them again. Or think about them again. I wasn't even sure of the names of several of the new dancers. To me, they were an interchangeable group of tall, long-legged Emmas and Emilias, partnered by a series of chiseled Ethans and Tylers.

I took a few steps in Ron's direction. "You said that people had come to you with their concerns. Are you saying that people are genuinely worried about—that they were worried about me?"

When I turned back to face my colleagues, only a handful had the courage to make eye contact. Several looked downright suspicious. The rest made surreptitious comments to their neighbors or checked their phones, determined to appear uninterested and to stay uninvolved. What on earth was the matter with these people? If anyone seriously thought I was the killer, he or she should have been the first to nod and smile and indicate unwavering support, if only to avoid having me murder them. Maybe dancers weren't as smart as I thought.

Mavis was the only person who was genuinely unmoved by the unfolding drama. She looked neither right nor left, and instead of engaging with the people around her she continued to admire herself in the mirror. Her total detachment was both chilling in its selfishness and admirable in its concentration. Not many dancers reach the pinnacle of stardom without a healthy measure of vanity, but Mavis's obsession with herself was as perfect as her body.

Ron, despite his theoretical grief, was as cool as Mavis, if not as obviously self-involved. He ignored me and said, "I'm here to let all of you know that you can come to me with your problems." He smiled, but the light reflecting off his glasses made his expression difficult to decipher. "My door is always open." With that seemingly unironic remark, he nodded and left the room.

Madame Maksimova came to my side. She spoke softly. "My darling Lelotchka, please to not derange yourself. I will help, of course." She turned to the rest of the dancers, who were watching her intently. "And now, please to begin." She demonstrated what she wanted us to do with her hands, as many arthritic ballet teachers do. "*Demi- plié. demi- plié, grand plié. Port de bras*. First, second, fourth, fifth."

The pianist improvised an introductory phrase for a Chopin waltz, and we began our day as most of us have since childhood, bending and stretching our joints. But even the most basic elements of ballet never got old. At least not for me. When I'm dancing, I literally can't think of anything else. It's impossible to concentrate on perfecting one's technique, or learning new choreography, if any irrelevant thought intrudes. At that moment, though, even the habits of a lifetime were insufficient to distract me.

When the class came to an end, we all curtseyed and bowed and applauded Madame Maksimova. She gestured to our pianist, and we curtseyed and bowed and applauded him as well. This ritual is sacrosanct to all dance classes.

Outside our beautiful world of ballet, flakes of snow softly fell, coating the Upper West Side of Manhattan with another layer of ice and slush. It was a winter morning like a thousand other mornings. Except that a man had been killed. And there was a good chance someone in that room—or at least in the building—had committed the murder.

Chapter Nine

If I could tell you what it meant, there would be no point in dancing it.
—*Isadora Duncan*

Olivia and I, along with most of the rest of the company, checked for changes to the rehearsal schedule as soon as class ended. When Mavis approached, the throng of dancers parted like the Red Sea. Their deference annoyed me, because she resembled a plague of locusts far more than she did an icon of spiritual leadership. I didn't budge an inch, other than a slight move that might have blocked her view.

Mavis pushed past me and jabbed at the bulletin board. "Bloody hell. Has everyone in this company gone barking mad?" She turned and stared at me with narrowed eyes and pinched nostrils. "Perhaps you'd like to explain how you got yourself into the first cast for Austin's ballet."

I kept my face a perfect blank. "I'll be delighted to discuss why you lost top billing. Perhaps it had something to do with your conversation with Ron this morning."

She put clenched hands on her bony hips. "You are beyond mad. You're the one who was politicking with Ron. Not me."

My heart beat faster. "How, exactly, could you know that unless you were there yourself?"

Mavis pressed her lips into a most unpleasant sneer. "I have friends in high places. This ballet will do your sorry reputation no good, of course. The choreography stinks, as does everything else in this foul place."

She'd made some good points. Chief among them was her assessment of

Austin's ballet. It was indeed terrible, and if I had the chance, I'd graciously allow someone else to take my role. However, her comment about American Ballet Company being stinky was unwarranted. If I let her get away with insulting the company, the situation between us would get worse, not better.

I sniffed loudly. "If anything around here stinks, I believe it's you. That powder you spilled all over the floor nearly wiped out half the company."

Her sallow cheeks flushed red. "My fans send me gifts all the time." She looked briefly at Olivia, to indicate my friend was also a target of her disdain. "Jealousy is such an ugly emotion. You couldn't possibly dislike me more than I despise you. So keep away from me. Far away."

I planted my feet and crossed my arms. "For once we're in agreement. If I had my way, I'd put the Atlantic Ocean between us."

Mavis threw the ends of her silk scarf behind her. "And I know why. You can't hack the competition. You should quit now. Before someone does it for you."

"Is that a threat?" I pointed to the crowd of dancers. "We do have witnesses."

She looked down her nose. "I'm *Mavis Ferris*, you twit. I don't have to make threats. Once this bloody gig is over I'm headed to Paris, where they understand art." She pivoted and pointed to Ann's bright red flyer. "I've heard the charming Ann Rothman is your stepmother. Maybe she can help you lose a few of those extra pounds. I'm rather busy, but if you want, I'll give you a few tips."

Her words elicited a gasp from those close enough to hear. There was no more devastating insult than to be called fat.

Except for one. There was one insult that trumped fat. "I hope you won't be too busy to celebrate your fortieth birthday. Or was that two years ago? You've given so many different dates for that happy event."

She stalked away to the sound of smothered laughter. Relieved of her presence, I snapped a picture of the schedule and retreated to the bathroom to examine it in private. Previously, I had been left out of the cast of *Precious Metals*, a ballet I dearly loved. Mavis, of course, had scored the prized part of Golden Lady. In another place and time, I would have been thrilled to dance the role of Silver Maiden. But not when my prop was the scrolled piece of metal that had been used to kill Pavel. I suspected Ron was behind this casting decision. Audiences would undoubtedly show up in droves to see a murder suspect dance while wielding a copy of the murder weapon.

That wasn't all. Ron had made good on his promise to cast me in a starring role in many ballets. Overnight, my rehearsal schedule had become brutally taxing. A headache bloomed behind my eyes and my knees started throbbing, in tense anticipation of the workout they'd be getting in the coming weeks. Before leaving the bathroom I tossed back two Excedrin with a black coffee chaser. With so many worries competing for attention, I didn't give a second thought about the risk of burning a hole in my stomach.

The next rehearsal was for *Les Sylphides.* This Romantic ballet, by the legendary Mikhail Fokine, was easy to dance, but difficult to dance well. It's without technical tricks, and instead demands perfect grace, control, musicality, and lightness. It also has approximately ten billion *bourrées,* tiny steps on pointe, which require as much effort as many more bravura moves.

Mavis was sitting in a corner, nibbling on carrot sticks, when I entered the rehearsal. She resumed her attack, presumably energized by the twenty-five calories she'd ingested. Her lips curved upward, but the smile never reached her marble-hard eyes. "One wrong move and I will bury you. Not the other way around."

I put a hand over my mouth to cover a fake yawn. "You really have been around forever. No one falls for that kind of intimidation anymore. Unless you mean it literally, in which case I'm the last person you should be confiding in."

Ironically, Mavis's monster talent for intimidation earned her the sort of respect and deference that kindness rarely inspired. The tendency to grovel in the face of meanness probably occurs in other workplaces, but it is endemic in ballet, where the actual age, along with the emotional age, of many dancers is at the high school level.

Olivia waited for Mavis to stalk off before she joined me. "I know you're upset with Mavis. But you should be happy with all the roles you're dancing."

My face burned. "I'd be a lot happier if it was my dancing that got me top billing."

"Try to avoid complete paranoia. So many dancers have been injured; it makes sense they've turned to you to fill in. You know all the steps, and you're a freaking phenom on stage." She sighed. "I wish it were me."

I tried to relax. "Thanks for the vote of confidence. But now that you mention it, it is weird that so many have gotten hurt this season."

Although no one was close enough to hear us, she kept her voice to a whisper. "Yeah. But no guys. All women."

I winced. "Except for Pavel."

"Maybe let's change the subject." She opened a bag of candy and chewed on a few gummies. "Who cares why you got those roles? The important thing is you're dancing the parts you love. I'd do anything to be in your place." A smile broke through her sober expression. "I'd be over the moon, even if all I got was a starring role in Austin's ballet."

My mood lightened in tandem with Olivia's. "I'm going to suggest he title it *A Study in Forty Thumbs and Zero Talent.*"

Olivia laughed. "Make it *A Study in Forty Winks.* Unless the composer adds a few cymbal crashes, the snoring might overshadow the music."

With several minutes to spare before the rehearsal began, I checked my silenced phone for missed messages. One was from my father, who confirmed our dinner plans for the evening. Barbara left two messages. The first informed me I would need moral support during dinner and had therefore invited herself. The second message bore the unwelcome news that her new boyfriend also was coming, which suggested her relationship with the handsome and charming Philip was improving.

Zachary Mitchell texted to say he'd pick me up at seven-thirty. Last, but certainly not least, homicide detective Jonah Sobol offered to meet me at Café Figaro after rehearsal. I refused his invitation with some regret and resigned myself to an evening with a most awkward combination of people.

I hadn't been this much in demand since I'd been accused of murder.

As one grueling rehearsal succeeded another, I cataloged the wear and tear on my battered body. At the end of a typical day, most of us were limp and exhausted and ready for our glamorous nightlife: ice packs and/or heating pads, carefully calibrated portions of food, and as much sleep as we could get. However, even if I'd been able to spend the day snoozing, I still wouldn't have felt good about the prospect of a dinner party that included my father, his current wife, my mother, her current boyfriend, and Dr. Zachary Mitchell, the man my parents hoped I'd marry.

During a brief break in the middle of a rehearsal for *Symphonic Moods,* I tried to explain how I felt to Olivia. "Is it weird I still hesitate to refer to Zach as my boyfriend? And even though he's met my parents multiple times, I'm not sure I want him to come tonight."

Olivia looked serious. "I have no problem referring to Horace as my boyfriend. So, yeah, I do think it's weird. And what do your parents have to do with how you feel about Zach?"

It was a good question to which I had no easy answer. "If you knew my parents better, you'd understand. My mother's been planning my wedding to Zach since the day we met."

Olivia polished off a bagel with cream cheese and rooted around in her dance bag for more food. I was envious of her ability to stuff herself without gaining a pound. At the same time, I knew all too well there were many ways to eat without gaining weight, and in the dance world, few of them are related to a super-charged metabolism. But while Olivia and I discussed, without filters, our relationships with men, our relationship with food was still too intimate a topic for the short period of time we'd been friends.

She looked thoughtfully at an apple and a chocolate bar and chose the chocolate. "I'm not sure your mother's feelings are the most important element in this equation. Does Zach want to get married again? Has he said how he feels? Because it sounds as if you have no idea how you feel."

I drained the last dregs of my black coffee. "I have no idea how Zach feels about a potential long-term relationship. He's divorced, and his relationship with his ex-wife seems a bit complicated. I've never even met his daughter. And, as you've guessed, I also don't know how I feel about it."

Olivia gave me a quizzical look. "I know you're close with both your parents, which is why your worries about them seem out of character."

I rolled my eyes. "Out of character for me or for them? Because my extremely modern, totally feminist, and forward-thinking parents can be surprisingly retro in their attitudes toward Melissa and me."

Olivia stood up and bent her knees in a deep *plié*. "I don't think I've ever met your sister. What's she like?"

This was not an easy question to answer. "I'll give you the short version. Melissa graduated from Brown and got her doctorate in philosophy from Harvard. She married a doctor and had two kids as perfect as she is. She's a bestselling author and the president of every socially conscious group in her enlightened corner of suburban New Jersey. In brief, she's perfect in every way."

Olivia adjusted her pointe shoes. "She sounds awful. I don't think I'd like her at all."

I shook my head. "I know what you're thinking. But Melissa is the nicest, most sympathetic, and best person I know. When I say she's perfect, I'm not kidding."

As soon as the words were out of my mouth, I mentally smacked myself in the head. When Savannah began her PR campaign against me, I'd shrugged off Melissa's many offers of help and downplayed my distress. It was time, however, to engage the smartest person I knew. Two seconds after my SOS message, she texted back.

See you at dinner. xoxo Bernie

Bernie was the code name she'd used the last time we conspired together. It was Melissa's way of saying she was ready to do battle.

Chapter Ten

Ballet is a dance executed by the human soul.
—Alexander Pushkin

O nce again, Austin's rehearsal was the last of the day. Despite the persistent Arctic chill that held New York City hostage, the studio was hot, and the windows were steamed over. It was an open rehearsal, which explained why it was the only one on the schedule that didn't get postponed or shortened. At open rehearsals invited guests, usually people who have donated large sums of money to the company, were allowed to attend. Their chairs lined the perimeter of the room, and I recognized quite a few faces from gala events and charity auctions. The more money they donated, the more access they had to events like this open rehearsal. It was our job to make sure they'd be back for more.

We pretended to ignore the audience and acted as if no one was watching our every move. In reality, we danced as if we were onstage, which is what dancers call "full out." Normally, we would give ourselves breaks by "marking" the steps. But we're always in the business of fundraising, and if shredding our muscles meant more money for the company, it was our responsibility to grind away until the only thing left of us was a puddle of sweat.

At our first rehearsal, Austin was highly critical of the soloists, but during this session, he targeted the younger dancers. Janelle, our talented apprentice, he completely ignored. At the halfway point, Austin once again had a fit over the position of our thumbs. With the fate of the free world hanging in the balance, I managed to execute a series of pirouettes and jumps with my thumbs in place, but Austin simply turned away from me and excoriated poor Olivia.

Mavis, of course, Austin deemed perfect. It was sickening to see him fawn over her. I was certain he was angling to get a commission to choreograph in London. Given the low level of talent Austin had exhibited thus far, it was more likely the New York City Transit Authority would decrease the price of a subway ride before another dance company would invite Austin to join them.

It pained me to admit this, but objectively speaking, Mavis was close to flawless. No one in her right mind could complain about the British dancer's skill and professionalism. She seemed to learn the movements even before Austin showed them, and she executed each step with precision and conviction. Mavis didn't have the freedom and flair of American Ballet Company dancers, but she had a finely tuned technique that served her nearly as well. I needed every ounce of willpower to keep up with her unflagging energy.

As I approached the furthest limits of my endurance, the session ended. When Austin dismissed us, the guests rose to their feet and applauded. While we dancers always applaud the teacher and pianist, we rarely do so for a nitpicking, second-rate choreographer. Nevertheless, we followed the guests' example. We didn't want to seem ungracious. Austin preened and bowed. Mavis curtseyed and blew kisses, acting as if the applause were for her alone. Which, curse her, it might have been.

Olivia turned to me and pretended to stick a finger down her throat, the universal signal of disdain that is popular with dancers of all ages. I shook my head slightly, to warn her that one of the invited guests, Jonathan Llewellyn Franklin IV, was headed in our direction.

Jonathan was in his mid-fifties but projected a younger and hipper vibe than the typical patron of the arts. Although not bad looking, he had a half-cooked look about him, as if his face needed more time to evolve into adult features from its fetal beginnings. He made up for his protruding eyes and receding chin with a smooth tan, black leather jacket, and space-age sneakers that whispered, *money, money, money* with every step he took.

Jonathan applauded longer than anyone else. He watched Mavis curtsey and then kissed her hand, to her evident delight. As she murmured something British and well-bred, Jonathan turned to Austin and said, "Fantastic work! Really genius. And this lovely dancer," Jonathan dropped Mavis's hand, walked over to Olivia, and put a proprietary hand on my friend's shoulder, "she is a breath of fresh air."

Unsure of how to respond to Jonathan's praise of his scapegoated dancer, Austin opened his mouth and then forgot to close it. After an awkward silence, he said, "Yes. Er, yes. Her talent is still a bit raw." He looked nervously at Mavis's glower and told Jonathan, "But I don't know what I'd do without this, er, prima ballerina. She is my inspiration."

Austin awkwardly approached Mavis. I think he was going to attempt a hand kiss, à la Jonathan, but Mavis's furious expression stopped him dead.

Jonathan persisted in his pursuit of Olivia. He placed his other hand on her shoulder, rudely forcing her to face him. He told Austin, as if Olivia weren't there, "I haven't officially met this pretty lady, but I'd love to get the chance to know her better."

Olivia ducked a bit, to get away from him, but like a prisoner in a very adult version of London Bridges, she found herself caught between the two men.

Austin said with a smirk, "I think that can be arranged."

Olivia was silent and her face was red, not from exertion, but from embarrassment. Since she seemed incapable of speech I, as her self-appointed guardian, spoke for her.

"I believe Olivia may be otherwise engaged."

Jonathan looked smug. "As Austin said, all things can be…arranged." He finally addressed Olivia directly. "You must allow me to tell you how much I admire your"—he stepped back and looked her up and down—"dancing."

Seemingly oblivious to the tension he'd caused, Jonathan waved a breezy goodbye and departed.

There was enough emotion in the room to blow out the windows. In an attempt to prevent the combustive situation from devolving into an international incident on par with the sinking of the *Lusitania,* I endeavored to interject some common sense into the conversation. "No one should take Jonathan too seriously. A few months ago, at the gala, he was all over Zarina Devereaux. At the New Year's Eve party, it was Kerry."

When I mentioned Kerry, I didn't realize how close she was to us. She alerted me to her presence with a furious look and said, "I was never involved with Jonathan. Quit repeating dressing room gossip."

I was slightly less abashed than I would have been had I named someone else. "I'm sorry, Kerry, if I misspoke. You, of course, are an expert in repeating idle gossip and ruining a person's reputation."

Daniel stepped in. "The point Leah is trying to make is that Jonathan has a very short attention span. This week it's Olivia. If she's not interested—"

"I'm not!" shouted Olivia.

"Okay," Daniel said equably. "Since Olivia's not interested, next week it'll be someone else. Let's not slit our ankles and cha-cha to death over this non-issue."

I put my arm around Olivia before answering Daniel. "You're right, of course, but this guy's attitude is obnoxious. Someone should inform him buying costumes for the ballet doesn't mean he can buy us."

Olivia's fury did not abate. "Who does he think he is? The Sun King?" She was referring to the French monarch, King Louis XIV, who invented the steps for what would later evolve into ballet.

I pulled her aside and spoke in a low voice. "Forget Jonathan. His only talent is his gift for inheriting money."

Olivia crossed her arms. "He's lucky Horace left early. Horace would have done a *grand battement* right between his eyes." She took out a hand towel and scrubbed her shoulder where Jonathan had touched her.

I bent down to untie the ribbons on my pointe shoes, giving myself some time to come up with a diplomatic response. Olivia's new boyfriend was beautiful, talented, and sexy, but not warm or loyal or smart. Horace was one of the first to turn against me last season, using our slight acquaintance to pretend he knew more about me than others did.

It's never easy, and rarely helpful, to tell a friend her boyfriend is a jerk.

An unfaithful jerk. But if I told Olivia my opinion of Horace, she might think I held a grudge against him. I did, of course, but that didn't make my assessment of his character any less valid.

Perhaps Olivia would come to her senses about Horace without my help. If Olivia were still friendly with Kerry, she'd have a better understanding of the kind of guy he was. Kerry and Horace were together for several months before he dumped her for Olivia. Maybe that was why Kerry despised Olivia so much.

The day had been packed with more drama than a PBS miniseries, and I was not anxious to raise the temperature any higher. I raised my eyebrows at Olivia and looked meaningfully in Austin's direction. I didn't want my friend to get on the wrong side of a political battle.

"Forget about Horace. He's not the right person for this situation. I'll talk to…" I paused, not sure who would be willing to curb Jonathan. Despite the progress the #MeToo movement had made in the dance world, we remained extremely vulnerable to abuse. Finally, I said, "I'll talk to Madame Maksimova. She'll know what to do."

Olivia flushed a deeper red. "No. You don't have to do that. Forget it. No big deal. No need to drag Madame M into this. I can handle it myself."

"You may think you can handle it alone, but it's complicated. This can easily get out of hand and end in a series of he-said/she-said accusations. If that happens, you can't win. Jonathan is as powerful as he's creepy. Let me talk to Madame. She won't be happy to hear that one of our donors is sexually plowing his way through the corps de ballet like Attila the Hun rampaging through Rome."

Daniel, who had been a silent partner to the latter part of our conversation, laughed before resuming his serious tone. "Don't do it, Leah. You won't help Olivia, you won't help Madame, and you certainly won't help yourself."

I watched him go through his post-rehearsal routine, untangling his muscles on a foam roller. Like me, he needed time to cool down as well as warm up.

I poked him. "How do you know? And more importantly, what do you know? I thought I'd heard every possible bit of gossip about Jonathan

Llewellyn Franklin IV."

Daniel zipped his bag, got to his feet, and lightly kissed me on the cheek. "I hate to echo Kerry, but I too think you're getting your gossip from the wrong people. My sources are a lot better." He lowered his voice to a whisper. "And my sources say that Jonathan will be named the acting artistic director."

I laughed out of sheer nervousness. "I don't believe it. How can the board hire someone with no background in ballet, other than giving money to the company? Even the dumbest of them knows better than to do something like that."

"Madame is going to be named the acting ballet mistress in chief. That's the one bit of good news." Daniel hoisted his dance bag over his shoulder. "I have to say, I'm getting out just in time. Things have been so weird and depressing, I'm not sure I'll even miss being with the company." He looked around to check once again no one could overhear him. "Jonathan has experience as a producer, although not with classical dance. He's got Broadway and Off-Broadway credits. The stuffed shirts on the board and the people at Artistic Solutions love his law degree from Yale. It's only temporary, of course. Really rich people don't like full-time commitments."

I swallowed hard to quash the sudden lump in my throat. "This wouldn't have happened if Pavel hadn't died. Hadn't been murdered."

Daniel shot me a warning look. "I suggest you stop talking."

I looked around at the nearly empty studio. "Why? You and Olivia aren't going to rat me out."

Daniel was wary. "I would never rat you out. But don't get in the habit of speaking your mind. It's a bad move under any circumstances."

I was sick of watching every word that came out of my mouth. "We now know Jonathan had an excellent motive to get rid of Pavel. That's worth talking about."

Daniel was impatient. "Right. But this is not the place to have that conversation."

Olivia listened intently. When Daniel was done talking, she left the room the same way she did at Austin's first rehearsal—without a backward glance or a single word.

Chapter Eleven

Dance every performance as if it were your last.
—Erik Bruhn

Daniel's gossip was troubling, if not downright terrifying. In the past, the post of artistic director of American Ballet Company had been held by giants of the dance world. The only choice worse than Jonathan Llewellyn Franklin IV would have been Ron Wieder. Or Austin Dworkin.

When I joined ABC at the age of seventeen, the legendary René Vernier was the chief ballet master, choreographer, and artistic director. He would have turned up his Gallic nose at the thought of hiring Artistic Solutions to help manage the company he'd remade in his image. He loved my dancing, which was no surprise since he and Madame trained me. I still missed him. Long after he left, I still heard his voice in my mind before every performance.

While dreaming of the past, I completely lost track of the time. It wasn't until I got to the dressing room that I realized I had a scant hour before Zach came to pick me up for my highly blended family dinner. I stripped off my sweaty dance gear and raced home but didn't break any speed records on the five-story climb to my apartment. My knees demanded a more leisurely pace and usually insisted on some rest when I got to the third floor, which was one of the reasons I feared Ann's evaluation of my physical fitness.

When I finally reached my tiny apartment I showered, slathered on some makeup, and faced the first challenge of the evening: what to wear? The original invitation was from Dad and Ann, but when the roster of participants expanded to include Barbara and her boyfriend, the list of potential restaurants, as well as appropriate attire, expanded exponentially.

As I scanned the closet for an outfit I knew Zach liked, he texted to say he'd be late and would meet me at whatever restaurant we chose. As an emergency room physician, he always had a good excuse to be late or not show up at all. In my opinion, no one needed an excuse to avoid the hike to my apartment. Or an evening with my parents and their odd-couple partners. Thankfully, my sister would be there as well. Melissa would help ease any awkward moments.

I arrived at Dad's apartment five minutes after the appointed time, figuring I wouldn't have to wait more than thirty minutes for my perpetually late mother. But Barbara surprised me. She was already ensconced in a shabby but comfortable chair that was familiar to me from the time before she and Dad got divorced.

Next to her, a man with hair so dark it looked polished rose gracefully to his feet. "Lovely to see you again, Leah." His manner was so formal, I half expected him to click his heels and bow, but he merely shook my hand with his clammy palm and chilly fingers. "I'm delighted we have the opportunity to get to know each other better. Though I do feel as if I know you well, having seen you perform many times."

Barbara looked fondly at him. "Philip is quite the balletomane. It's a big reason we connected."

Philip took Barbara's hand and pressed his lips against it. The gesture reminded me of Jonathan, another guy I didn't trust. A slight movement and clattering sound from the drinks table interrupted their tender moment. Dad's face was redder than the drink he was pouring. It was a bottle of Malbec, Mom's favorite wine. Whether his distress was due to Philip's attention to Barbara, or anxiety about me, was not immediately clear.

Barbara's boyfriend was as different from my father as Ann was from my mother. Philip was charming, suave, stylish, and a hand-kisser. Dad looked exactly like the philosophy professor he was—bookish, kind, and partial to rumpled shirts and ill-fitting jackets. My father was more likely to turn cartwheels than kiss a woman's hand.

I hugged Dad and Barbara and waved a greeting in Ann's direction. He offered me a drink, but I declined in favor of a glass of water.

Ann nodded approvingly at my choice. "I can put some vitamin powder in the water that will make you feel like a million bucks."

I'd had some experience with Ann's ability to turn a refreshing glass of water into sewage sludge, and I declined the offer. She shrugged but didn't take the refusal personally. I suspected she'd given up on me, which under other circumstances would have been a welcome development. However, now that she was a member of the Artistic Solutions team, I was less complacent about her resigned stance regarding my aversion to her pills and potions.

Ann's attitude wasn't the only new thing about her. For as long as I'd known her, she'd favored yoga pants, sneakers, and a face bare of makeup. That night, however, she was clad in tight black jeans, a silk shirt, mascara, and lipstick. I glanced at my father, but he seemed abstracted. Perhaps he was thinking about Schopenhauer. That often gave him a headache.

Although I had steeled myself to a long debate over where we were going to eat, Dad forestalled any argument by telling us he'd made reservations at Palmyra.

My mother was not pleased. "Really, Jeremy! I think that's extraordinarily insensitive of you."

Dad looked confused. "I thought you liked Palmyra. That's why I picked it."

Barbara set her lips in a straight line and gazed meaningfully at him. "Don't you remember the last time we were there? I still have very painful memories of that night. And I'm sure Leah feels the same way."

Dad looked at me. "How do you feel, Leah? I can make reservations someplace else if you want. I'll call Melissa and tell her of the change in plans."

I gave him a hug. "No worries, Dad. Palmyra is fine."

He breathed a sigh of relief. "In that case, let's go." He picked up a small overnight bag and explained, "I'm spending a few days with Melissa and

David. Can't wait to see Ariel and Benjamin. They're growing up so fast."

Ann said, "I feel terrible I can't go too."

As we headed uptown, Barbara explained in a low voice to Philip that the last time we were all at Palmyra I was facing murder charges.

That scary time ended several months ago, but Barbara was right. I thought I'd be fine, but as we entered the restaurant my heart started beating with uncomfortable intensity. Perhaps I wouldn't have been so emotional if weren't for Pavel's death and Savannah's cruel accusations. Her relentless criticisms and innuendoes had hurt me more than I wanted to admit. They reminded me of the last time I faced public censure.

My sister and her husband were already seated when we arrived. Once settled at our table, Dad leaned over and asked me, "Where's the good doctor? I thought Zachary was joining us."

"He's still at the hospital. He said he'll get here as soon as he can, which I can tell you from experience might not be until after we've left."

Barbara gave a small, self-satisfied smile. "As Melissa well knows, a doctor's wife has to get used to irregular hours. Luckily, your whole life is a tangle of irregular hours. You and Zach are a perfect couple."

I had no immediate desire to fulfill Barbara's dearest wish, which was my marriage to Zach. Nothing in the last few months had dented her conviction that we were meant for each other, although she did occasionally ask me about Jonah, whom she called "that detective." She liked Jonah well enough, but it's tough for a cop to compete with a doctor in my hyper-educated, hyper-accomplished family.

As soon as the waiter took our order I turned to Dad and Ann. Waiting for coffee and dessert might have been a less awkward time to address the real reason I wanted us to meet, but I cared more about getting answers than I did about their digestive processes.

I attempted a pleasant tone. "I have to tell you, Ann, I was pretty surprised to see you walk into rehearsal. Why on earth didn't you tell me you'd taken this job that would so directly affect me?"

Ann let Dad speak for her. He had a pleased look on his face. "That was

Ann's idea. She thought you'd really get a kick out of the surprise."

Barbara's wineglass did not shatter when she slammed it into the table, but her composure did. "In my opinion, it was quite thoughtless. How would you like it if I showed up at your job, and your supervisor explained that I'd be evaluating your effectiveness? How charming would you find that situation?"

Dad sputtered. "As usual, Barbara, you've let your emotions get in the way. And that's a terrible analogy. You don't know anything about what I do. Ann is an expert in her field."

Barbara didn't back down. "With all due respect to Ann, I'm not convinced she is capable of judging Leah, or any other ballerina."

Dad came very close to raising his voice. "You don't understand Ann's position, because your mode of thinking is flawed. You should not believe a proposition when there are no grounds for supposing it true."

She fixed him with a steely glare. "Don't you dare quote Bertrand Russell to me! I'm not one of your philosophy students."

Dad didn't flinch. "Ann can help Leah, and all the other dancers, prevent injury. Someone needs to do something, since according to Leah, several dancers are on disability."

While he spoke, Ann meditatively chewed on one of her vitamins. In her usual phlegmatic manner, she said, "The people at Artistic Solutions are quite confident in my abilities, and that's all that matters. Injured dancers hurt the bottom line. And frankly, I can't see that it makes much difference when Leah found out. Like Jeremy said, we thought it would be a nice surprise. It's too bad she didn't take it that way."

I'd practiced many times what I would say during this conversation, but the dialogue I'd written in my head failed to play out in real life the way it had in my imagination. My father's support of his wife I expected. Ann's clever reversal, blaming me for my failure to appreciate her nice surprise, I did not.

I ignored Ann and concentrated on my father. "I appreciate the fact that you didn't realize how I might feel. But think about it now. Ann is going to be evaluating me, which may have a profound effect on my future with the company. Surely you can see that this is a major problem for both of us."

Dad crinkled his forehead. "I'm not sure I understand you, sweetheart. No matter what, Ann will always do the right thing."

Melissa intervened. "Right or wrong, she should never have accepted the position. But now that she has, she is facing a classic moral dilemma."

Ann spoke with mild interest. "How so?"

For my father's sake, I tamped down the hostility. "This is how your new job presents us with a dilemma. If you don't give me a good evaluation, I will never speak to you again. If you do give me a good evaluation, but only because we're"—I struggled with the next few words but managed to choke them out—"related by marriage, then you will have broken trust with your employers. People in the company will think it's favoritism." Looking at Dad, I said, "Frankly, I'm baffled that you've failed to understand the ethical ramifications of Ann's job." I was tempted to add a sarcastic comment regarding the philosophy of morality, which was his specialty, but refrained.

The waiter returned with a bottle of wine. This time I accepted the drink. The night was already a nightmare. My father immediately signaled for another bottle.

Dad sipped from his wine while Ann stirred a packet of powder into her cup of hot water. It looked like dirt and smelled like camphor. He gave me a reassuring look. "I think this is all a big misunderstanding. Ann has been hired as a health and wellness coach. I thought you'd be pleased." He turned to Ann. "What's this about evaluations? I thought you were going to be working with the dancers to help prevent injuries."

Ann spoke to a spot on the table. "That was the original idea. Then I was asked to take an expanded role. I couldn't easily refuse the higher-level position."

Barbara was terse. "Conveniently, you have employed the passive tense in your answer." Because Ann did not appear to understand this insult, Barbara hammered home her grammatical and moral point. "Stop equivocating and tell us who offered you this higher-level position."

Philip's interjection surprised all of us. "Is that really important? Pavel

Baron is dead. What difference does it make who introduced Ann to him?"

Barbara turned to him in astonishment. "I think it's quite relevant. The relationship between Ann and Leah is the issue here."

She leaned across the table, a Viking ship ready to head into dangerous waters. "Let me remind you the police don't know who killed Pavel. Thanks to Savannah Collier's campaign against Leah, her position is already difficult. I will not allow you to make it worse."

Before Ann could respond Philip again broke in. "If that's the case, perhaps Ann can help Leah. It sounds as if she could use some support."

Zachary Mitchell entered the restaurant at that fraught moment. He seemed unaware of the tense mood, kissing me and Barbara, and greeting Dad, Ann, Melissa, and David with an easygoing smile. He extended a hand to Barbara's boyfriend. "You must be Philip. Nice to meet you."

Philip, who had watched our back-and-forth conversation like a spectator at a close tennis match, greeted Zachary with his customary formal politeness, although he could not repress a sigh of relief. The arrival of our food provided another distraction, which everyone welcomed except for Barbara and me. We had ordered the same minimalist meal, although my mother mostly ignored the food in favor of the wine. I, however, was starving and ate every scrap of kale. When I was done, I moved the breadbasket to the other end of the table. I was still hungry and didn't trust myself to resist the siren song of carbohydrates.

Unencumbered by an appetite, my mother did not let any concerns about diplomacy slow her down. She fixed Ann with a stare powerful enough to pinion her to the banquette. "I'm still waiting for your answer. But maybe we should start over. To whom do you report now that Pavel is dead?"

Ann looked at Dad, who was no help. He appeared as interested in his lasagna as he was in his wife's answer. She muttered, "My role is new. The details are still being ironed out." She stopped talking, shook her head, and drained the rest of the muddy-looking fluid from her glass.

I was bewildered by her refusal to answer us. "Surely you're not working in a vacuum. Who's your immediate boss?"

Two vertical lines appeared inside her eyebrows, but she continued her silence.

Finally, when Ann didn't answer, Dad prodded her. "Tell them about what happened to your practice. I don't think Barbara or Leah understands the situation."

Ann was not happy, but with everyone's eyes upon her, she had no choice but to respond. Unlike my high-strung mother, she rarely betrayed emotion, but on this occasion, her voice wavered, and the words came with obvious difficulty. "My practice wasn't doing well. It wasn't just me. All the partners were struggling, and we had been for a while. The job offer from Artistic Solutions came at a critical moment, and I, well, I didn't hesitate to take it."

I tried to sound sympathetic. "That is unfortunate, Ann. But you haven't responded to either of Barbara's questions. What we—what I—want to know, is who you currently report to and whose idea it was to have you evaluate the dancers."

I then hit her with the real reason behind my queries. "These questions are a lot more imperative now than they were before Pavel was murdered. Savannah told me you and Pavel spoke nearly every day. You might know something that will aid in finding his murderer."

Ann ignored my reference to Pavel. "I report to Ron Wieder. It was his idea to have me evaluate the dancers. He came up with some metric he had his people work up at Artistic Solutions. He sold the idea to Pavel. I didn't like it any more than you do."

Barbara was colder than the February weather that howled outside. "If you don't like it, then quit."

Dad's tone matched Barbara's in frostiness. "Barbara, that's enough. I don't like your attitude or your insinuations about my wife."

Barbara was defiant. "Jeremy, if I have to choose between your wife and our daughter, I don't have to think long about who to pick. But maybe you do."

I broke the furious silence that followed. "Once again, we all need to remember there's a lot more at stake than Ann's gig at Artistic Solutions. Savannah Collier has been trashing me, implying I had a hand in Pavel's murder. So far, she's not impressed the police with her accusations, but

I need to stay at least two steps ahead of her. That's why I need to know Ann's position in relation to the people at AS. Because Pavel is dead. And that changes everything."

Chapter Twelve

A dance performance is rather like going out into a battlefield.
—Yamini Krishnamurthy

The icy winds barreling down Amsterdam Avenue were less frosty than the atmosphere inside Palmyra restaurant. My sister and her husband, my parents and their current partners, and Zach and I finished eating in uneasy silence. When the waiter cleared the table and asked if anyone wanted coffee, Philip looked longingly at the dessert menu. He did not, however, have the necessary grit to challenge Barbara, who informed us that she was going to forego coffee and dessert for the first time in her life.

That statement was not completely accurate. My mother, who taught me all too well, regards with horror any food more calorie-laden than a celery stick. On the other hand, no one could challenge her declaration that she drank coffee at every meal. Not only does my mother drink it at every meal, much of the time it is her meal.

Barbara rose to her feet and threw down her napkin as if throwing down a gauntlet. With a disdainful look in Ann's direction, she announced, "I think I'm done here." Her gaze softened when she looked at me. "I have a car coming in a few minutes. Are you and Zach ready to leave?"

Zach was quick to get to his feet, but Philip took his time, murmuring to no one in particular, "We must do this again sometime."

Melissa rose as well, but my brother-in-law was even more unwilling than Philip to skip dessert. David stayed seated and told the waiter to bring him

75

an order of tiramisu.

My sister was impatient. "Get it to go. I want to go home. Dad looks exhausted. The kids are really excited about his visit, and they're sure to get him up at sunrise."

With a sour look, David complied. Ann again professed regret at her inability to visit with them and the grandkids, a sentiment none of us took at face value. My sister smiled slightly. She put her thumb to her ear and pinky to her mouth, to let me know she'd call me later.

Despite the miserable weather, Barbara waited outside the restaurant to snatch a few puffs of a cigarette. When the car pulled up she tossed the butt, and Zach and I scrambled into the cab to escape a sudden icy downpour of sleet mixed with snow. Philip hung back.

He reached into the car for my mother's hand. "*Cara*, I fear I must leave you here. I forgot to mention I have an important conference call with the Sydney office. I'll get myself home. Forgive me?"

Barbara's hatred of cold weather easily outweighed her passion for Philip. "There's nothing to forgive. But for heaven's sake, close the door!" He did so, but not before blowing a kiss in our general direction. I watched Philip cross the street and head to the entrance to the subway.

While Barbara gave the driver meticulous directions on her preferred route, Zach bent his mouth to my ear. "What exactly does Philip do?"

I shrugged. "No idea. Why?"

Zach whispered, "Because it's Saturday in Sydney. All the Aussies I know are way too laid back to be at a business meeting when they could be on the beach."

I had too much on my mind to think about office schedules in Sydney. "Surely there must be at least a few workaholics in Australia." As the car idled at a red light, I peered through the rear window to watch Philip. "Now, that's interesting. He crossed the street again and went back into the restaurant. Maybe you're right, and coffee and dessert were on his agenda, and not a work meeting."

Zach glanced at Barbara, who was busy with her phone. "How well does Philip know Ann?"

His question surprised me. "Not at all. They hadn't met until tonight. Surely you don't think he's having a clandestine affair with her."

Zach craned his neck as the car moved forward. "I suppose it could have been the cannoli that drew him back to Palmyra. But if I were a betting man, I wouldn't put money on it."

I put my finger to my lips as Barbara settled back into her seat. She joined us in peering through the back window. "What are you looking at?"

I turned and faced forward. "Nothing. I thought I recognized an old friend, but it was too dark to tell."

As if she were reading my mind, Barbara said, "Mark my words, That Woman is hiding something. What it is I'm not yet sure, but trust me, I'll find out."

Zach was calm and reasonable, as always. "I admire your persistence, Ms. Siderova, but how are you going to go about doing that? You may not like it, and Leah certainly doesn't like it, but Ann's employment seems completely aboveboard."

My mother sat up straighter. "Please, Zach, it's Barbara, not Ms. Siderova."

In the dim glow of a streetlamp, we saw a smile break through the tense expression on her face. "My plan could not be simpler. I'm going to contact American Ballet Company and tell them I'm writing a major article on the recent tragedy. I'll find out all there is to know about Ann if it's the last thing I do."

I was horrified at my mother's plot to stalk Ann. "Barbara, you're a fiction writer. That's never going to work."

For once, my mother incorrectly gauged how I felt. She was genuinely pleased with herself and certain I would feel the same way.

"Don't worry about a thing. You can trust me to uncover the facts. I've spent my whole life writing about character and motivation. I'll find out the truth, even if I have to excavate it with a drill. Who knows? I might uncover the murderer as well."

I cast about for a way to dissuade her. "You're crazy. Pavel's murder was no joke. I can't let you put yourself in danger."

This, of course, made Barbara even more determined. "You see, Leah, you were wrong when you said the company had no need of a mystery writer. I'll do a true-crime story about what happened. This is exciting! While I'm at the studio I'll investigate using the same techniques as Professor Romanova."

I nervously jiggled my foot, trying to expel excess energy from an overload of anxiety. "Nice try, but that's never going to work. Professor Romanova is a fictional character. A fictional character you made up." When she didn't respond, I added, "Professor Romanova's technique is to use literature to solve the crime. How is that going to work in real life? Are you going to threaten people with a recitation from *The Canterbury Tales* and hope they confess their guilt to avoid expiring from boredom?"

Barbara was shocked. "*The Canterbury Tales* is brilliant. And a hoot. I'm ashamed of you for that piece of sacrilege." Shaking her head sadly, she said, "I've failed as a mother."

I didn't debate the point, because my mother has a closer relationship with Professor Romanova than she does with the real people in her life. Instead, I argued, "The last thing the company wants is more talk about dead people."

Zach broke in. "Don't be too sure. Didn't you tell me Ron Wieder liked the fact that Savannah was trashing you, because it brought more attention to the company? Barbara's idea is way better than what Savannah is doing. I think it sounds like a win-win. You two can look out for each other."

My mother looked at him with even more approval than usual. "Yes. I'll give the company all the publicity they could desire. More importantly, I'll move the focus away from Leah. Maybe I can even turn the tables on Savannah. Give her a taste of her own medicine. Ron Weasel won't know what hit him."

I choked between laughter and despair. "You might want to remember that his name is Wieder. Not Weasel."

Barbara patted my shoulder. "I know, dear. I tried to make a joke, which I should never do. I'm not funny in real life. Only in print." She leaned forward to explain to Zach, "On the page, I'm hilarious. My detective is a scholar of medieval literature, but lately she's more into Shakespeare." She chuckled. "Did I ever tell you about her riff on Lady Macbeth? It's priceless!"

The car slowed as we arrived at Barbara's apartment building, so Zach was spared a reply. I grabbed Barbara's sleeve. "Even Ron is not going to want that much publicity about the murder. And once they hear your last name, all bets are off. There aren't many Siderovas out there. They're going to guess we're related."

Barbara didn't skip a beat. "Are you kidding me? The fact that I'm your mother will make a great story."

Zach laughed. "I'd read it, for sure."

My recent meal felt like it wanted to climb back up my throat. Was it possible that both my mother and stepmother would be following me around at work?

One glance at Barbara's determined expression and I had my answer.

Chapter Thirteen

There comes a point when you have to say what you mean, which makes you
scream louder when you dance.
—Suzanne Farrell

Two days later, Barbara showed up at American Ballet Company. This amused several of our younger company members, whose hypervigilant Ballet Mothers still followed them around, knitting legwarmers and bragging about their kids to anyone who would listen. But the joke was on them. Barbara had never been a typical stage mother. The few times she talked to me about future careers she insisted I had more talent in my head than in my feet.

When Barbara made her entrance, Olivia was the first to greet her. She'd only met my mother a few times, and Barbara doesn't love close contact. Nonetheless, my mother was clearly gratified by Olivia's embrace. To my surprise, Olivia wasn't the only one delighted to see Barbara. Several dancers, when they realized who she was, shyly asked for her autograph. Barbara couldn't have been happier.

She traversed the length of the lobby and entered the office as if she owned it. I walked in with her, although she was doing fine on her own.

Savannah was seated, which gave my small, slight mother an atypical physical advantage. Barbara looked at the younger woman, and, as if disappointed with what she saw, blinked and sighed. "I'm Barbara Siderova, here to see Ron Weasley. Please direct me to his office."

I didn't know if Barbara's mispronunciation of Ron's last name was deliberate, but I couldn't help laughing.

Savannah, appalled by this heresy, sharply corrected her. "It's Ron *Wieder.*"

Barbara was unfazed. "Very good, dear. Now direct me to his office."

Savannah was smug. "Mr. Wieder is on an important call. You'll have to wait."

Ron's power-play pleased Savannah, who seemed to feel she'd regained the upper hand.

I whispered to Barbara, "Did you bring those copies of *Troilus in Trouble?*"

She opened her bag to show me the dozen paperbacks inside. I texted Olivia: **Asap! Tell everyone B is giving away copies of new book.**

In less than three minutes, several dancers had gathered outside the glass-walled office. At my signal, Barbara got up and told Savannah, "When Mr. Wheezer is ready to see me, please let me know. I wouldn't want to keep him waiting. That would be rude."

By the time Barbara autographed five of the books, word had spread to the farthest reaches of the building. She told the crowd she wanted to interview them and put them in her next book. Then she handed out branded pencils and bookmarks, to general acclaim.

Savannah emerged from her lair and tried to get Barbara's attention, but my mother was studiedly blind to her waves and watch-tapping. It wasn't until Ms. Crandall joined Savannah that Barbara looked away from her new fans.

Ms. Crandall carried the hardcover version of Barbara's latest book and wore an expression of atypical good humor. The office manager, who was even less prone than Barbara to initiate physical contact, warmly shook my mother's hand. The rest of us fell silent before Ms. Crandall's smile. It was like seeing a gargoyle step away from its rooftop perch to wave at a float in the Macy's Day Parade.

Savannah watched the unaccustomed proceedings with her mouth slightly open as if she'd forgotten how to close it. I knew how she felt. If there were a contest to determine whether it was easier to stop a cannonball or Barbara, I wouldn't bet the farm on the cannonball. Ms. Crandall ushered Barbara back into the office. Neither of them appeared to notice Savannah, whose heavily made-up face was crimson with rage.

Olivia looked at me with respect. "I was going to mock you for having your mom here. But now that I've seen her in action, I take my hat off to you. Barbara is a force of nature. I've never seen anyone, other than our biggest donors, get a smile out of Ms. Crandall."

I continued to keep my eye on the office, but Savannah had disappeared. I texted Barbara to warn her that Savannah might be listening in. She texted back a breezy **Kk. Np**

I turned back to Olivia. "Turns out Ms. C is a huge fan. She's read all of Barbara's books multiple times. I doubt Crandall would have been moved to give the Dalai Lama that level of red-carpet treatment, unless he'd written an academic murder mystery."

Olivia peered over my shoulder. "Don't look now, but the second meanest person at ABC is right behind you, breathing fire."

Bobbie, for once, hadn't descended from the costume room to threaten the staff at Artistic Solutions. She came in search of her team of seamstresses, a group of die-hard mystery fans, who had deserted her en masse to meet Barbara.

I didn't doubt the seamstresses' adoration of my mother's writing, but I was cynical enough to question Ms. Crandall's devotion. Our office manager seemed sincere, but I had to consider the possibility that her warm welcome was inspired by her desire to annoy the Artistic Solutions' office staff. We all loathed their corporate incursions into our daily lives, but Bobbie and Ms. Crandall were even more angry, and threatened, than the rest of us. The management of the wardrobe department and the office were more vulnerable to our corporate masters than any other part of the company.

Olivia looked enviously at me. "My mother worked in a real estate office, and she used to drag me with her on Take Your Kid to Work Day. I always hated it. But I might not have minded if Barbara was the one showing me around."

I shuddered in mock horror. "I was spared that particular bit of childhood trauma. As a writer, Barbara's always worked at home. And forget about my father. I'm not sure he even knows that Take Your Kid to Work Day exists or is a thing other parents do."

Olivia did not appear to understand how frazzled I was, for she laughed again. "You'll have to keep me posted on how Take Your Mom to Work feels when you're doing it every day." A text message from her phone interrupted us, and her amused expression faded. "My wellness appointment with Ann is also a thing. I'm scheduled to see her at the end of the day. And you know what that means?"

I held up a hand to stop her. "Can we change the subject?"

Olivia regained her good humor. "It means that after all those years of being spared the boredom of going to work with your parents, you now have to work with both your mother and your stepmother. That's hilarious."

I rooted around in my dance bag. "And now you know why I've decided to take Excedrin for my headache instead of Advil for my muscles."

Olivia became more sympathetic. "If it was me, I'd definitely opt for the Excedrin. Working with Austin is all the reason you need to prioritize headache relief."

"Good point. Given the way rehearsals have been going, I should have brought the economy-sized bottle."

She took the bottle from me and shook two tablets into her hand. "I agree. His face should be on every label. They'd sell a million tablets right here at ABC."

I looked anxiously at Olivia. "Speaking of major headaches, have you been able to avoid any more awkward encounters with Jonathan? I'm worried about you."

Olivia didn't appear to hear me. She was distracted by another text, and by the time she finished tapping the rehearsal had begun.

I took a few quick chugs from my water bottle and joined Daniel, who was marking through our pas de deux. Most of Austin's choreography wasn't technically challenging, but Daniel and I had a few tricky lifts that depended, as all lifts do, on perfect timing. He stood behind me, placed his hands on my waist, and swung me in the air. At the very top of the lift, I arched backward and extended both legs. He briefly let me go on the way down, and then caught me and turned me upside down. A split-second hesitation on the part of either of us would be dangerous for both of us. We did it twice. No problem, other than a dull ache where he caught me. From the audience's perspective, it would look as if I were flying. From my perspective, it would add a few more areas of intense body pain.

Daniel grabbed a towel to wipe the sweat from his face and arms. He kindly did not mention the extra weight he had to carry. "Not bad. Give me a minute and we'll do it again."

The moment we ceded the small area where we'd been practicing, Horace and Mavis took over. Not content with the modest amount of real estate we'd used, they pushed everyone else out of the way as well. The evicted dancers were mostly junior members, who respectfully retreated to the edges of the studio. When the two paused to regroup, Horace drew Mavis close, in an unchoreographed embrace. Olivia studiedly ignored them. I hoped she wasn't too heartbroken over her boyfriend's sudden desertion.

Kerry was less circumspect than Olivia. At the sight of Horace embracing yet another woman, Kerry practically ran them over in her eagerness to demonstrate how she and Max, her newest partner, were better than they. It was clear Kerry's friendship with Mavis, which had been predicated on self-interest and not affection, had frayed badly.

Although Kerry smiled at Max and was lavish in her praise, her off-stage resentment of him was an open secret. Max was an exciting new dancer, who'd been getting rave reviews for his dancing, as well as for his outreach to young Black dancers. Unless someone put a gun to her head, or threatened her supply of illegal diet pills, Kerry wouldn't lift a finger for another human being.

I was happy to have an excuse to avoid further repetitions of the lift and was practicing pirouettes when Jonathan unexpectedly entered the studio. The atmosphere in the room, which had been chatty and casual, instantly became formal and careful. Jonathan walked with a purposeful stride in my direction. I smiled pleasantly at him, but he looked at me in the way people do when they don't really see you. He kept going until he reached the corner of the studio where Olivia was stitching ribbons to her pointe shoes.

His back was to me, and I couldn't hear what he said, but I clearly saw the expression on Olivia's face. It startled me. She looked teasingly at him and put out her hand. He grabbed it and drew her to her feet, pulling her close to him. And she didn't step back.

I wasn't the only one shocked by their flirtation. Austin peered nearsightedly at the pair, and Daniel, Kerry, and Mavis also watched closely. Olivia giggled at whatever Jonathan was whispering into her ear.

Kerry responded by banging her pointe shoes on the floor as if she wanted to beat them, and not the faithless men in her life, into submission. In full view of the company, both her former lovers were in hot pursuit of other women. And she couldn't even pretend a romantic involvement with Max, because her new dance partner was in a long-term relationship with a hedge fund guy.

I was stunned and worried about Olivia's sudden change of heart regarding Jonathan, but my dance partner was philosophical. "You can't blame her, Leah. She's smarter than you are." Daniel gazed pointedly at Horace and Mavis, who were standing so close together it would have taken the Jaws of Life to separate them. "Horace is doing the same thing with Mavis."

I was too distressed to be either catty or bitter. "It's one thing to hook up with someone when you're on the rebound. It's quite another to let a predatory louse like Jonathan into your life. Olivia stands to lose a lot more than she'll gain, even if she's only doing it to get back at Horace."

Daniel was unmoved by my argument. "That might be true for you. But not necessarily for Olivia. It's quite possible she's more interested in her career with the company than in teaching Horace a lesson. Plenty of people, and not only dancers, will do anything to get ahead. And anyway, how well do you even know Olivia? She hasn't been with the company for very long." He tilted his head to one side and smiled to take the sting out of his next words. "I know you miss Gabi. So do I. But you and Gabi go back a long way. I have nothing against Olivia, but the company tests people and their relationships, sometimes to the breaking point. Not everyone passes."

I struggled to answer. "Olivia stuck by me when I most needed a friend. She was too nice and too fair to follow the crowd. I value those qualities, and we ended up becoming real friends."

Daniel didn't argue. "She's young, and people change." He looked at Olivia and Jonathan and amended his statement. "Or maybe they don't change, and we simply get to know them better."

Olivia watched closely as Jonathan approached Austin, who practically genuflected at the sight of him. "And what can we do for you today, Jonathan? It's not an open rehearsal, but we'll make an exception for you."

The older man nodded. In his entire privileged life, he'd probably never found himself in a situation when people weren't willing to make an exception for him. "As a matter of fact, there is something you can do for me. I've asked this lovely lady," he pointed to Olivia, "to accompany me on some, ah, company business. I assume you have no problem letting her leave a bit early?"

Austin's lips puckered, as if he were sucking on a very sour lemon. "It's very irregular, of course, but, well, you're the boss."

Jonathan laughed and briefly put his finger to his lips. "Not yet, buddy, not yet."

He drew Olivia aside and muttered a few words to her. Horace nearly knocked Mavis off her feet as he scrambled for a better vantage point to watch the unfolding drama. Olivia ignored her former lover and resumed her place in the corps de ballet.

Without bothering to lower his tone, Jonathan said to Austin, "I figured you wouldn't mind if Olivia left early. Especially since she's only the understudy, and according to her, she's unlikely to ever get the chance to perform any of the big roles."

Austin's glasses slipped down his sweaty nose. "No! That's not true at all. I'm always looking to give a young kid a chance."

Jonathan nodded. "That's a good policy to have. Especially when you have someone as talented as Olivia. You're going to want to make sure you get her a few performances. In the big roles."

In the silence of the studio, Jonathan's unmistakable threat hung in the air. Even after he left, the tension remained.

Despite the awkward start to the rehearsal, it was business as usual once we began dancing. After about an hour, Olivia left. She paused as she got to the door, looking at Austin for permission to leave. With an expression on his face that was more a scowl than a smile, Austin waved her off.

Toward the end of the two-hour rehearsal session, Daniel and I got ready for one last repetition of our pas de deux.

I could tell Daniel was tired. So could Austin, who yapped, "Full out, people! No more marking!"

We neared the end of the duet and prepared for the lift that closed our section of the dance. Even before Daniel propelled me into the air, I could sense our timing wasn't quite right. Under my breath, I muttered the counts and hoped for the best. I tensed the muscles in my back and abdomen as tightly as I could, so that Daniel would have an easier time grabbing me midair.

Savannah burst into the studio, screeching wildly, just as Daniel was flipping me upside down. Her intrusion caused him a split-second lapse in concentration, and he hesitated before catching me. In a heroic move, he saved me from taking the full force of the fall. He lowered me to the floor and collapsed, frozen with pain. I was too shocked to realize my arm and hip were on fire.

I was the only one to minister to Daniel. Everyone else crowded around Savannah, who yelled, "They're at it again! They need to be locked up!"

An ambulance came to a screaming stop outside the window.

Savannah shuddered with theatrical intensity. "Poor Ms. Crandall! She's been attacked!"

Several girls screamed. The rest pelted Savannah with questions. She pushed them aside and approached me with her arm outstretched, pointing a fingernail lacquered in blood-red polish. "You can ask your mother what happened. She did it."

Chapter Fourteen

Dance for yourself.
—Louis Horst

W hen Savannah burst into the studio with the appalling news that Ms. Crandall had been attacked, and that Barbara was the prime suspect, a throng of screaming dancers huddled together and threatened to displace her from the center of attention. She responded to the challenge by flapping her arms and yelling even louder. Later, when I told Zach what happened, he thought the scene, for all its horror, was funny as well. I failed to see the humor in the situation. We were in shock, unnerved by the blaring sirens, Savannah's hysterics, and Daniel's collapse.

Horace put his arm around Savannah. As he murmured a few soothing words, Savannah buried her face in his shoulder and sobbed with theatrical intensity.

He patted her back. "There's nothing to be frightened of. I'm sure the police will figure out what happened. In the meantime, I'll make sure you're safe." He looked up and stared at me so intently, the force of his gaze compelled the other dancers to direct their attention to me. Following physical prompts is second nature to dancers, and I wondered, for a brief, hysterical moment, what they would do if Horace demonstrated the best way to jump off the window ledge. Probably, like the children following the Pied Piper, they would march, zombie-like, to their own deaths. Or maybe they'd test the waters by pushing me off first.

Austin, unnerved at how easily he was upstaged, squeaked ineffectually,

"People, calm down. I'll find out what's going on."

A police officer appeared in the doorway. "I'm Officer Morelli. Which one of you is Savannah Collier?"

Savannah stepped forward. "Officer, thank God you're here. There's the person you need to interrogate." Once again, she jabbed her index finger in my direction.

Officer Morelli gave her an unfriendly look. "Thank you, Ms. Collier, but I'll take it from here." She put her hands on her hips. "The first thing I want to know is why you left the office. You were supposed to stay with the others."

Savannah gasped for breath and fanned her face. "I wanted to warn everyone. No one here is safe, least of all me."

Morelli curled her lip. "If you were that worried, you would have stayed where you were. As for protecting people, that's my job." She surveyed the rest of us. "Everyone needs to take a seat. You're going to be here awhile." The policewoman's tone hardened as she looked again at Savannah. "And that includes you." She pulled up a chair and installed herself in front of us. "As you may have heard, there's been an unfortunate accident."

Savannah lost whatever composure she had left. "That was no accident! Ms. Crandall was pushed! And *her* mother did it!" Her voice rose again to hysterical heights. "That's why I ran away! The whole family is a bunch of homicidal maniacs. No wonder the mother writes about murder!"

Officer Morelli's lips tightened. "Ms. Collier. Stop screeching. This building is now a crime scene." Her New York accent thickened. "In other words, sit down and shut up."

I longed to point out the inconsistencies in Savannah's tirade, but Morelli didn't look open to parsing anything we had to say.

Everyone who wasn't already sitting quickly followed the police officer's direction. Savannah swallowed hard and looked wildly around the room. In her tight skirt, sitting on the floor would have been uncomfortable, if not impossible. She finally fixed upon the piano bench, daring the pianist to object. He did not fight her for the seat and instead used the opportunity to park himself in the middle of a group of very pretty dancers.

In a whiny voice, Savannah insisted, "I need to talk to someone in charge. I saw the whole thing. Let me talk to Detective Sobol." She looked around for Horace, the only one to have come to her aid. He ignored her appeal for sympathy and sat next to Mavis. His body was as finely chiseled as a marble statue, but his affections were not nearly as firm. Horace was endlessly willing to adopt the courage of other people's convictions.

"If you wanted to talk to Detective Sobol, you should have stayed where you were." Morelli stood up and scowled from an imposing height. "I'm in charge here. And you'll talk to me when I tell you to." Looking around at the rest of us, she said, "No one's goin' anywhere. So make yourselves comfortable."

I texted Barbara over and over, but she didn't answer. I tried calling, but the phone went immediately to voicemail. I was so worried about her I forgot about poor Daniel until his agonized attempt to sit up got my attention.

I kneeled next to him. "Can you get up if I help you? I'll tell Morelli you need a doctor."

He tried to grin. "Tell her I need a really good-looking doctor with a taste for stylish, blue-eyed male dancers. In case anyone asks."

I waved at Morelli, who reluctantly relinquished her post in front of the room. She needn't have worried anyone would rebel. Dancers are excellent at following directions.

"Officer, we need to get Daniel some help. He's badly injured."

Morelli sat back on her heels to talk to him. "Daniel, can you stand up?"

He grimaced. "Probably. But I'm going to need some help." He put one hand on the police officer's shoulder and one on mine and tried to get to his feet. Sweat poured down his face and his eyes were red and watery.

Morelli gently placed him back on the floor. "Sorry, man. I'll get someone in to see you." She withdrew her phone and retreated to a corner but did not relax her constant surveillance of us. After what looked like a brief argument, the officer hung up and told us help was on the way.

The hurried buzz of conversation slowed, and the early evening shadows of February crept across the room.

A few minutes later, Ann walked in. The perfect end to a perfect day.

CHAPTER FOURTEEN

Assuming, of course, the day was indeed at its end.

Chapter Fifteen

I don't want a childhood; I want to be a ballet dancer.
—Billy Elliot

Ann entered the rehearsal studio wearing a white coat and an expression of clinical detachment. Instead of a stethoscope and doctor's bag, she carried a tie-dyed cloth sack, embroidered with peace signs, yin-yang symbols, and flowers. She spoke in a low tone to Officer Morelli, who nodded her assent.

My stepmother barely glanced in my direction. "Daniel, explain to me what you were doing and how you got hurt."

While he talked to Ann, I tried to engage Officer Morelli, speaking in a friendly, we're-all-pals-here way. "So, Officer, when did Ms. Crandall's, um, accident happen?"

Morelli shook her head. "You're the one who has to answer questions. Not me."

I dropped my casual tone. "Please. My name is Leah Siderova. My mother is upstairs, and I'm worried about her. She's not answering my texts or calls. I'd like to wait with her."

Again, the officer shook her head. "I know who you are. No can do."

I nodded docilely but made up my mind that nothing, including the full force of the New York City Police Department, was going to keep me from breaking out of that room and finding Barbara.

First, though, I had to make sure Daniel was taken care of. I crouched next to him, opposite Ann. His eyes were shut tight against the pain. She asked him, not unkindly, "Have you taken anything by mouth?"

I answered for him. "He took some anti-inflammatories a few minutes ago."

Ann rolled her eyes at me and returned her attention to Daniel. "I'm going to apply some pressure to your back. It won't be fun, but it won't be worse than what you're experiencing right now."

Daniel was frozen with pain. "Do whatever you can." A ghost of a smile crossed his face, and he opened his eyes. "I promise not to sue until I'm feeling better."

Ann didn't smile, not because she was unfriendly, but because she had no sense of humor. I'm sure she would have smiled, had she known Daniel was trying to make a joke. She rolled him onto his stomach, and he muffled a cry of pain. I held his hand until she impatiently pushed me away.

Ann pressed her stubby fingers into different sections of Daniel's back, shoulders, legs, and feet. His body lost some of its tightness, and his breathing became steadier.

Ann, still kneeling next to him, asked, "Better?"

Daniel whispered *yes*. I was somewhat surprised at Ann's skill. All I'd ever seen of her professional side was an unhealthy obsession with vitamins and minerals.

I smiled at her. "Thanks so much, Ann."

As coolly as if we'd never met, she said, "I believe I'm wanted elsewhere. Leah, you have my number. If his back seizes up again, let me know."

My knees were stiff, and my hip bone was sore. The worst pain was from my wrist, which had taken much of the force of my fall. I showed Ann the swelling joint.

She looked at my arm without interest. "You should ice that."

It was some consolation to know my appraisal of her personality was still accurate, even if my assessment of her professional skill was flawed.

Ann got permission from Morelli to leave, but I stopped her. "Wait! I can't get in touch with my mother. Have you seen her? Is she okay?"

My stepmother, always so phlegmatic and unemotional, could not quite mask the look of gratification that crossed her face at the thought that

Barbara might be suffering. "Your mother has told me many times about how capable she is, so I have no doubt she is fine, even after finding Ms. Crandall, unconscious, at the bottom of the stairs."

Although I was horrified at this news, I understood Ann's indifference to Barbara's distress. My mother is a hard act to follow. Also, while Barbara has never treated Ann badly, her attitude of amused detachment probably grated on Ann. To Barbara, Dad's second wife was a woman without taste, style, or wit, whom he, for some unfathomable reason, married. Until our recent dinner together, Ann never fully registered as a human being to Barbara. With a start, I realized Savannah might harbor the same feelings toward me, and for the same resentful reason. Until Savannah forced herself into my life, I'd given her no more thought than I would an inconspicuous piece of furniture that you don't notice until you trip over it.

I was too worried about my mother to mimic Ann's detached attitude. "Ann. Please tell me what's happened. I'm really anxious about Barbara."

Ann sighed, but she was far from sad. "The police are questioning her. Like I told you already, your mother found Ms. Crandall at the bottom of the stairs."

I whispered, "The same place I found Pavel."

Ann's voice was dry. "Yes. That's quite the coincidence." She shook her hands to release the tension, but the impression I got was that she was shaking me off as well. "I believe I'm needed elsewhere. The police, of course, need to talk to everyone in the building."

"Will you text me? Let me know what's going on? And tell Barbara I'm okay but really worried about her?" I was burning with more anxious questions.

Ann's pointed look at her watch told me she was unlikely to divulge any more information than what she'd already so reluctantly delivered. "I doubt I'm going to get the chance to talk to your mother. And it's quite unlikely the police will tell me anything."

I grabbed her sleeve to keep her from turning away. "Talk to Jonah Sobol."

She jerked the fabric from my hand. "Why don't you call him yourself?"

I was done with waiting patiently. Without asking permission from

Morelli, I circled the room and pulled open the door.

"Get back here!" roared Morelli.

Over my shoulder, I assured her, "I'll be right back!"

In my haste to leave, my large dance bag caught in the closing door. I snatched it free before Morelli could catch up with me. She was strong, but I was quick, and I would have made a clean getaway if I hadn't knocked the breath out of myself by crashing into Jonah. In life, as in dance, it does help to look where you're going.

Jonah was at the top of the stairs, which at ABC had become a most dangerous place to be. Happily, despite the extra pounds, I still didn't weigh enough to send us both to the same crushing fate as Ms. Crandall. Jonah gave no overt sign he'd ever seen me before, other than holding me slightly longer than was necessary.

Officer Morelli charged into the stairwell. She was furious. "I told her to stop, but she ran out anyway."

Jonah was stern. "Ms. Siderova, what do you think you're doing?"

I tried to edge past him. "I'm checking up on my mother, which I already told Officer Morelli."

"Your mother is doing fine. I'll let you see her in a few minutes." He took my arm and steered me back into the studio. "Ms. Siderova, you will follow Officer Morelli's directions, or we'll be forced to bring you down to the precinct for questioning."

Back in the studio, Morelli handed Jonah a list of people in the room. He announced, "As most of you know, I'm Detective Jonah Sobol. Officer Morelli and I will be taking statements from all of you. At that point, you will be free to go."

Austin stepped forward. "Can we continue our rehearsal? We've had so many interruptions already, and we have to get cracking if we're to make our Lincoln Center debut."

As I suspected, the young choreographer was tone-deaf, in more ways than one.

Jonah said, in an even tone, "Someone in this company, perhaps someone in this room, attacked Ms. Crandall." Still mild, he added, "I respect the importance of your job. For now, however, mine takes precedence."

Daniel, who was still pale, recovered enough to murmur, "He's smart, and he's a hunk. If I were you, I'd ditch the doctor for the detective. I'll bet there are plenty of dancers here who'd be more than willing to get him inside a locked room."

I held his elbow as he tested his back with a few cautious steps. "If you're well enough to be sizing up handsome men, you must be feeling better."

"If a guy this good-looking walks into the room and I don't react, it's because I'm dead." I flinched, and he draped his arm across my shoulders. "I'm sorry, darling. Bad choice of words." Despite his flip response, his face was stiff with pain.

I tried to keep him moving, but every time he put his left foot on the floor he winced. "I gotta get to the doctor. Like, now. I think I'm going to need a cortisone shot, or something radical, so I can get back on my feet."

Ann, whose exit was delayed by Jonah's entrance, was not pleased. "That's the way you dancers operate. Always with the drugs and the medicines, instead of letting your body do the work of healing itself."

I was furious, but Daniel wasn't in so much pain he couldn't handle the situation himself. With some effort and a good deal of restraint, he said, "I appreciate the help you've given me. I've had some training in physical therapy, so I understand what you're talking about. But I do have a doctor who's helped through much worse, and I trust him."

Ann shrugged. "You should trust your body. Doctors are in bed with big pharma. They don't know how to treat the whole person."

Daniel's blue eyes turned steely. "You know, you're right. And to prove it, I'm going to need a hammer."

Ann was confused, but I knew where he was heading, having heard his spiel before. Daniel continued, in the same pleasant manner, "When I get the hammer, if you don't mind, of course, I'm going to ask you to put out your hands—you know, the hands you need in order to do your job and earn a living—and I'm going to smash a few fingers."

Ann's mouth opened, but Daniel didn't let her answer. "After you're finished writhing in agony, we can continue our discussion on natural healing and pain management."

She sputtered, "That's not the same thing! You don't understand what I'm trying to do around here."

Jonah joined us. "Is there a problem?"

Daniel was grim. "I'm hurt. It's pretty bad." He stuck out his hand and said to Ann, in a more conciliatory tone, "I very much appreciate your help. And I feel a lot better, thanks to you. But I need to see my doctor. The longer I delay, the worse it's going to be for me."

Jonah rubbed his forehead. "Do you have someone who can help you get to the doctor?"

Daniel looked from Jonah to me. "Maybe Ann could help get me in a cab." He practically winked.

Jonah addressed Officer Morelli. "Ann still has to give a statement, as does Leah. I need you to get Daniel in a cab and take his statement while you're waiting." He looked back at Daniel. "If we need further information, we'll be in touch. Feel better."

I waited until the others left before questioning him. "What are you doing here? I thought you were off the case?"

He grinned. "Change of plans. I explained to Farrow and the higher-ups that you and I hardly know each other."

Jonah's hard-nosed partner was not prone to changing his mind. "I'm surprised Farrow caved so easily."

Jonah coughed slightly. "It's possible there are other reasons for his change of heart, which I would be happy to explain to you at another time. Right now, we have a very suspicious accident and another Siderova woman in the thick of it."

My chest tightened at the thought of my mother being interrogated by the police. "How is Barbara? I can't reach her."

"After the initial shock, she recovered enough to take notes for her next book. I promise you, when I left her, Farrow was a whole lot more uncomfortable than she was."

His words made me laugh, but I couldn't still the anxious beating of my heart. "Can I see her? Speak to her?"

"I'm sorry, Leah. We are treating this as an attempted murder, and the whole building is once again a crime scene. But be patient. We'll try to get the two of you out of here as soon as possible."

I was out of patience. "I still don't know what happened."

He was brief. "At this point, neither do we."

Savannah approached us with weak, halting steps. "Detective Sobol. I do hope we can meet again, under better circumstances." She put a hand on his arm and looked into his eyes. "I find that I am simply overcome with emotion. Can't we talk tonight? Or tomorrow? I can give you my address and phone number."

Jonah smiled. "Why thank you, Ms. Collier. But we have your contact information already. As soon as Officer Morelli returns, she will take your statement and escort you out of the building."

Savannah's voice lost some of its honeyed sweetness. She jerked her head in my direction and said, "Don't be fooled by her innocent expression. She and that mother of hers are two of a kind. Nasty, scheming liars, with no regard for human life." She sniffed loudly and wiped her eyes. "First, Pavel, and now poor, dear Ms. Crandall. The two of them belong under lock and key."

Jonah gently plucked her hand from his arm. "Thank you, Ms. Collier. I have heard your views on Ms. Siderova already, and I appreciate your additional insights about her mother."

To his evident relief, Morelli returned. Jonah said, with even more sympathy, "And now, if you could go off with Officer Morelli? I promise, she'll take good care of you."

Savannah persisted. "I'm sure Officer Morelli will do an excellent job interrogating the other people in this room. But what I have to say is too important for someone of her rank."

Morelli stood, stony-faced, as Savannah executed her well-rehearsed mean-girl routine. After pretending to shudder at the sight of me, Savannah regained her hold on Jonah's arm and said, "Far be it from me to improperly accuse anyone, but I have information about those two that I think will change your mind."

Jonah appeared to reconsider. "Very well." He pointed to the opposite side of the room. "Wait there for me." He bent his head and trained his dark brown eyes on her vacant blue ones. "I'll come and get you as soon as I've finished with the others."

She hesitated. "Um, yes. But could we make it later? I, uh, let's say, eight o'clock instead." She gave him a brilliant smile and a long look before crossing the room.

I was not pleased. "How could you let her push you around like that? You know what kind of person she is. She'll do anything to trash me, and now, she seems to be gunning for Barbara as well."

He watched her swing her hips. "That's why I'm the one who needs to talk to her. If she gives even one false statement, she'll regret it for a really long time."

Chapter Sixteen

Dance is a song of the body. Either of joy or pain.
—Martha Graham

Outside the main office, Barbara was deep in conversation with Detective Farrow. For the first time ever, she looked her age. Her eyes were half-closed, her skin ghostly in its pallor. Tiny lines appeared from underneath her makeup. Despite her obvious distress, when she saw me, she gave a brave approximation of her usual breezy attitude.

"Leah, my darling, you must get me out of here," she murmured. "I'm late for a Pilates class, and my abs will never forgive me if I miss it."

I turned to the detective. "You know where you can find us. My mother has had a terrible shock, and I have to get her home."

Farrow was unmoved by my plea and uninterested in Barbara's attempt at humor. "Not yet."

She attempted a smile. "Detective, if you let us go now, I'll give you a starring role in my next book. But if you don't, I'll sic Professor Romanova on you." Her tired eyes and obvious weakness belied the light words.

Clearly, while the detective knew Barbara was a writer, he hadn't read any of her books. This was not surprising. For reasons obscure even to her, my mother's mystery series featured an amateur sleuth who was a professor of medieval literature and hailed from St. Petersburg. Russia, not Florida. English teachers love her.

However enervated Barbara was physically, her wit remained sharp. "Detective Farrow, I bet you prefer hard-boiled detectives." He looked confused, so she clarified it for him. "Philip Marlowe? Sam Spade?"

I was ready to conk both of them over the head, Barbara, for living in a fictional time zone, and Farrow for his indifference to her plight. Despite my irritation, I tried to help the detective understand my mother. "Barbara thinks you might prefer detectives like Harry Bosch. Or Jack Reacher. Ring any bells?"

Farrow's expression lost none of its testiness. "I guess. Were they friends with Ms. Crandall? And what does that have to do with what happened today?"

Barbara shrugged. She too had no idea where the conversation was going. I gave up and texted Jonah.

Thirty seconds after I sent the text Farrow's cell pinged, and after a brief conversation, presumably with Jonah, he gave us the go-ahead to leave. He watched as Barbara walked with slow, tentative steps. She leaned heavily against the wall as we waited for the elevator, which was now back in service. Many minutes elapsed before the clanking, wheezing contraption arrived.

The moment the elevator began its reluctant journey, Barbara's eyes popped open, her spine straightened, and ten years dropped away. "We're on the trail of a ruthless killer. But she picked the wrong person when she tried to finger me for the crime."

My head was spinning, not only by what Barbara said, but by her transformation from frail victim to vibrant pursuer. "She? You know who did it?"

Barbara was impatient. "Of course. I know who did it, and so do you. It has to be that little Southern sweet potato."

The creaky door opened onto the icy lobby, and for once the cold air felt good. "Did you hit your head? Or is this craziness as much an act as that pathetic performance you put on for Detective Farrow?"

Barbara huddled against the building to light her cigarette. "I had you fooled as well. Don't deny it! I was a pretty good actress in my day. Did I ever tell you about the time I played Beatrice in *Much Ado About Nothing* in high school? I don't want to brag, but I think I could have given Emma Thompson a run for her money."

I'd had enough. "Stop changing the subject. I'm on fire to find out what happened. What did you see, or hear, to make you so sure Savannah is the killer? She burst into Austin's rehearsal to announce that you were the guilty party."

Barbara could barely contain her emotion. "When I found poor Ms. Crandall, I realized exactly what happened."

I waved away the smoke. "Start at the beginning. I'm in no mood for flashbacks."

Barbara sniffed at my inartistic preference for a straightforward narrative but agreed nonetheless. She began again. "I was talking to Ron when he cut me off to answer a text. He got up and left, quite rudely, in the middle of our conversation, saying he'd forgotten something. I tiptoed down the hall and heard him tell Savannah to get the elevator fixed. She said she'd already called someone. Then she told him she was going to post a sign for people to use the stairs."

I felt sick. "The same thing happened the day Pavel was killed. Someone reported the elevator broken, even though it was working as well as it ever does."

Barbara was so excited, a tinge of color returned to her cheeks. "That 'someone' was almost certainly Savannah herself. But it gets better. She told Ron she wanted to kill Ms. Crandall for leaving her to do all the work while Ms. Crandall took all the credit!"

"That's it? That's all you have? Because I think it's a bit on the thin side for any jury in possession of half a brain."

She barreled on, impervious to my objections. "Savannah left the office. In order to push Ms. Crandall down the stairs, of course. She was hysterical, not for any of the reasons she gave, but because Crandall somehow survived the fall."

I took a lungful of icy air. "First of all, it was Ron who told her to put up the sign. But let's say, for argument's sake, Savannah is the killer. How could she possibly ensure you'd be the one to find the body?"

Barbara smoothed her forehead to avoid wrinkling it in thought. I could almost see the gears of her brain working. After a moment she snapped her fingers. "She has the master schedule. She knew when Ron had his next appointment and put up the sign right before I was due to leave."

Barbara moved farther from the entrance to the studio. "Of course, it might simply have been dumb luck that I found Ms. Crandall. But you're missing the essential point. Savannah, who is obviously unhinged and dangerous, said she wanted to kill her, and then she did her best to make it happen. We can only hope the poor woman recovers. And when she does, that's the end of Savannah Collier."

Although I welcomed any evidence of Savannah's guilt, Barbara's argument remained unpersuasive. "That's ridiculous. People don't tell other people they're going to commit murder and five minutes later do it. Unless they're fictional characters in a very improbable murder mystery that features a Russian-born detective."

Barbara pinched my cheek. "Very funny. You should write for television. But in the meantime, we have work to do. Poor Michelle Crandall is in the hospital. She didn't deserve to suffer, and it's up to us to help her. Let's also not forget that the odious Detective Farrow treated me like I was a suspect. Me! It would serve him right if we showed him up."

I stepped into the street to search for an unoccupied taxi. "You were the one to find her. That kind of places you, as they say on television, at the scene of the crime."

She shook her head, perhaps regretting she'd given birth to so dim a daughter. "You're still not seeing the big picture. Savannah plotted the whole thing. And she's trying to pin the murder on me in the same way she tried to pin Pavel's murder on you." For a moment, her pallor returned. "It was all quite shocking. I don't think I ever realized how brave you were." Somewhat shamefaced, she admitted, "I did feel quite faint. It wasn't all an act."

I stepped back from the curb to avoid getting hit by an overeager cabbie. "Go home. I'll come over later to check up on you."

She hung back. "Why aren't you coming with me?" Her voice lowered dramatically, even though the only people close enough to hear us were busy picking over half-price vegetables set out in front of the adjacent grocery.

"Are you plotting an investigation? If so, you'll need my help."

I murmured an apology to the impatient cab driver and practically pushed Barbara inside. "I don't have any plans. I'm going home."

Barbara got out of the cab and slammed the door. "I know when you're lying to me, and I refuse to move until you tell me the truth."

I pulled the car door open to the great distress of the driver, who thought he was finally free of us. "If you must know, I'm meeting Jonah. I'm going to pump him for information and call you later."

She closed the door, planted her feet, and crossed her arms. "Try again, Leah. If you want to catch a killer, you're going to have to up your game."

My injured wrist ached as I pulled open the car door for what I hoped was the last time. "I'm going to wait for Savannah. I don't think she's the killer. But she might know something even she doesn't realize. There's a very good chance I'll be stuck waiting in the cold for a long time. I swear I'll call you if anything interesting or exciting happens."

Barbara was relentless. "What makes you think following her will lead to anything?"

Having inherited the Siderova Relentless Gene, I remained firm. "Savannah has been trying to wrap her tentacles around Jonah since she first laid eyes on him. But when he offered to see her after he finished his interviews, she put him off. She told him she wouldn't be free until eight o'clock. The only way she would postpone meeting him is if she already had an appointment with someone else. I want to see who that is." Anticipating further objections, I said, "It will be easier to follow her if it's just me. I don't want a parade."

She finally assented, undone by the cold and fatigue. "I'll wait for your call."

The moment the car pulled away I rang Gabi, and as economically as I could, explained the situation.

As always, whenever I needed her, my best friend found a way to help. When Gabi quit dancing and got married I feared our friendship would fade, but, if anything, we got closer. She spoke quickly. "My parents are already babysitting Lucie. I'm on my way."

Ten minutes later, I spotted Gabi's long, lanky figure as she turned the corner. She jumped over a puddle, squeezed between two cyclists, and sprinted across Broadway.

She hugged me. "Sid, I don't know what I'd do without you. My life would be so boring."

She was more sober after I told her about Ms. Crandall. "Is she going to make it?"

I pushed aside the rush of dread. "I don't know. But we have to do something. Despite what Barbara thinks, Savannah is not likely to have murdered anyone. But that miserable woman has accused and threatened both of us. I think she knows a lot more than she's let on. I know the odds are against us, in terms of learning anything new, but it's worth a shot."

Gabi scanned the crowd of people waiting at the corner bus stop and moved farther away from them. She spoke softly. "Savannah might not be a killer, but she might be covering up for a killer. From what you've told me, she's not the sharpest crayon in the box. Is it possible she doesn't know she's being used?"

I pulled my scarf up around my face. "I don't know. But we're going to do our best to find out."

Gabi was nervous. "I won't let you down."

My mind was racing. "I let myself down. I've been sitting around while Savannah, or someone else, has been directing this horror show." I swallowed the lump in my throat. "I have to protect myself. And my mother."

We found the perfect place for a stakeout, diagonally across the street from the studio. Positioning ourselves behind two concrete planters, about four feet high and two feet wide, we had a nearly unobstructed view. Had we taken refuge in the spring, the concrete planters would have been filled with flowers, but in this gray season, they were barren and empty. We crouched behind them whenever anyone from ABC exited. A few passersby looked curiously at us as we dodged and weaved, but we ignored them.

There were few women in the tri-state area less likely to garner suspicion than Gabi and I, but after fifteen minutes of creeping around the planters a shopkeeper emerged with a most skeptical expression on his face.

He looked at us, his hands on his hips. "Can I help you two?"

I said *no* at the same time Gabi said *yes*.

With no increase in friendliness, he said, "Make up your mind, ladies. But no matter what you decide, quit lurking around my store. No one's gonna wanna come in if there's two loonies playing hide and seek outside."

Gabi turned and peered through the plate glass window behind us. "You're not exactly doing box office business. Maybe you shouldn't be so unwelcoming."

He took out his phone. "Loitering is against the law."

While Gabi sparred with the owner, I kept to my command post, and when a bright pink pouf of a down jacket, topped by an equally bright head of blonde hair left the studio, I grabbed her. "Let's go!"

Despite the cold, Savannah moved slowly, stopping often to stare into shop windows. I took advantage of her slow pace to call Melissa.

My sister, like Gabi, wasted no time. "Where are you? I'll call the babysitter now and get on the next train to Penn Station."

"Half a block from your old apartment, which I wish you hadn't left. Get the sitter, and I'll keep you posted. If this doesn't pan out, I'll meet you at Barbara's."

I missed the days when Melissa still lived in the city, but after the twins were born she and David traded their cramped city digs for a posh suburban house with central everything. Their kitchen was bigger than my entire apartment. I wished they'd move back, but every time I broached the topic, Melissa launched into a boring litany of reasons why life in New Jersey was better for Ariel and Benjamin.

Gabi whispered, "Leah, it seems as if she has nothing better to do than window shop. How long do you want to follow her? I'm hungry."

Despite my weariness, I resisted the temptation to give up. "She just checked her phone and her watch. Let's hope her appointment isn't with a hairdresser."

We continued our slow crawl, in contrast to every other person on the street, who was hurrying to get out of the cold. On the corner of Eighty-

Ninth Street, I stopped short and shaded my face. "If you stick around a few more minutes, I can guarantee you, at the very least, a drink."

Gabi rushed to follow Savannah across the street and into a dimly lit bar. I held her back. "Slow down. It looks like Savannah will not be drinking alone."

Austin Dworkin and Jonathan Llewellyn Franklin, coming from opposite directions, entered the bar a few minutes after Savannah.

I pretended to study my phone and waited to see if anyone else was going to show up. We were lucky to have had such bad weather. Thanks to our winter hats and woolen scarves only a few inches of our faces were visible, and we were both dressed in generic down jackets. Jonathan was the only one to check to see if anyone was watching, but unlike both bareheaded men, we were indistinguishable from every other Upper West Side shopper.

Gabi edged into the crosswalk, trying to see farther down the block.

I pulled her sleeve. "What are you looking at?"

Gabi stepped back onto the sidewalk. "I was trying to catch sight of the woman Jonathan was with."

I peered down the street. "I didn't see her. I was watching Austin. What did she look like?"

"Short, with dark hair and a long puffy coat. I think she got into a private car."

"Sounds like a description of me, other than the part about the private car. Maybe it was Jonathan's mother. She's the only person I know, besides Jonathan, who has a driver."

Gabi was doubtful. "Maybe. I only saw her from the back, but I got the feeling she was young. And she was skinny. Like, dancer-skinny."

Chapter Seventeen

Dancing can reveal all the mystery that music conceals.
—Mikhail Baryshnikov

G abi and I lingered before entering Bar Bleu, to make sure no one was following us while we were following Savannah. Inside, we kept our hats pulled down to our eyebrows and our scarves pulled up over our noses while we did a quick sweep of the room. Savannah, Austin, and Jonathan weren't at the bar, or at any of the tables near the door. We followed the sound of Savannah's high-pitched voice to the back of the room. At the last booth in the aisle, the back of Austin's head, with its floppy blonde hair, was visible. The waitress wasn't pleased when we declined the clean tables she offered and opted instead for the only one with dirty dishes on it. I knew she'd be much happier once we left. My parents were extreme over tippers, which helped them resolve their guilt over leaving their working-class roots. They trained me and Melissa to do the same.

We were in luck. Austin was tall enough to see over the back of the booth, but he was facing away from us. Next to him, another tall man with very dark hair had his head bent over a menu. Jonathan and Savannah were completely absorbed in their conversation and looked as if they wouldn't notice a Mack truck barreling down the aisle.

The waitress chatted as the busboy cleaned. We ordered by silently pointing to the menu, and she finally left. I stretched my head back as far as I could. Gabi, wide-eyed, waited for me to report what they were saying, but all I could decipher was a low murmur of sounds, punctuated by the occasional snort, which was Austin's idea of a laugh.

I leaned away from them and toward Gabi. "I can't hear a thing."

Gabi whispered, "Do you have some kind of earphones with you?"

I pulled out wireless earbuds, and she pointed to an app on her phone that would amplify their conversation. I was stunned, since I'd never known her to be on the bleeding edge of technology. She grinned. "Don't ask. Really dumb party game."

Despite the amplification, as the bar filled up it became increasingly difficult to hear. I took out a notebook and a pen. As I wrote, Gabi followed every pen stroke.

Jonathan said, "Obviously, this was another terrible tragedy. A truly awful accident. But every dark moment has its silver lining. Crandall was a drag on the organization. We needed new blood. With her out of the way, at least temporarily, there's literally nothing stopping us."

Savannah was quick to follow. "I agree. It's all quite, quite, terrible, but I can't pretend I'm not happy about the opportunity to get out from under her thumb. And who knows? After such a traumatic episode, even if she recovers, she might not return. Ms. Crandall was not what I would call a team player." She sighed noisily. "Of course, I'm praying she makes a complete recovery." She continued more matter-of-factly, "I'm finally going to get to take charge of that office, which would have happened already if poor Pavel hadn't been murdered. He was going to fire her and promote me, first chance he got."

I jotted Savannah's comment and showed it to Gabi. She bit her lip. "I'm surprised it wasn't Savannah who got pushed down the stairs."

Austin didn't bother with platitudes. "That's all very well and good, but let's get down to specifics. I want my new ballet to be front and center of all PR promotions. And I need you, Jonathan, to put in a good word with Mavis Ferris. I'd love to spend six months, or a year, in London. She can help."

Jonathan let out a honking laugh. I couldn't catch the beginning of his answer, but the end of it came through loud and clear. "You two aren't the most popular kids on the block at ABC. And I don't do anything unless there's something in it for me."

The voice that answered Jonathan sounded familiar. The tall, dark man sitting next to Austin said, in a clear tone that cut through the ambient noise, "I can take out anyone who stands in the way. Legally, of course." This silenced the others' chatter. The man continued, "I'm here because of you, Jonathan. These two are useless. You'll get nowhere without me. I've done quite a few, shall we say, favors for most of the board. If you want to be artistic director, I can guarantee you the votes. At a price. I don't come cheap. If you want to subsidize anyone else, that's on you."

Jonathan grunted. "Listen, Philip, if it's one thing I've got, it's money. As for them, they're simply along for the ride. But don't underestimate having them do the dirty work. They have their uses."

I clutched Gabi's hand. In big letters, I wrote: *PHILIP IS WITH THEM*

Gabi raised her shoulders and held her hands wide. I forgot she didn't know who Philip was. I pressed the pen with so much force each letter formed a shallow groove in the paper. *BARBARA'S NEW BOYFRIEND!!!*

In times of great stress, Gabi reverts to Spanish. She mouthed the words, "*Dios Mio.*"

Gabi and I sat in tense silence, anxious to hear if the conspirators behind us would explicitly reveal their involvement in the murder of Pavel and the attempted murder of Ms. Crandall.

For the next few minutes, the foursome spoke too softly for me to hear what they said. I folded and refolded a corner of the paper. Gabi placed her hand on mine to calm me down.

Finally, Austin spoke loud enough for the sound to carry. "Not so fast. You can't shove us aside. I have an inside track with the dancers, and Savannah has the media hanging on every tweet. We can bring public opinion wherever we want it. And when we do, we want our payoff. Same as you."

Austin reminded me of a barking dog. People will do anything to shut him up, but not because they respected what he had to say.

Jonathan sounded impatient. "If you want to earn your keep, do something about that Ann person. She's Leah Siderova's stepmother, and I don't trust anyone in that family. For God's sake, her accursed mother was there today as well."

Savannah sounded pleased. "Yes, she was. Turned up just in time to find the, uh, to find Ms. Crandall. We're two for two, where those conceited women are concerned. I'm still hoping to see them behind bars. As for Ann, I'll talk to Ron about her. That's something else, gentlemen, that I can bring to the table. Don't overlook my relationship with Ron."

Philip's voice was cool. "You overestimate your value, Savannah. If it makes you happy, you can keep up your campaign against Leah. But don't kid yourself. You're already last week's news. As for Ron and Ann, they're employees of Artistic Solutions and will do what they're told. I got them in. And I can take them out."

The jangle of a cell phone interrupted them. Jonathan answered it and responded to his caller so cryptically, I couldn't figure out if he was talking to an ex-lover or his cleaning service. After several minutes of hearing him deliver an increasingly impatient series of assents to his caller's demands, he hung up and told the others, "I have to go. We'll talk later."

Philip's voice again cut cleanly through the chatter. "Inform your girlfriend, or whoever, that you're busy. We still have important matters to discuss."

Jonathan sounded bitter. "I agree. But that call was from my mother. I'm afraid I must leave to attend my dear little brother's latest celebrity showing. Laurence did an absolutely hideous design job for some minor art museum in the Bronx, and now I have to brave this filthy weather to cheer him on. Not exactly my usual stomping ground."

Philip's tone was sharp. "Get out of it."

Jonathan raised his voice. "I can't. The press is going to be there, and my job is to stand around and look proud. The nauseating thing is that he's guaranteed to get rave reviews as New York's youngest starchitect, no matter how crappy, or derivative, his work is."

Austin sounded impressed. "Wait a minute. Your brother is Laurence Melville Franklin? Are you kidding me? He's famous."

Philip's tone was cold. "He's an overrated hack." After a pause, he added, "As are you."

Savannah tittered and Jonathan honked. I slouched down as far as I could without inflicting permanent spinal damage. From the corner of my eye, I saw Jonathan stand up and impatiently motion to the waitress. She hurried over and serendipitously positioned her comfortably proportioned body so that Gabi and I were shielded from view. I took out a compact and angled the mirror to get a better look behind me.

Jonathan was about to swipe his credit card when Philip stopped him. "No records, please. Don't you have any cash?"

Jonathan huffed. "What's the problem? We're not doing anything illegal. Just happened to run into each other."

Philip was brief. "This meeting never happened. I have no knowledge of, or personal relationship with, any of you."

I too wondered why he was so insistent Jonathan pay cash. If Philip's motive was to escape leaving any record of their visit to Bar Bleu, that plan failed spectacularly as soon as the waitress checked the total amount of the check. Her cool expression of thanks was a clear indication of a very cheap tip. According to Barbara, who waitressed her way through college, no server forgets a cheap customer. Mrs. Franklin had probably not instilled in Jonathan the same generous impulses my parents had inculcated in me. Typical rich guy.

After Jonathan left, Philip spoke again. "I am leaving. You two will do nothing until you hear from me. Stay where you are for at least ten minutes."

I whispered to Gabi, "That's our cue." I waved to the waitress who returned to our table with the check.

That's when our luck ran out.

Chapter Eighteen

Dancing is a sweat job.
—Fred Astaire

U nlike the rest of the patrons at Bar Bleu, Gabi and I weren't taken by surprise when Savannah shrieked and Austin cursed.

I knocked over the sugar bowl in my haste to accuse them before they could accuse me. With feigned anger and surprise, I said, "What are you doing here? Are you spying on us?"

Gabi didn't miss a beat. She stared with disdainful composure at Austin and asked, "Why on earth is your girlfriend yelping like that? Is she not well?"

Austin was a sickly green and looked as if he were about to faint. He never was very good at controlling his emotions. To his credit, he managed to gulp out an answer. "She's not my—we just—we were surprised to see *her*." He jerked a nervous finger in my direction. "What are you doing here, anyway?"

Savannah chewed her lip. "Yeah! What are you doing here?"

Thankfully, neither of them could hear the beating of my heart. "It's none of your business what we're doing here. This is a private party, Savannah. Move along and quit bothering us."

Her voice rose. "You can't fool me! You were spying on us!"

Austin shushed her. "People are staring. Let's get the hell out here."

Gabi smiled sweetly. "Good idea, especially since I believe the management is coming over to escort you to the door."

Without checking to see if her words were true, they hurried out.

Gabi took a napkin and fanned my face. "Are you going to faint?"

"I'm not going to faint. I'm sick over the possibility Barbara's dating a killer. And that Austin and Savannah will inform said killer I was spying on him."

Gabi wasn't looking too perky either. She murmured, "*Que desastre.*"

I started to shake. In any language, this was, indeed, a disaster.

She placed her hand over my tapping fingers. "Let's not jump to conclusions, Sid. Come back to my place. You look like you're going to puke."

Gabi is the only one who calls me Sid. After my parents' divorce, Barbara changed our last name from Feldbaum to Siderova, partly in homage to her Russian ancestors, and partly because it looked better in print. I was uneasy about getting rebranded, but Gabi made me own it and love it.

I gave Gabi her phone and took out mine. "I'm not going to puke. I'm going to call Madame. We need to enlist her. And warn her."

Madame insisted we come immediately to her apartment. My next call was to my sister, to tell her of our change in plans. I waited for the long screech of brakes to end as her train came to a stop. "Don't bother calling Barbara. I'll let her know to meet us."

Melissa agreed and rang off. My next phone call was more challenging. In the end, I simply told Barbara to meet us at Madame's apartment.

She demurred. "Philip is on his way. He's bringing dinner. Let's talk tomorrow."

I panicked. "No! Don't—you shouldn't. Come to Madame's right now. Tell Philip you're not feeling well."

Barbara sounded bemused. "Darling, that's why he's coming over. I spoke to him not ten minutes ago. He said he wanted to take care of me after all I'd been through." She laughed. "I told him you were tailing Savannah, and he thought that was hilarious."

I felt a sick lurch of anxiety. Ten minutes earlier, I'd heard Philip promise to take care of people who stood in his way, and the chilly tone of his voice indicated his mission wasn't to bring them chicken soup. "Get out of the house. Now. For once in your life, do not argue with me. Go immediately

114

to Madame's and I'll explain when I get there. Don't tell Philip where you're going. Make some excuse to get out of it."

After I told her Melissa was coming, she reluctantly agreed to meet her two daughters and cancel her plans with Philip. Gabi and I plowed through slushy streets and freezing rain to the apartment building where Madame lived in pre-war splendor. Not many former ballerinas could afford a "Classic Six" New York City apartment, but Madame had married and amicably divorced three men, each richer than the last. She refused multiple marriage proposals from suitor number four, claiming she's too old to live with anyone else again. I didn't know how old she was, but Madame was still beautiful and elegant enough to turn heads.

The journey wasn't easy. Unlike my mother, who made taxis and Ubers materialize out of thin air during peak times of demand, I was unable to summon a single ride. Gabi suggested we wait for the crosstown bus, but the people at the bus stop all had an air of hopelessness about them. I checked the NYC bus app for the next arrival time, which explained their misery. Walking was our third and only option.

Gabi and I arrived half-frozen and dripping wet from an icy mix of snow and rain that pelted us throughout most of our trip. Madame's apartment was warm and fragrant. It was filled with ornate furniture and draperies in deep shades of red and gold that echoed pre-Revolutionary Russian charm. My ballet teacher was no minimalist; every surface was covered in silver-framed pictures, mostly of her in her prime.

Madame greeted us with thick towels, wooly socks, and a seat by the fire. Knowing my preferences, she did not offer tea from the silver samovar that held pride of place on a mahogany sideboard in the dining room. Instead, she pressed a cup of steaming hot coffee on me. Barbara was already there, despite the greater distance she'd had to travel. She rose to greet me but didn't get close enough to risk marring her cashmere sweater with what would have been a very damp hug.

Madame had no such compunctions, and she warmly embraced me and Gabi. Dressed all in black, she wore a thin, pale pink belt to emphasize her still-tiny waist. She gestured toward the silver ice bucket. "Wine and champagne later, yes? But for now, we relax with hot drink and wait for Melissa, your so very nice and smart sister."

While Barbara regaled Madame with tales of Melissa's Ivy League education, degrees in philosophy, and bestselling books, Gabi and I exchanged nervous looks. Gabi said, in an undertone, "I don't want to be in the room when you tell Barbara you think Philip is a killer. I'm going to hide in the bathroom. Or maybe in a bomb shelter. I can't believe your mother is dating that guy."

I made sure Barbara was fully occupied with Madame before answering. "Let's try to look on the bright side. He might not be a hitman. Maybe he's blackmailer. Or an upscale con artist. He did say the board members owed him favors. I shudder to think of what he did to get their support. The only thing we know for sure is he wants Jonathan to pay him for some unspecified services."

Gabi was too overcome to express herself in English. *"Esto es una pesadilla!"*

Before I could request a translation, Melissa walked in and said, "Who's having a nightmare? And in Spanish, no less!"

I had been so intent on my conversation with Gabi, I hadn't heard the doorbell. I answered in a voice that sounded artificial even to me. "The weather. It's the weather that's a *pesadi*—what she said. A nightmare."

Melissa put some crackers and cheese on a plate. "I'm starving, and this is lovely. Thank you so much, Madame."

My sister looked with some amusement at Barbara, who was regarding her with a mix of affection and exasperation. Melissa returned the exact same look and asked, "Would it kill you to eat a cracker? You're skinnier than ever."

Barbara stepped back from the tray. "You just ate thirty-seven calories worth of carbohydrates and fat."

Melissa remained cheerful. "Keep count for me. I'm not done eating. And you should eat something too."

Despite our mother's borderline eating disorder, my sister had a healthy attitude toward food. She takes after our father. My life was very different from Melissa's. Thanks to the skeletally thin requirements of life as a ballerina, as well as my mother's paranoid fears, I have yet to ingest a crumb of food without first calculating the exact number of calories and carbohydrates in each bite. I'm an expert at adding three-digit numbers in my head. With less frequency, I also calculate the emotional cost.

Barbara didn't argue the point. She poured some wine into one of Madame's charmingly mismatched crystal glasses and ate half a cracker to demonstrate her acceptance of Melissa's thirty-seven calorie splurge.

Madame settled into a gilt and velvet chair. "Lelotchka, you must first to tell us all what you know. And then Barbara will explain all what happened this afternoon to poor Ms. Crandall."

I studied my scribbled notes, but all I could think about was how I would tell Barbara about Philip.

Gabi nudged me. "Leah has important information."

I steeled myself for the coming storm. "We have reason to believe Philip was involved in the murder, if not directly, then indirectly."

Barbara reddened. "What does Philip have to do with all this? Where did you get this crazy idea?"

I took a deep breath. "As I told you this afternoon, I waited for Savannah and tailed her."

Melissa whooped. "That's my girl!"

Buoyed by my sister's response, I continued with more confidence. With the help of my scribbled notes, I managed to relate most of the conversation between Philip, Jonathan, Austin, and Savannah.

Melissa was thoughtful. "We need to think carefully about everything they said. Here is how I see things at this point. One of them might be guilty of murder and the others unaware of that fact. One or more could be guilty of aiding, abetting, or concealing that crime. It's also possible they're completely innocent of any legal transgression, and they simply suffer from a profound absence of any moral compass."

I looked again at my notes. "That's true. But they all have credible and interconnected motives. Jonathan's family is rich and powerful, but even they can't buy him the position or the prestige he seeks. If Pavel hadn't died so suddenly, it's unlikely the board would have appointed him director of the company, even on an interim basis. Jonathan is quite jealous of his younger brother, who is a very successful architect."

Gabi nodded. "Laurence is quite the prodigy. And yet, I can't imagine sibling rivalry rising to that level."

Barbara gripped the arms of her chair. "Jonathan, along with the rest of the Franklin family, is loathsome. But that has nothing to do with Philip. I don't understand what part you think he played in Pavel's death. Nothing you've told me indicates he's guilty of anything, other than using his considerable influence to help Jonathan secure a coveted post at the company. There's no law against that."

Melissa, our resident genius, clarified the matter. "Philip isn't helping out a friend. He's squeezing Jonathan for what will probably be a hefty sum of money. He has promised, for a price, to pressure the ABC board members to hire Jonathan. We don't know what that pressure entails, but it sounds rather unethical."

Barbara gave Melissa an impatient rap on the knuckles. "You sound like your father. Ethical this and ethical that. I suppose you're going to drag Aristotle into the discussion."

My sister remained unperturbed. "If I sound like Dad, it's because I'm also a philosopher. He and I do tend to think alike."

Barbara was still defensive. "You're also a writer like me. You should be more sympathetic."

Melissa was careful in her response. "Let's not get distracted by side issues. I'm not passing judgment on your love life, and I don't want to jump to conclusions any more than you do, but let's be clear about the facts of the case. There is a reasonably strong possibility Jonathan paid Philip to kill Pavel or have him killed, possibly with the help of Austin and Savannah. All they had to do was make sure Pavel was in the right place at the right time. The narrow time frame for the murder indicates a highly coordinated effort."

Barbara seemed to be wavering. I added an argument I thought would clinch the deal. "Philip said he's the one who got Ann her job at Artistic Solutions. I suspect their relationship is more complicated than a simple business connection."

Barbara got a stubborn look on her face, but I didn't let that stop me. "On the night we all had dinner at Palmyra, Philip acted as if he and Ann had never met. But we now know that was a lie. And when we left the restaurant Philip ditched us, saying he had to talk to a client in Sydney. That also was a lie. He didn't go home. He went back into Palmyra, where the only person still there was Ann. You said yourself, on the day Pavel was killed, that there was something fishy about those two. You were right."

Barbara reached for a vape pen, her comfort of last resort when she can't have a cigarette. "How do you know he didn't go back to retrieve a lost glove? Let's not go too far down this conspiracy hole."

When pressed, I could be as tenacious as my mother. "Face facts, Barbara. He lied. And that's not the worst of it. Because the only occupation that fits in with what I overheard him tell Jonathan is blackmailer, con artist, or killer."

Barbara remained calm. "Always so dramatic, Leah. Philip is a consultant. A very successful consultant." She puffed more energetically at the vape. "Jonathan is one of his clients. It's as simple as that."

Melissa interjected with a dose of common sense. "Leah is not being dramatic. And you haven't told us exactly what service, or type of consulting, he does."

Barbara got up to examine a photograph, as if questions about Philip's highly suspect business dealings were insufficient to hold her attention. "He probably told me, but I can't quite remember. I'll ask him about it tomorrow."

"No!" Melissa and I shouted at the same time.

Her charming good humor still intact, she said, "If the two of you gang up on me, I will not argue any further. Philip is now history. Let's move on to the next item on our agenda."

Madame spoke in somber tones. "Ms. Crandall must have suspected who is this killer. Which reason it was she was attacked. I called Ms. Crandall's aunt, who is with her at hospital. Not look good."

Melissa and I exchanged glances as Barbara put down her vape pen and ate an entire cracker. With cheese. She wasn't nearly as composed as she pretended.

Ever the pragmatist, my sister said, "The most important job we have right now is to prevent another attack." She turned her gaze back to Barbara. "Embarking on a murder investigation will be dangerous. I'm worried about you."

Barbara, even in the most extreme circumstances, is rarely without wit. "If Philip is implicated, I'm going to write a strongly worded letter to *TheNew York Review of Books*. The quality of their journalism must have seriously declined if they're attracting criminals to the Personals column."

As we laughed and raised our glasses to toast her, the doorbell rang. A server from one of Madame's favorite restaurants delivered several platters of savory food.

Barbara followed Madame to the dining room. With my mother safely out of the way, I was able to talk freely. "Aside from Philip, I think Barbara is in for a lot more trouble than she's ready to handle. She has no conceivable motive to hurt Ms. Crandall, but she was the last person to see her before she was pushed down the stairs. And she was the one to discover her in the stairwell. In other words, by some bleak fate, we both were at the scene of two different, but related, crimes."

Gabi poked at the fire. "The police would never believe Barbara was a killer, and since Barbara didn't do it, we have to figure out who else was there."

I grabbed the bottle of wine Madame had discreetly left with us. "Exactly. Someone who was on the scene for both crimes and who might now target Barbara. Or me."

Melissa said, "The more I think about Savannah, the more I have to wonder if she's the driving force and not the pawn we've assumed her to be. It took real skill to go after you as effectively as she has. From what you've told me about her, as well as what I've observed, her personality alone makes her a strong suspect. She's got a monster ego and an almost pathological lack of empathy."

I tried to get the wine past the lump in my throat. "That does make sense. But as much as I want her to be the killer, I can't get past the fact that she loved Pavel. She literally worshipped him."

Gabi looked at me. "You could be right *and* wrong. What if she loved Pavel and he rejected her? Perhaps humiliated her? She could have killed him in a fit of rage. Then she became desperate to pin the deed on someone else. I'm not saying her grief isn't real. It probably is, but it also could be mixed with fear and guilt. That combination is enough to make anyone do desperate things. Like push a middle-aged woman down a flight of stairs."

Melissa tugged at my sleeve. "What's the name of the dancer who was going to replace you?"

I huddled closer to the fire. "Kerry Blair. But after the murder, I got all my roles back. I'm still waiting for Savannah to use that choice piece of information to get herself trending again. It's a miracle she hasn't gotten around to it yet."

Gabi put her arm around me. "Kerry isn't half the dancer you are."

Melissa snapped her fingers. "Exactly. So why did Pavel promote Kerry and not some other dancer?"

My mouth went dry. "Having sex with Pavel was Kerry's bargaining chip. If you're right, we can remove her from our list of suspects. Kerry had better watch her back. She could be next."

I was nearly overpowered by weariness. "Savannah has three very powerful men backing her up. They appear to think they can use her to further their own ends. But they might be underestimating her, as men often do when faced with a young and pretty woman. Let's not make the same mistake."

Chapter Nineteen

The art of ballet chooses the dancer, not the other way around.
—Kevin McKenzie

T he dining room table in Mme. Maksimova's apartment gleamed with gilt-edged platters, delicate wine glasses, and a crystal vase filled with vivid red roses. A tureen of soup and a tantalizing array of vegetables and salads beckoned us. When Gabi and Melissa finished eating, and the rest of us finished pretending to eat, we returned to the living room.

Madame showed me a legal pad, filled with her spidery black writing. "*Regardez*, Lelotchka! I have already begun with investigation. You tell me all what you think."

I squinted. The handwriting was beautiful, but not completely legible, and was peppered throughout with French phrases and letters from the Cyrillic alphabet. Madame's first language was Russian and her second, French. She was the reason so much of my high school French stayed with me, since she sometimes forgot to speak in English. This occurred with some frequency during ballet class, because all the steps are in French. We *glissade* when we glide, *jeté* when we jump, and pirouette in two directions: *en dehors* and *en dedans*.

Unsure of how well I understood what she'd written, I handed it back. "You write beautifully, Madame, but I'm a little rusty. Why don't you read it aloud to us, and we can all take notes?"

Madame put on her reading glasses. Probably even she had trouble figuring out what she'd written. "First, I think to myself, sounds like Philip is killer. But then I think, too soon to decide that. Other people wanted Pavel to be dead. Who most of all?"

She tapped the pen on the side of her head. "And then I think of the so very sad answer. Many dancers and teachers, that's who will benefit, because Pavel, he bring Artistic Solutions into company." She had a rueful expression on her face. "Maybe killer is thinking, if Pavel dies, all my problems with Artistic Solutions, they go away." She glanced in Barbara's direction. "So maybe your friend, he not a killer. We must keep the open mind."

Barbara ran a nervous hand through her hair, mussing its usual perfection. "It's possible someone from the dance company is guilty, but I don't think we should take anyone from Artistic Solutions off the list of possible suspects. I can assure you Professor Natalya Romanova would not agree. In my book, *Blades, Bodies, and Beowulf*, the detective assigned to the case makes the same kind of mistake, and Professor Romanova has to set things right."

Madame shrugged. "*Je ne sais pas.* I hope you are right. Would prefer killer to be one of the business people, not ballet people. Feel bad to say this, but must admit, is already better for me and all people I love with Pavel gone. Dearest Lelotchka, you get many new roles." She hesitated. "I not supposed to announce this yet, so please to keep to yourself, but the board already tell me I will be the ballet mistress in chief. Jonathan, he will be business side. I will be artistic side."

We raised our glasses to toast Madame's ascension to the post she dearly desired. I kept private my uneasiness, reluctant to mar her pleasure. She had more than earned her right to the job, but was that the reason she was chosen? I already knew my new performances were a consequence of Ron's desire to capitalize on my notoriety. Perhaps Madame's appointment also had less to do with merit than with politics or public relations.

Everyone adored Madame, from the dancers to the seamstresses. If Jonathan had a hand in the decision to put her in charge, or pretended it was his idea, he would garner strong support from the company.

I mentioned neither of those worries. "I agree that many people in the company are better off with Pavel gone, but I'm not sure life at ABC will be better without him, especially if Jonathan becomes artistic director. I'm so happy for you, Madame. But we can't rule anyone out, and at this point, Philip, Jonathan, Austin, and Savannah remain our prime suspects. They're all either a part of Artistic Solutions or in bed with them."

Gabi leaned over my shoulder. "I agree they're our most likely suspects. But I also think Madame is right about looking inside the company, as well as outside." She pointed to Mavis's name, which I included only because I didn't like her. "You've got Mavis and Horace on the list. What about your friend Olivia? Where was she when Ms. Crandall was pushed?"

I got up and stretched my aching joints. "Olivia left early to meet Jonathan. I'm sorry to report she seems to have succumbed to his slimy charm. I'll ask her tomorrow how long she was with him. She might be his alibi for the time Ms. Crandall was murdered, in which case I will regretfully cross him off the list."

Gabi tapped her fingers with a nervous beat. "Be careful how you approach Olivia. I'm as interested in her whereabouts as I am about Jonathan's." Echoing my thoughts about Savannah, she said, "Given Jonathan's reputation, it makes sense he was exploiting her. But what if it's the other way around? Let's not assume she's the innocent one. Behind the scenes, she could have been using him. Maybe she was the woman I saw with Jonathan, before he went into Bar Bleu."

Barbara wasn't buying it. "Jonathan preys on vulnerable dancers less than half his age. He's got quite a reputation. I agree with Leah. A kid like Olivia couldn't possibly be involved."

Gabi didn't give in. "We shouldn't dismiss a dancer on the make. What I know about her so far is this: She's friends with Leah, who has much more status than she does. She recently dumped her boyfriend for someone rich and powerful."

I put up a hand to stop her. "Horace dumped Olivia, not the other way around. Olivia is probably on the rebound."

Gabi remained skeptical. "That's what she told you. Doesn't make it true. When was the last time you had a heart-to-heart conversation with Horace? Maybe he was the one on the rebound."

I found myself getting angry with Gabi, which almost never happened. "After you retired, Daniel was the only person left I could trust. And then, when I was going through a really tough time, Olivia stood by me when no one else in the company wanted to talk to me. I trust her as much as I would you. She also happens to be a fabulous dancer, who doesn't need the help of a predatory creep like Jonathan to get ahead."

Gabi spoke softly. "People change. If Olivia doesn't get her promotion soon, some fresh-faced seventeen-year-old, who also is a fabulous dancer, is waiting in the wings, ready to take her place. You know that as well as anyone."

I didn't agree with her but was too emotional to argue. Gabi didn't know Olivia. I did. Barbara stood over me and smoothed my forehead. "Don't frown like that. It makes wrinkles."

Melissa rolled her eyes at this pronouncement. With a conciliatory smile, she said, "I don't know Olivia, so I can't speculate about her motives. What I do know is that she's playing a dangerous game. Jonathan Llewellyn Franklin IV is not someone to trifle with."

I drained the last of my water and poured some more. "Yeah, I vaguely remember reading something about that. His ex-wife accused him of…what was it? Mental cruelty?"

Barbara narrowed her nose, a gesture she saves for people she finds contemptible. "Not just mental cruelty. There were allegations of physical abuse as well."

I felt shaky and ill. What if Gabi was right, and Olivia was the woman Gabi saw with Jonathan? It made sense, since she did leave rehearsal early to meet him. She could be in danger. "I'll tell Olivia about Jonathan. Maybe that will make her think twice about having a relationship with him."

Melissa was grim. "Wealth and power can be irresistible." She looked earnestly at me. "For the moment, I agree with Gabi. Stay clear of Olivia, until we know for sure she's legit. She might be using you, and Jonathan, for her own ends."

I blinked back tears. "Please don't say that. It's hurtful."

Melissa was unrelenting. "I'm trying to protect you. I don't want to hurt your feelings. I know you think she's your friend. I hope I'm wrong, but in the meantime..."

I squared my shoulders. "In the meantime, we use her. Not the other way around."

I palmed two Excedrin and gulped them down, willing them to work their magic on my banging headache. "Enough of theorizing. We need a plan of action." I turned to my mother. "Barbara, the first thing you do is ditch Philip. Ghost him if you must. Tell him you met someone else. Or tell him you're getting back with Dad. That should do the trick."

Barbara huffed. "I'll do no such thing. If you can pump Olivia for information, I can do the same with Philip."

I would have smacked myself in the forehead if the headache didn't hurt as much as it did. "Do not, under any circumstances, let that man in your house. This isn't a game. Pavel is dead. Ms. Crandall is in the hospital. I don't want you to be the next victim."

With her usual clarity, Melissa observed, "We're all victims now, directly or indirectly. The police are doing all they can. But we can't afford to sit on the sidelines like helpless females, hoping we get saved. The only way to get free of this mess is to fix it ourselves."

Intent on our conversation, we barely registered Madame's disappearance. While she conducted a conversation in Russian in the bedroom, we cleared the table. When Madame ended her phone call, she stopped us. "Olga come in morning to clean. She get upset if we not let her do everything her way."

I put down the plate. "Is Olga your cleaning lady? Or your housekeeper?"

Madame paused. "Olga clean houses, yes, and offices too, but she is my friend. She come from Odessa. Not a dancer, but she have artistic sensibility."

A germ of an idea came to me." Would you—would Olga—be interested in temporarily working at the ballet studio? Ron said he fired one of the cleaning staff. Maybe Olga could get the job and we could pay her extra to spy for us."

Barbara interrupted before Madame could answer. "You can't do that, Leah. You can't put an innocent woman's life in danger. It's one thing for us.

We're already involved. But we cannot allow another person to put herself in harm's way."

Madame bit back a smile. "Not to worry about Olga. She very good at taking care of herself. This is the idea I have myself. Is why I called her."

Gabi laughed and spoke in an exaggerated New York accent. "What am I, chopped liver?"

My unjustified anger with her disappeared. I love it when Gabi uses expressions she picked up from my family. "Yes. You're the best chopped liver from the finest deli on the Lower East Side."

Barbara hugged Gabi. "You are unique. We bend the rules for you. But also, you wouldn't face the danger that someone at the studio would." She grabbed Gabi's shoulders. "All the same, never meet any of our suspects in private. We're tracking a killer, and the studio isn't the only place that's dangerous."

I stared meaningfully at Barbara. "That goes for you too."

Madame said, "Then all is settled. I talk to Olga, but I know already this she will do. I will send the email tonight to Ron." She clasped her hands together. "Very exciting time. We have mole. Like KGB."

Madame walked us to the elevator. "We must never forget most important thing. Is killer going to murder someone else? Or is there more people going to be attacked?" She held me close. "I worry. You need be careful. Look behind two backs!"

Madame's Russian idioms didn't often translate well into English, but this time we knew exactly what she was talking about.

Chapter Twenty

You dance love, and you dance joy, and you dance dreams.
—Gene Kelly

The morning after our dinner at Madame's apartment, in the early hours before ballet class, I set out for a diner near Carnegie Hall. Not to eat, of course, but to meet Madame. Ensconced in her usual booth, Madame spoke intently to a large woman with red cheeks and bright blue eyes. As I approached the table, the woman leaped to her feet.

She wrapped thick arms around me. "I am Olga. I will help." She drew back and searched my face. "But I think you are Russian, no?"

I sat down to recover from the unexpected enthusiasm of her embrace. "Yes, Olga, but not for the last few generations. My great-grandparents came here from Odessa."

She squeezed both my hands. "But I! I too! From Odessa!" She burst into a stream of Russian. Madame placidly drank her coffee while Olga chattered away. I opened my mouth to explain I knew exactly four Russian words, but Madame wagged her finger to stop me. While I waited for Olga's flood of Russian reminiscences to stop, I flexed my fingers to check if Olga had broken any major bones.

I put my hands in my lap to avoid further injury. "I'm pleased to meet you, Olga. Has Madame explained what you're going to be doing at American Ballet Company?"

Olga gave me a two-thumbs-up sign. "But yes, of course. I am there to spy on people. This, I can do." She looked meaningfully at Madame. "Have had some experience, yes? I am a cleanup expert!"

Madame laughed. "Yes. I'd say so." She then spoke a few words in Russian that made Olga so happy she pounded the table in delight.

I texted Barbara to assuage her worries about Olga's safety. Ballet dancers pride themselves on their strength, but Olga looked capable of crushing anyone at American Ballet Company foolish enough to get in her way. Her physical power, combined with her benevolent demeanor, made her look like the offspring of a Sherman tank and Glinda the Good Witch.

The waitress filled our coffee cups and placed a basket of rye toast in front of Madame. Olga dug into the Carnegie Hall Breakfast Special: eggs, toast, home fries, sausage, and pancakes. She offered me one of her pancakes, but of course, I couldn't accept.

The scent of all that food made me so hungry. If Madame hadn't been sitting across from me, I would have ordered my own Breakfast Special. Instead, I mentally repeated my new diet mantra, which was a combination of self-flagellation and cheerleader-type pep talk.

Madame said, as if apropos of nothing, "Austin's new ballet is getting costumes today. It will be a leotard ballet." She looked at me with kindness and concern.

Upon hearing those words, the scent of pancakes and toast became much less appetizing. Leotard ballets mean the dancers are clad only in that. Sometimes we wear tights, but often our legs are bare. Onstage, leotards are brutally unforgiving, especially under bright lights. They don't simply reveal flaws. They magnify them.

I groaned. "I'd rather dance in a tent than in a leotard." I tried to stay optimistic. "Maybe the leotards will be black."

Madame was all business. "Not for women. Men in all black. With black masks. Women, all white. With white headbands."

She didn't have to explain further. I would have to lose the extra weight or face the mockery and cruelty of the critics. Or I might be removed from the ballet altogether. Over the years I'd been a sympathetic and horrified witness to the effect that even a modest weight gain had on dancers' careers. Puberty, for example, ended many girls' dreams of a life onstage, if they had the misfortune to grow breasts, or if their thighs expanded past the dimensions of a popsicle stick. The girls who made it safely through adolescence were required to maintain a pre-pubescent body until the day they retired. I had my retirement dinner already planned: a pastrami sandwich on rye with extra mustard, followed by at least one, possibly two, black and white cookies.

Still painful to me was the memory of watching a rehearsal director chastise a ballerina for gaining weight. She had dazzled audiences in her role as the Sugar Plum Fairy in *The Nutcracker,* and as a young student, I idolized her. The year I joined the company, the rehearsal director began publicly referring to this red-haired dancer as Plumpkin. He wasn't the only one. The former critic of *The New York Times* was especially brutal, speculating on the exact number of pounds the poor woman had gained. It was a cautionary tale I never forgot. One day you're on top, and the next you're teaching kindergarten classes at Dolly Dinkle's School of Ballet.

In lieu of eating, I took a deep cleansing breath. "Thanks, Madame. Don't worry about me. I'll lose the weight."

She smiled at me. "Good girl, Lelotchka. Best to stop eating as much as possible. Very effective. Will not kill you."

Madame was not urging me to a life of anorexia or bulimia. She was simply telling me the most efficient method to lose weight. I got the message and was grateful to get it from Madame and not from someone far less sympathetic.

Having made her point, Madame concentrated on the business of the day. "Lelotchka, I make phone calls already. Olga doing one-week trial as substitute cleaning lady. She start today. What is plan?"

Olga's blue eyes got even brighter. "Yes! We make plan."

I was exhausted after a sleepless night, but Olga's enthusiasm was infectious. "You should pretend you have a hard time understanding English. Whenever someone tells you something, repeat it slowly, like you're trying to mentally translate the directions. Maybe ask them to explain a particular word. That will make people more likely to talk in front of you. If you hear something suspicious, or if the people you see talking look as if they're telling secrets, record the conversation on your phone. Do you know how to do that?"

Olga was amused. "Yes. Have much experience with this."

I considered the unfortunate fact that most of the world communicates electronically. "Since we're not going to be able to access anyone's computer or phone, we should review any written material we can find. Olga, if it's not too much to ask, don't throw out any papers. In fact, don't throw out any of the trash. It'll be easy enough to get papers from the recycling bin, but if anyone wants to bury a literal paper trail, they're more likely to throw it in the garbage."

Olga didn't assent with the same degree of enthusiasm. I hastened to reassure her. "If this is asking too much, let me know. We'll figure something out that doesn't require so much time."

Having recklessly left my right arm on the table, Olga gave me another of her bone-crunching squeezes. "No! Not too much work! Not enough work! Because I do other cleaning jobs too if you want. Not just garbage. I am also good fisher. No cleaning lady does fishing like Olga." She puffed out her chest, proud of her skills.

Madame, who is so technologically insecure she refers to her tentative forays into technology with the trepidation others use when discussing a trek to the top of Mount Everest, intervened to translate. "Olga, as she say, is cleaning expert. She also fish. On internet. She can fish. Or maybe she hooks the fishes? Not certain how it works."

I wasn't sure I understood what they were telling me. Did Olga fish? Or did she phish?

Olga explained. "I am good spear phisher. That mean once I am inside company, I can get information for who you like. No problem."

I asked, as delicately as possible. "Olga, if you have all these, er, skills, why are you cleaning houses?"

"Madame is dear friend. I clean for her, yes. But we are friends." Mindful of Madame's frailty, Olga did not hug her, but put both her hands to her mouth to mimic a hearty kiss. "Madame help me get started in my little side business. In Brighton Beach. In Brooklyn. You know this place?"

I knew Brighton Beach very well. My grandmother was born there, after her parents fled the Soviet Union. Huge numbers of Russians emigrated to Brighton Beach, which gave it its nickname, Little Odessa. I also knew it was a center for the Russian mafia.

Olga looked concerned. "You are worried about me? Not to worry. You can trust Olga. I only work for good guys." She gave me a quizzical look, perhaps thinking I would disapprove. "Mostly good guys. After all, must pay bills!"

I considered the possible risks of using Olga to infiltrate American Ballet Company. Olga might be a member of the Russian mafia. Or the KGB. Or the CIA. Or some other organization with three letters in its name and about which I knew nothing. I didn't care. I already liked her and trusted her. Looking at her earnest, open, face, which was probably a terrific asset for a woman who phished and spied, I couldn't help laughing. Seeing me laugh made the other two laugh as well.

Olga pounded the table to try to contain her mirth. When the silverware stopped dancing and the plates settled down, we made a few minor adjustments to our plan. Madame said she would alert Olga via text message if she saw anything suspicious. She is quite proud of her texting skills and recently sent me her first emoji, which she followed with seventeen hearts. I was nervous, though, about having her communicate via text. Madame's vanity doesn't allow her to wear glasses, and the font on her text messages is large enough to be legible from a football field away.

"Great idea, Madame. But don't take any risks. Make the text short. Olga will know what to do."

Madame is not easily fooled. "What you think? I not good spy?"

I tried to appease her. "I think you're a wonderful spy. Look how you helped me out last year. I couldn't have investigated without you."

She nodded. "Yes, I give you much help. But not worry about text messages. Or anybody knowing. We text in Russian. Like a secret code. No one there know Russian. Only me and Olga. We get fishing together." She spoke briefly in Russian to Olga, who again became so overcome with laughter she could contain herself only after pounding so hard the coffee sloshed from our cups.

Olga translated for me. "If we mushrooms, we jump in basket."

Another bit of Slavic wisdom lost in translation.

Chapter Twenty-One

When the music changes, so does the dance.
—African proverb

I left Madame and Olga to finish their breakfast and hurried to the studio. With more than an hour to go before Madame began the daily company class, I was hoping to do a bit of sleuthing myself. I was already wearing my leotard and tights under my street clothes, as an extra layer of protection from the icy weather that continued to torment the denizens of New York City.

I made a pit stop in the dressing room, where I swapped jeans and a sweater for leg warmers and a sweatshirt, and then quietly roamed the halls of the studio. Because I wanted to escape notice, I drew inspiration from one of my favorite ballets, *Giselle*. The frail, seemingly helpless title character, who dies of a broken heart in Act I, was not as unlikely an inspiration as one might think. She returns in Act II as a powerful, if ghostly, incarnation of her earlier self. She appears only when she wishes to be seen, which was my goal as well. I silently hummed Adolphe Adam's music to give me courage.

The main office was off-limits. Savannah was already at her desk, and there was little I could do with her standing guard. Investigating the office would have to wait for an after-hours visit with Olga for protection.

I went upstairs to the costume room, which took up the entire top story of the building. Floor-to-ceiling windows let in the pale February sunshine, which wasn't yet bright enough to take the chill out of the room. I examined Bobbie's desk. It was covered with swatches of gleaming fabric.

Underneath layers of material was a clipboard, with a printed invoice covered in handwritten notes. I bent closer and flipped through the papers beneath the invoice. A printout from Artistic Solutions, marked Private and Confidential, was on the bottom. It was titled *Restructuring the Future!*

I focused the camera on my phone to record the information. A nearby door slammed with unnerving force, and I dropped my phone onto the desk. A chilly gust of wind, scented with cigarette smoke, blew in my direction, and a gravelly voice demanded, "What the hell are you doing here?"

Because temperatures outside hovered below zero, it hadn't occurred to me that Bobbie was still taking her cigarette breaks on the roof. The nicotine had not improved her temper, perhaps because the calming effects of her cigarette were muted by incipient frostbite.

I put a hand to my chest. "You almost gave me a heart attack! Do you always sneak up on people like that?" Despite my nervousness, I had the presence of mind to move a few of the fabric samples so they covered the memo from Artistic Solutions.

Bobbie got close enough for me to smell the lingering smoke on her breath and her clothes. She pointed out, with some reason, "This is my room. You're the one sneaking around. Now get the hell out of here before I call the police."

I casually slipped the phone in my bag, sat down in her chair, and crossed my legs. "Don't be ridiculous. We both work here, and I'm scheduled for a costume fitting. However, should you decide to make a fool of yourself by calling the police, make sure to ask for Jonah Sobol in Homicide.

She slammed her hand against the bulletin board. "Get out of my chair this instant. You're not supposed to be here until four o'clock. Until then this room is off-limits to you. I'm giving you five seconds. Then I'm calling…I'll call, uh, Madame." Seeing my amused expression, she amended her threat. "Ron. I'll complain to Ron and…" Her voice trailed off. She knew perfectly well it would do her no good to complain to Madame or Ron. Madame loved me, and Ron cared about nothing and no one except himself and his precious plants. It was a sad state of affairs at American Ballet Company when the only person nominally in charge was a third-rate administrator whose green thumb was bigger than his brain.

"You're going to look like an idiot if you try to report me. Although now that I think about it, that's never stopped you before. In fact, while you're at it, why not make a citizen's arrest?"

I held out both wrists, and in doing so, knocked several swatches of fabric onto the floor. This enraged her beyond what was normal. As she gathered the swatches, I replaced the Artistic Solutions memo in its original position.

"Get out! And don't come back!" She pushed me aside and deposited the swatches on the desk. I walked toward the exit but turned to look at her one last time.

Bobbie's rage continued unabated as she muttered dire imprecations against me, American Ballet Company, and Artistic Solutions. Her wrath, while somewhat justified, was unnerving. I'd known her for years, but for the first time, I felt threatened.

It didn't take a genius to understand that Bobbie's anger cloaked an insecure and weak personality. She terrorized her husband with fits of jealousy, believing every woman secretly harbored an unquenchable desire for that chubby, mild-mannered, middle-aged man. She was brutal to her staff of seamstresses, who trembled at her fits of temper. And yet, even for her choleric temperament, the depth of her emotion seemed extreme. Bobbie was hiding something important. She wasn't simply angry. She was nervous, even more nervous than I was. Perhaps she was afraid of becoming the next victim. Maybe she was afraid of her own capacity for violence. Someone slammed Pavel with a silver, scrolled ballet prop. That attack, like the push that sent Ms. Crandall down a flight of stairs, might not have been premeditated. Both attacks could have been acts of impulsive violence.

I retreated to the bathroom. After checking under each stall to ensure privacy, I called Ms. Crandall, as I had each day since she was taken to the hospital. Still no answer. I had better luck with the floor nurse, who said I would be able to visit for a short period of time during regular hours. We'd had no news about her condition, other than that she was grateful for the flowers, gifts, and cards. I was relieved to know she was on the mend.

As soon as I could, I would visit her and take Barbara with me. In the few hours my mother had spent with her, she'd gotten closer to the office manager than those of us who'd known her for years. For my other plan, I needed a different type of assistance. I tapped a message to Olga. Time for her first mission.

After ballet class, I headed to the first rehearsal of *Precious Metals*. With Pavel gone, whatever influence Mavis once had was now much diminished. Unfortunately, this turn of events made our guest artist an even more unlikely suspect. I looked forward to the day Mavis exited the company, and I didn't much care if it was in handcuffs or on the next flight headed to Heathrow Airport.

Our fractious relationship was grounded in more than the usual competition between ballerinas. During her last stint with ABC as a guest artist, critics compared her interpretation of the Swan Queen unfavorably against mine. She was incandescent with rage, and her veneer of gentle cooperation cracked. Mavis was friendly only to dancers who didn't threaten her, so theoretically I should have been pleased by her enmity.

As I entered Studio C, the opening bars of the music for *Precious Metals* greeted me. The Mozart clarinet concerto was one of my favorites, but it had three movements. With Mavis and Kerry by my side, sixteen bars would have been ample.

Madame was in charge of coaching us. My role, Silver Maiden, had originally been choreographed on her. Ballerinas take seriously the responsibility of keeping alive the choreography of previous generations. Despite the ubiquity of film, no digital version can replace this sacred tradition.

Olivia was already warming up when I arrived. I put my dance bag next to hers. "I'm glad you're here. What role are you dancing?"

She put her leg on the barre and bent over it. "Bronze Girl."

The role of Bronze Girl was second only to the Golden Lady and Silver Maiden. It was reserved for the most promising young dancers. "Congratulations! Why didn't you tell me? I'm so happy we'll be dancing together. I thought Kerry was cast in that role."

Olivia switched legs so that she no longer faced my direction. "I didn't find out until this morning. I was supposed to be dancing in the corps and understudying Kerry. I was as surprised as I'm sure everyone else it."

I glanced at Kerry, who was deep in conversation with Mavis. Their recent squabble over Horace's affections appeared to have ended. This was sensible. Horace wasn't worth the sacrifice of even their shallow friendship. The two dancers strode over in perfect unison.

Kerry snapped her fingers at Olivia, who remained face down over her outstretched leg. "Hello? Anyone home?"

Olivia straightened. "Not to you."

Kerry was unlikely to dispel the myth that dancers are dumb. Mavis, seeing her minion's blank look, took over the attack on Olivia. "You're not the only one with friends in high places. I'd watch my back if I were you." She swiveled to face me. "Same goes for you. This time, when you're swinging the murder weapon, you'll have witnesses."

I knew this was coming. There were several copies of my prop for the ballet, an intricately scrolled piece of silvered metal. By this time, the whole world knew the killer had used one of them to kill Pavel. I'd spent two sleepless hours worrying about having to touch it, let alone wield it in a series of technically challenging turns and jumps.

Playing defense doesn't work with bullies. I stared directly into Mavis's eyes. "Brilliant observation. You're quite the mental giant. I guess the extra free time on your rehearsal schedule has really paid dividends for your IQ level."

She practically spit her words at me. "I will bury you. Onstage, of course." She flipped her hand in Olivia's direction. "And that goes double for your conniving little Mini-Me."

It's true Olivia looks a lot like me, and not at all like most of American Ballet Company's new recruits. We're not a very diverse group. In a ballet company full of tall dancers, we are tiny; amid many blondes we're dark-haired with large, dark eyes. In only one way were we like most dancers, and that was in the color of our skin. After Gabi retired, we had only five dancers of color, which had earned the company several biting commentaries. At least no one has to powder over dark skin anymore. In the world of ballet, that counts as progress. When it comes to body types, only size zero and under need apply.

I stood my ground. "Old-school ballerinas like you have been scheming and backstabbing other dancers for many years. In your case, many, many, years."

Mavis's sallow skin was marred by white and purple patches of rage. She hissed, "Bugger off. Not only can I take care of myself, I can take care of anyone who crosses me."

Few dancers reach the summit of professional ballet without grinding their pointe shoes into every hapless soul who gets in their way. I didn't know if Mavis was talking about me or Olivia or someone else, but in any case, I believed her. I smiled sweetly. "I'm so sorry you feel this way. I can imagine how tough it's going to be for you to go head-to-head against me and Olivia. I'm not surprised you're so nervous about it."

Kerry finally piped up. "That's what you think! It should have been me showing her up."

The idiocy of her words put a temporary check on both Mavis and me.

Olivia laughed. "Watch out, Mavis. I think Kerry just said she wanted to be the one to dance you off the stage."

Madame interrupted with three short claps, and we leapt to attention. The respect we gave her sprang from our appreciation of her talent and was very different from the fear Pavel had inspired. All of us had seen grainy videos of Madame's acclaimed performance in the same ballet we were rehearsing. As always, she spoke from a deep well of experience. Her love of ballet, which she fervently believed was the epitome of all the arts, was evident in every word and gesture.

Madame called the principal dancers and the understudies to the center of the room and discussed the nuances of each part. Mavis and I had danced all the roles in this ballet many times. Olivia, who had understudied Bronze Girl the previous year, had spent hours on YouTube, reviewing every step. The corps de ballet, however, needed a lot of attention. This should have rendered dancing in that rehearsal as easy and enjoyable as eating chocolate chip cookies dipped in ice cream, but I found myself fighting for space each time Mavis danced next to me.

I was relieved when it came time to run through the first solo. Normally, I wouldn't have danced it full out, time after time. But that day I did, because I have my pride. The individual variations for the lead ballerinas are not explicitly framed as a contest of skill, but that's how Mavis and I danced them. Every nailed pirouette was a stab in the other ballerina's eye, and every jump was an attempt to leap over and crush each other's ego.

The spillover of our personal lives into our dance lives was not the norm. Most times, the ballerina who dances Princess Aurora isn't in love with the guy who dances Prince Désiré. She might, in fact, want to bash her pointe shoes over his head. Nor does she hold a grudge against Carabosse, the cross-dressing Wicked Fairy who dooms her to sleep for one hundred years. Once the curtain comes down, they might be best friends or in a long-term relationship. Nonetheless, the whole time Mavis and I were in that rehearsal, we might as well have been locked in a fight to the death. We already loathed each other, and every moment we had to share the stage turned into a balletic rendition of a professional wrestling tournament. No blood, but plenty of sweat and pain.

The drama of our fierce desire to outdo each other had everyone in the room spellbound. Ron and Jonathan, who watched from the sidelines, conferred quietly as they watched us.

I finished a series of rapid-fire turns that circled the floor and ended in an arabesque. My knee stayed strong, and I held the balance for several seconds, which is an eternity for that pose. A few young dancers clapped and squealed, and Madame nodded her approval. Her opinion mattered more to me than a standing ovation. I gasped for air, conscious I had only a few minutes to gather myself before the next grueling section of the work.

Olivia's role did not require her to dance with me or Mavis. She led the corps de ballet and had two short solos, one when she summons them onstage, and another, when she dismisses them. She swooped into the space I vacated, and sixteen bars later the corps de ballet followed her. As strenuous as the rehearsal was for me, it turned out to be the least taxing, and least threatening, part of the day.

At the end of our allotted time, we curtseyed and clapped for Madame. I picked up my dance bag, which, as usual, I'd left open and unattended for most of the day. A tightly folded note peeked out from the tangle of pointe shoes. I smoothed it out.

In block letters, it read: BEWARE

Chapter Twenty-Two

Dance for me a minute, and I'll tell you who you are.
—Mikhail Baryshnikov

After receiving the threatening note, I was afraid to go to the dressing room alone. In the dark days of winter few dancers lingered after hours, and I was taking no chances without a friend by my side. I'd texted Jonah, but no death threat was potent enough for me to meet him without first taking a shower and applying makeup. I might be the target of a killer, but thanks to Barbara, I had my standards. No amount of vanity, however, was sufficient to make me risk a *Psycho*-type moment in the process. I was grateful Olivia was willing to wait while I primped.

In a corner of the dressing room, away from prying eyes, I showed Olivia the scrap of folded paper, holding it by the corners.

"Have you called the police?" She reached for the paper, but I snatched it away. I didn't want her fingerprints to mar any evidence I hadn't already muddied.

I tried not to shriek. "Of course I called the police! I'm terrified I'll end up at the bottom of the stairs with blood pouring out of my head."

She hovered near the door. "What do you need me to do? I, uh, I have plans, but I'll cancel them if you need me."

I took a deep breath. I never questioned Olivia's relationship with the horrible Horace, as much as I'd loathed him. but the stakes were much higher where her new boyfriend was concerned. "Do these plans include Jonathan? I'm worried about you, Olivia. If you really like him, that's fine.

But you don't need him. If you're feeling pressured by him, talk to Madame. Or Ron. Or anyone. I don't trust Jonathan. Believe me, I have my reasons."

She was bitter. "Do you seriously think it's a good idea for me to complain about Jonathan? I might as well kiss my career goodbye. As for Ron, don't kid yourself. He acts like he's running the show, but he's in the Franklin family's pocket. And those pockets are very deep. Ron's number one job is raising money. He will strip me of every role I have if I alienate Jonathan. As for Mrs. Franklin, I've heard she's even more vindictive than Jonathan. And more powerful. I wouldn't be so casual about their influence if I were you."

I shook my hair free from its bobby pins. "You're not wrong about the Franklin family, but I'm not sure you realize the kind of danger I'm talking about. One person has been murdered. Another is in the hospital after being brutally attacked. That scares me more than possible blowback from the Franklin family."

I realized, as soon as the words were out of mouth, that I was neither as brave, nor as independent, as I wished I were. My career was still as much a matter of life and death for me as it was for Olivia.

She exhaled an exasperated sigh. "The last person to annoy Jonathan and his devoted mommy was Wendy Severin, who is now pirouetting to her heart's content in Wyoming. And here's a fun fact: More people audition for ABC than live in Wyoming."

Olivia, like many New Yorkers, has a deadly fear of living in a location that lacks twenty-four-hour access to bagels, lox, and public transportation. Like me, she doesn't know how to drive, and her culinary skills are limited to making coffee. She continued to detail the misery of Wendy's life. "Unless you've developed a taste for chicken fried steak and minimum wage contracts, I'd keep my mouth shut if I were you."

She broke off and looked impatiently at the clock. "I don't have much time. Tell me what you need me to do."

I stripped off my sweaty leotard and tights. "I need you to stand guard while I shower. I'm meeting Jonah, and I don't want to look as frazzled as I feel. I won't be long. Make sure no one tries to kill me while I'm washing the soap out of my eyes."

She sat down and pulled out a sandwich and a banana. It was good that one of us wasn't completely panicked. But maybe she was stress-eating.

The smell of peanut butter, which is usually more appealing than perfume, sickened me. "How can you be so calm about this?"

She ate with undiminished appetite. "I'm being supportive, and it won't help you one bit if I start freaking out. I'm trying to stay logical and unemotional, and I can't do that on an empty stomach."

I took out a bag of toiletries. "How do you manage to eat so much and stay so crazy skinny? My sole ambition at this point in my life is to eat what you eat and weigh what you weigh."

From the corner of my eye, I saw her cheeks flush. She stuffed the sandwich back in her lunch bag, and said, "Just lucky, I guess. I've always been this way."

With some remorse, I assured her, "Don't let me stop you." I feared overstepping any boundaries Olivia might have erected concerning food. For many dancers, eating, or to be perfectly honest, eating disorders, are far more delicate a topic than discussions about sex.

I kept my tone lighthearted. "You're not doing anything you shouldn't, are you?"

She gave me a mocking look. "Why, whatever are you talking about? Surely you don't think I'm doing anything unhealthy?"

I hesitated before answering. She continued, with an undertone that sounded resentful, "You don't think I'm hiding anything, do you? Or maybe you're suspicious because you're the one who's hiding something from me."

This time I was the one whose cheeks flushed. I wasn't sure if she was referring to eating or to Jonathan. I hadn't told her I was investigating him with the help of Gabi and Madame Maksimova, and I was certain none of my co-conspirators would have told her of our plans. But she must have guessed something was going on. I wondered if Madame had questioned her. I was sorely tempted to confide in her, despite my sister's warning.

I angled my body away from Olivia and texted Madame, Olga, Gabi, and Barbara. **New development! Put everything on hold for now—will txt ltr Stay home & safe- xoxo**

Olivia said, "Maybe the note wasn't meant as a threat. Maybe the person who wrote it was a friend, someone who wanted you to be careful." She put both hands on the wall and stretched her Achilles tendons.

I stuck my hand in the shower to test the temperature. "I don't have your faith in humanity. If it wasn't some sick joke by Mavis or Kerry, I think it was the killer. Hence my request to have you literally watch my back. I'm afraid to be naked and alone."

She considered this. "Not Mavis. She is too self-absorbed, and she's going back to London soon. Kerry is a better bet. Unless, as you said, it was the killer. And while I wouldn't put it past either of them to take out the competition, neither one had any reason to murder Pavel or Ms. Crandall."

I amended her statement. "Neither of them had any reason to kill Pavel or Ms. Crandall that we know." I stepped into the shower, but that gentle remedy didn't do much to relax me. I was so nervous, the tube of body wash slipped out of my hands and through a gap in the shower curtain. I retrieved it in time to see Olivia bend over my open dance bag.

She smiled at me without a trace of nervousness or guilt. "Don't look so shocked. I'm not stealing anything." She took a gold bottle from my bag. "I couldn't help but notice you got the same gift I did, presumably from the same secret admirer. Mavis has one too."

A wave of fear made me dizzy. "I don't know where that came from. What's inside?"

She resumed eating. "It's a bottle of that foot powder. I threw mine away. The label said it's supposed to be good for your feet, but I didn't like the smell."

I stepped out of the shower, got dressed, and put my makeup on with an economy of motion that would have made an efficiency expert proud. "Please be careful. I'll walk you back to your place and tell Jonah I'm going to be late. I don't want you to be alone."

Olivia took out a brush and ran it through her long hair. "Don't worry about me. I'm not going to be alone. As I said, I have plans."

My meeting with Jonah did not qualify as a date, even without the death threat. We were simply having coffee together at my favorite place, Café Figaro. He offered to buy me a drink, but after an early start at the diner with Olga and Madame, I needed a booster shot of caffeine.

As usual, all the tables at Café Figaro were full. Several people looked at me for a longer period of time than is normally considered polite, but at the Café Figaro, that was also typical. The owners' daughter, an aspiring photographer, had used me as a model for her college portfolio. Her work and my image lined the walls.

Jonah didn't immediately see me walk in. I watched him read through his notes and then look up at a picture of me in Central Park, in a tutu, in the middle of winter. I preferred the more polished studio portraits, where my hair, makeup, and costumes were without blemish. But I knew that picture of me, with my hair around my shoulders and no lipstick, was Jonah's favorite. Not for the first time, I wondered if he had a girlfriend. He rarely talked about his personal life.

Mrs. Pizzuto greeted me warmly and led me to his table. She, like my mother, was heavily invested in getting me married. Unlike Barbara, she'd chosen Jonah over Zach.

She nodded to her husband, who began brewing two double espressos. "How 'bout some cannoli, Detective? Or pignoli cookies? They just came out of the oven." She circled my wrist with her fingers. "So skinny! Have the cookies, for once. They're very small. Practically dietetic."

Jonah laughed. "Thanks, Mrs. Pizzuto. Bring us a plate of cookies, and I'll do my best to persuade Leah to eat one or two."

I smiled in assent, although I was so anxious about my weight, I would sooner eat soap than cookies. When Mrs. Pizzuto left, I handed Jonah the note.

In an instant, his mouth went from smiling to grim. "Do you have any idea who committed this obscenity?"

"Yes. I have good reason to believe either Austin or Jonathan placed it in my bag. Or maybe Ron. You should arrest all of them. Arrest Savannah too, to be on the safe side." I didn't mention Olivia. She had the best opportunity to plant the note, but I couldn't bring myself to seriously consider her a suspect.

Jonah took out his notebook and pen. "I'm assuming you have some basis for this deduction. Is it because they had a good opportunity to place it in your bag? Did any of them approach you? Threaten you?" His eyes narrowed. "Or did you do something to threaten them?"

I hesitated before answering. I wasn't quite ready to reveal the plans I'd made with Madame and was especially anxious to hide Olga's involvement. Judging from the little she'd told me about her life, it seemed likely she was involved in dealings that weren't strictly legal. She didn't need law enforcement prying into what she euphemistically called her cleaning service.

I could have saved myself the trouble of dissembling. Jonah looked long and hard at my face. I found it difficult to meet his gaze and focused on the wall behind his head. He tossed his pen on the table. "Are you and Madame and Gabi back in the amateur detective business?"

I swallowed hard and suppressed the urge to cry. "Don't be angry. We—it all started in response to Savannah and her social media onslaught against me. I wanted to clear my name. And then, after Ms. Crandall was attacked, Savannah went after Barbara. We had to do something to protect ourselves."

He didn't respond, so I kept going. "After Ms. Crandall had her—well, I guess it wasn't an accident—but anyway, after she was attacked, I waited around for Savannah to leave the studio. I figured if I caught her off-guard, she might explain why she'd targeted me and Barbara in her smear campaign." I rushed through the rest of my feeble, and not entirely truthful, explanation of our adventures at Bar Bleu.

Jonah's tone was not friendly. "Bar Bleu is a good half-mile from the studio. So you and your mother decided to spy on four people you already suspected might be dangerous?"

I cleared my throat. "Not exactly. Barbara wasn't there. Gabi was with me."

His words dripped with sarcasm. "That makes all the difference in the world, knowing that Gabi was there for protection." He clenched his fist. "Someone in American Ballet Company is a murderer. And you've decided to put a target on your back. Is there anything I can say that will make you back down? Or is my next visit to the studio going to be an investigation of your death?"

I was not quite as angry as he was, but my temperature was on the rise. "I was going to tell you, even without the note. Is it so hard for you to understand that this is personal? My career is on the line. My reputation is on the line. And now my mother is also involved."

"Is your career worth your life?" He gripped his coffee cup so hard I worried the porcelain cup would crack. "You haven't mentioned your doctor friend. Is he the one you're confiding in? Do you, for some insane reason, think he can protect you better than I can?"

I got up. "I don't need a man to protect me. Not now. Not ever."

It was my exit line, but Jonah hadn't read the script. He tossed some money on the table and followed me out into the street. "Where are you going? Don't you understand anything?" He grabbed my shoulders and forced me to look directly at him. "I'm not just anyone. I'm a homicide detective. And I can't do my job if I have to worry every second about you."

I shivered in the cold. "Then stop worrying and let me help you. Maybe if you'd confide in me, I'd be better able to protect myself."

I tried to pull away, but he held me tighter. "Be reasonable. You know I can't do that."

"If you won't tell me anything, why should I talk to you?"

"I'm a cop. You're a ballerina. Surely you can see the difference."

I broke free and handed him the gold bottle, which I'd wrapped in a paper towel. "This was also placed in my bag. Other ballerinas have gotten it as well."

The color drained from his face. He placed it in a clear plastic bag. We stared at it, instead of each other, before parting.

Chapter Twenty-Three

Fine dancing, I believe like virtue, must be its own reward.
—Jane Austen

Hospitals make me queasy, even when I'm not the patient, and I enlisted Barbara's support for my visit to Ms. Crandall. The smell of disinfectant and the soft beeping of machines followed us as we traversed the hushed corridor. Ms. Crandall lay in a dimly lit room. An older woman rose from her chair as we entered, blocking our way. Even without her introduction, I could see she was a close relative.

Mrs. Talbot was no friendlier than her niece. "I hope you don't mind if I stay." Her granite expression made it clear she couldn't care less if we minded. Or if we left.

Barbara held out her hand. "I'm Barbara Siderova, and this is my daughter, Leah. I'm so sorry about what happened."

When Mrs. Talbot heard who we were her expression changed from unwelcoming to overtly hostile. She folded her arms and left Barbara's hand hanging in midair. "Michelle wanted to see you." Clearly, Mrs. Talbot didn't share the sentiment.

It took more than a single deliberate snub to quash my mother. "I found Michelle and called the ambulance. I stayed with her until the medics arrived. You can trust us."

We edged around Mrs. Talbot and approached the bed.

The change in Ms. Crandall shocked me. Her cheeks were sunken, and her face was still bruised. I spoke softly. "I'm happy to see you."

149

She nodded slightly. In a weak voice, she said to my mother. "You...you were there. I remember you came to the studio. What happened to me? One minute I was at work. The next thing I knew, I was in the hospital." Her eyes filled with tears. "I've lost a piece of my life. I want it back. Can you help me do that?"

Barbara and I exchanged glances. Mrs. Talbot said, "My niece has been through hell. You are not to ask her any questions that might upset her."

I was quick to soothe her. "We're here because we're worried about her."

She remained hostile. "Michelle doesn't remember what happened. She doesn't know who attacked her. You'll excuse me if I'm protective of her. The person who did this is still at large."

Barbara was sober but undaunted. "If you think I can't imagine how you feel, you're wrong. I can."

She placed a pile of books, tied in a festive red bow, on the nightstand, and I put a bouquet of flowers on the crowded windowsill. Two large baskets took up most of the space, one from American Ballet Company and another from Artistic Solutions. Smaller bunches of flowers bore cards from many people I didn't know and a few I did. Jonathan, Savannah, Ron, Gabi, Daniel, and Madame Maksimova had all sent personal gifts.

Mrs. Talbot picked up Barbara's books and shoved them into the closet. "Michelle can't read. She can't watch tv. She can't be around anyone or anything that causes her distress."

Barbara took Michelle's hand. "I understand. We'll be back when you're feeling stronger. Take care of yourself." She turned to Mrs. Talbot. "You too. Take care."

I was sickened by the damage done to both. "We didn't mean to intrude. But you can trust us. We pose no threat to Michelle. Quite the opposite. We won't rest until the person who did this is brought to justice."

Before leaving, we stopped by the nurses' station. I addressed the friendliest looking nurse. "When will Ms. Crandall be released? We're good friends with her, and we want to plan a nice party when she gets out."

The guy behind the desk was sympathetic. "Couldn't say right now."

Fishing for good news, I said, "She must be getting better, since she can have visitors."

He looked puzzled. "Um, yes. Uh, yeah. She's uh, she's okay to have visitors."

We stayed silent until we were outside the hospital. Barbara lit a cigarette. "Well, that was weird. Why do you think the nurse gave us that look?"

"Maybe it wasn't the doctors who decided to restrict visitors. Maybe it was her aunt."

She took several thoughtful puffs. "Or the police."

I should have been exhausted, but the tension and emotion of the day had me so wired that when I got home I cleaned the apartment in record time. Zach was coming over, and our relationship had not progressed to the point I felt comfortable having him see it, or me, looking less than perfect. He brought a bottle of wine and a stack of sandwiches.

I told him about Michelle, hoping for some medical insights.

He examined his sandwich with as much attention as if he were about to perform surgery on it. "Without seeing her it's hard to say. Sounds like a low-grade bleed. Depending on the severity of the bleed, it could be quite some time before she recovers."

I discarded the top slice of bread and picked at the vegetables. "She doesn't remember what happened. She doesn't know who pushed her down the stairs."

Zach finished his first sandwich and started on a second. "That's typical. She might not ever remember anything that happened in the hour or so before she fell. Not great, in terms of identifying the attacker, but not necessarily serious from a health perspective."

It felt as if years had passed since my morning meeting with Madame and Olga. Thinking over all that had transpired, I didn't immediately realize Zach was still talking. With an effort, I forced my attention back to him.

His eyes were creased with concern. "Stop poking at your food and eat something."

I looked down at the dismembered sandwich. "I think I'll take advantage of the fact that I'm not hungry."

"I'm worried about you. What's on your mind that you don't want me to know?"

I told him about the anonymous note I'd received. He was furious. "What is going on with the NYPD, that a girl like you is left unprotected?"

I pointed out, with some reason, that I wasn't a girl. This did not mollify him. "I apologize. Of course, you're a woman." He caressed me. "Very much a woman. But there's a killer loose at American Ballet Company. This Sobol guy and his partner are useless. Have they gotten anywhere yet in the investigation? Or are they counting on you to once again come to the rescue?"

Zach's comments irritated me. "They're working on the case. I trust them."

Zach took my hand in his. "I don't have your faith in either of them. You should take a sabbatical, or a leave of absence, or something. Nothing is worth putting your life in danger."

I pulled my hand away. "I can't just walk away. Ballet is my life."

He turned away as his phone buzzed a text. "I'm sorry, Leah, but I have to go. An emergency. I should be free in a few hours."

I never asked Zach if it was a medical or marital emergency that so often pulled us apart. Nor did I ever suggest that he take a leave of absence. He's an emergency room physician, and the hospital is often short-staffed. He's also divorced, and his relationship with his ex-wife is even more complicated than the one between my parents. He and Sloane have joint custody of their daughter, whom I had yet to meet.

He checked his watch. "I won't be gone long. I can be back in a few hours."

The offer was tempting. Despite many loving people in my life, there were times when I felt quite lonely. I did not doubt Zach's interest in me, but I couldn't yet commit to a relationship with him. Despite his divorce, he was far from unattached. "Not tonight. My rehearsal schedule tomorrow is a beast, and I need my beauty sleep."

He opened the door. "You're beautiful enough without the sleep. I'll call you when I'm done. In case you change your mind." He kissed me, but I could tell he had other things on his mind.

So did I. I restlessly tuned into my favorite mystery series and chose an episode I'd seen twice. The first two times I watched it, the show delivered the desired soporific effect, but the third time was not the charm. Random thoughts and worries charged through my brain and refused to let me relax.

I remembered, as if it had been ten years ago, instead of ten hours ago, Bobbie's fury at seeing me standing at her desk. Her anger was perfectly justified, and at my costume fitting a few hours later she took revenge by stabbing me several times with her dressmaker pins.

I turned off the program. I already knew who committed the fictional crime on the cop show, whereas I had no idea who'd committed the very real crime of killing Pavel. Restless, I called Olga. If she was still at the ballet studio, we could investigate together.

I could have gone alone, but I'm not brave. In addition to the very rational fear of violent killers, I also was afraid of rodents, high places, and many species of insects. Few people inspired me with as much confidence as Madame's friend, whom I already considered my friend as well.

Olga answered with booming enthusiasm. "Lelotchka! Is okay I call you that?"

Madame nearly always referred to me with that affectionate Russian nickname. "Of course, Olga. I'm happy to be Lelotchka to you, as well as to Madame."

She laughed. "Perfection, then. What you need, Lelotchka?"

I took a deep breath. "If it's not too late, I'd like to come by the studio. We can search the place together."

Olga spoke so loudly, I had to hold the phone away from my ear. Anyone within a football field of her would have been able to hear every word. "Perfection. Yes. Please to come now. I am still here and finding nothing good. Where to meet?"

I was already in my coat and hat. "Meet me in the costume room, on the top floor. We can work our way down from there."

"You got it! Will finish cleaning floors and meet you there. Please to wait for me."

I stepped out of the elevator and into the open space of the costume room.

The place was illuminated only by the dim glow of night lights, and spooky shadows lurked in every corner. I texted Olga to let her know I'd arrived but didn't turn on the lights. The large windows that gave out onto Broadway and to the buildings across the street would place me in a most unwelcome spotlight. While I waited for Olga, I returned to Bobbie's desk. The Artistic Solutions printout was no longer in the mess of papers scattered across the surface. I pulled open several drawers, which held nothing of apparent interest. The center drawer was locked. Perhaps Olga would know how to pick it.

While I waited, I decided to attack the lock myself. I located a sharp, hooked, dressmaking tool and got to work. The creaking and grinding sounds that emanated from Bobbie's drawer, as I tried to pry it open, echoed in the silent room. My woolen gloves made manipulating the lock difficult, but I didn't want to leave any fingerprints. Finally, I tossed the tool and jammed and ground the blade of a pair of scissors in the keyhole. The mechanism didn't unlatch, but with one final twist, the entire lock popped out. Underneath a pile of invoices, I found the Artistic Solutions printout and took several pictures. Bobbie was not going to overlook the fact that someone had broken into her desk, but at least she wouldn't know for certain the intruder had found evidence of her motive to kill Pavel.

I texted Olga again. Nothing. No response.

When she didn't answer my call, I panicked. The logical person to contact was Jonah, but if he knew what I was up to he would kill me, if the actual killer didn't get to me first. I tried to still the beating of my heart, which felt as if it were bursting out of my chest.

I walked softly to the elevator and nearly fainted when a loud clanging noise emanated from its depths. There was someone else in the building. That someone was not Olga, who would have answered my text if she could.

With the horror of the last time I took the stairs fresh in my mind, I opened the door and began my descent. I couldn't get out of there fast enough. If only I hadn't had to worry about Olga as well.

Chapter Twenty-Four

In life, as in dance, grace glides on blistered feet.
—Jean-George Noverre

The Marines pride themselves on never leaving a man behind. That goes double for dancers. Olga was willing to protect me, and I could do no less for her. With scissors in one hand, and my silenced phone in the other, I prepared to do battle, which I defined as calling nine-one-one if we were in danger. I was consoled by the fact that whoever else was in the building was in the elevator and heading up, while I was in the stairwell and on the way down.

I walked silently down the darkened stairs. Like the rest of the building, they were lit dimly after hours. Good for the environment. Bad for me. On the main floor of the ballet studio, however, the slit under the exit door glowed brightly. I stood before that door, trembling with indecision. What was behind it? I put my hand on the knob, and with excruciating slowness, began to turn it. The door banged open with the force of a hurricane and whacked me in the head.

Olga grabbed me and put her hand across my mouth to keep me from screaming. Her cheeks were even redder than the first time I met her, and her body was rigid with fear.

She whispered in my ear, "No talking. We go now."

The sound of the elevator pierced the silence. Olga and I ran down the stairs and into the street. I wanted to stop to call the police, but she refused to slow down, and we darted across four lanes of traffic to the other side of

Broadway.

She stopped by the steps of a brownstone building directly across from American Ballet Company and sat down, as if her sturdy legs could no longer keep her upright. "Give me the one minute."

I waited in an agony of impatience as Olga caught her breath. She stared fixedly at the windows of the studio and said, "I hear noise. I get broom. I stand behind door. I get ready to pounce." She shook her fist. "But this lady, she is big, and she is quick. She not open door. She kick open door. She take broom and put across me." Olga pointed to a scarlet line across her throat. "I push her back."

I grabbed Olga's shoulders. "We have to call the police!"

Olga sprang to her feet. "No! This you cannot do! I not...I prefer not to talk with *politsiya*."

I didn't know why Olga feared law enforcement, and I didn't ask. "Olga, I know someone we can trust in the police. You don't have to worry."

I followed the line of Olga's gaze. The dim form of a woman appeared in a window and surveyed the street. Olga got up and dodged behind a parked delivery truck.

I crouched behind the same concrete pillar I'd used in stalking Savannah. Big as it was, it would not have been sufficient to hide Olga. I waited and watched. The woman left after a few seconds and did not reappear.

I turned back to Olga. "You're so brave. How did you escape?"

Olga was shamefaced. "Olga not escape. The woman, she let me go. She say she is nighttime cleaning lady, and what I'm doing here? I pretend, like you say, that I not understand English too good. But I do what she say, because she have gun."

My legs buckled and I had to hold onto the planter to stay upright. "She pulled a gun on you?"

Olga was quick to reassure me. "No. But I see it under uniform."

I took Olga back to my apartment. She groaned at the steep climb to the fifth floor and collapsed, breathless, when we made it to the top. After three glasses of water, followed by two shots of vodka, she was much recovered.

I badly wanted to call Jonah, but, aside from Olga's fears, I was worried about how to explain the evening's exploits in a way that sounded reasonable. I sank into the comfort of the sofa and put my aching feet on the coffee table.

"Olga, that was no cleaning lady. Describe her to me, and maybe we can figure out who it was." I already knew it wasn't Savannah. She couldn't have pinned Olga against the wall if her life depended upon it. For the same reason, it couldn't have been any of the dancers.

Olga frowned. "She big. Not so big as me, but strong. And quick. Dark hair, dark skin. And under her clothes, the gun. She say, like she very angry, what is day cleaner, by which she mean me, doing there? I explain it take me long time to learn. That it my first day. Then she say I must go and she will do work. I say, 'Yes, lady, no problem!'"

I was ill with anxiety. "You can't go back to the studio. It's too dangerous."

She protested. "But yes! Maybe later is better. Next time, we wait until this lady leave. Then we go."

I rubbed my forehead, where a large and painful bruise was taking shape. "We're not going anywhere near the studio after hours until we figure out who this mysterious woman was. I don't know what we'd find at this point, anyway. She'll have scoured every corner of the studio by now."

Olga smiled. "Not everything. No." She pulled out a sheaf of papers with the Artistic Solutions logo. One was a severance agreement, made out to Savannah, and signed by Pavel. The other was a copy of the same document I'd found inside Bobbie's desk. It was a plan to restructure the costume department, with a much-diminished role for Bobbie.

"Where did you find these?"

Olga said, "Inside hot room with the big plants."

On the day Pavel was murdered, Savannah cried and Bobbie raged. But the two together didn't add up in any coherent way. Savannah and Bobbie were unlikely to have conspired together, despite their common enemy. Also, while Bobbie knew about her coming demotion, Savannah might have been unaware of Pavel's plans to fire her. Still, we were much further along than we had been. I didn't want to upset Olga, but I had to get this information to Jonah as soon as possible.

I opened the freezer, got out an ice pack, and placed it over the egg-sized lump on my head.

Olga said. "Feel bad about crashing door into your head. Good news is we get closer. Very soon now, we find killer. But so worried about you, Lelotchka. What if this lady see you? She may suspect."

I didn't share Olga's optimism about finding the killer but was in perfect agreement with her anxiety about our future health. "You're right, in that we know a lot we didn't know before. But we've still got a long way to go before we nail the killer." I put my head back to balance the ice pack. "One of the many things we don't know is the identity of the woman at the studio. My guess is not many custodians pack a gun. Was she wearing a nametag?"

Olga frowned and inspected the lanyard around her neck. "Not sure. She was wearing uniform like me. Did not notice tag."

My head was throbbing. "I can't think any more tonight. We have to figure out a way to investigate that doesn't involve going to the studio at night. Early morning might work if we can get there early enough. Savannah arrives at dawn."

She stuck out her bottom lip, like a petulant child. "I much disagree. Next time we do nighttime visit, Olga will be ready."

After inspecting the contents of the refrigerator, Olga refused my offer of either the bedroom or the sofa, despite the long journey to Brighton Beach on the D train. "Lelotchka, I starve to death here."

I was sympathetic. Sometimes I too felt as if I were starving. "I'll order some food. Tell me what you want, and I'll have it delivered."

Olga demurred. I scanned the street below, which was deserted. Even the teenagers who normally occupied the stoop on the corner were absent.

Despite the apparent safety of the street below, I was still anxious for Olga. "If you don't want to spend the night here, why don't you stay with Madame? You can tell her what happened, and this way we can meet tomorrow and figure out what to do next."

Olga agreed, and five minutes later I saw her safely into a cab. With only my thoughts to keep me company, I sat down to write a precise and detailed account of everything that had happened from the day Pavel was killed to the evening's events at the ballet studio. As the daughter of two writers, and the sister of another, committing ideas to paper is an ingrained habit. I didn't inherit the family talent, but for my purposes, I didn't need it.

Bobbie. Savannah. Austin. Jonathan. Philip.

Each entry for these suspects raised more questions than answers. I'd known Bobbie for many years. She was a woman of harsh words, but her episodes of physical violence were limited to the occasional stab with a safety pin. Bobbie had two passions: her husband and her work. There was an outside possibility she would kill someone for love. But not for money. Not for a job.

At first, Savannah was an unlikely suspect. Her anguish over Pavel's death seemed too genuine to question. But her tears on the day Pavel died occurred before our discovery of the body. I now knew, thanks to the severance agreement Olga had found, Pavel was planning to fire her. Had Savannah been mourning the end of her career, the betrayal of her lover, or the death of her boss?

Austin was the least likely person to commit any kind of crime, mostly because he was incapable of hiding his emotions. He might have had the mental capacity to plan Pavel's murder, but he could not have shoved Ms. Crandall down a flight of stairs. When Savannah interrupted his rehearsal to report of Ms. Crandall's plight, his unfeigned surprise and general dithering appeared completely genuine. Nothing in his manner indicated he was a killer who had just found out his latest victim might live long enough to implicate him.

As I took careful notes on both Jonathan and Philip, I realized how much of this investigation was, by sheer chance, tied to my mother. Barbara had been with Ms. Crandall shortly before someone pushed her down the stairs. Barbara had been in a relationship of some intimacy with Philip.

My mother lived in a fictional world of crime writing, where she had total control over the twists and turns of the plot. This gave her an unrealistic view of her ability to solve crimes. She had cast herself as the protagonist of a novel. From my perspective, she was a better candidate as victim.

I put down my pen and picked up the phone. Barbara's voicemail responded before the end of the first ring. *I'm busy killing people. When I'm done writing I'll call you back. Leave a message, preferably in code.*

I left a message and waited, sleepless, for a very long time.

Chapter Twenty-Five

Dance is a transformation of space, of time, of people, who are in constant danger of becoming all brain, will, or feeling.
—Saint Augustine

I fell asleep, in my clothes and on the sofa, waiting for Barbara to call me back. I woke with a start at about five in the morning. The bathroom mirror revealed puffy eyes and a face without color, other than the purple and green bruise on my forehead. I covered my skin with the kind of makeup I usually reserve for the stage, hoping to hide the toll the last twelve hours had wrought. I gulped down a cup of coffee and made my way to Barbara's apartment. This was also my childhood home, which Barbara had retained in the divorce settlement with my father.

Not much about the building had changed in the years since I'd moved out. Gerald, the daytime doorman, was at his usual post. He adored my mother, who never failed to send gifts to him, his family, and now, apparently, a new granddaughter. After admiring pictures of the newest member of his extended family, I made my way to the apartment. He announced my arrival and waved me to the elevator.

The reason behind Barbara's failure to respond to my phone call was made clear when Philip answered the door, in pajamas and a silk robe. He clasped my hand in his clammy fingers and drew me into the living room. Barbara emerged from the bedroom, also clad in silk loungewear.

I felt as if I'd walked into the set of a 1940s screwball comedy starring Katherine Hepburn and Cary Grant. Or, more darkly, a Hitchcock movie, starring Ray Milland and Grace Kelly. Either way, it was an awkward moment for me. Philip and Barbara, however, were completely at ease.

"Coffee?" Philip held out a cup.

I took it, happy to give my mouth something to do other than hang open in shock and dismay.

Barbara frowned. "What on earth has happened to your face?"

I fingered my forehead. The ice had done little to bring down the swelling. "Oh, just a silly accident." I looked meaningfully into her eyes. "I could use an ice pack."

She ignored my transparent desire to get her alone. "You know where to find it, darling!" Barbara smiled forgivingly and said to Philip, "Dancers are notoriously clumsy when they're not onstage."

He spooned sugar into his coffee. "I've heard that but didn't know if it was true. I find it hard to believe Leah could ever be clumsy."

I didn't have much time before morning class and was on fire to get rid of him. "Well, now you know." I walked into the kitchen and called out, "I can't find the ice pack. Can you help me?"

Barbara wasn't happy with my tartness. She walked into the kitchen, took out an ice pack, and steered me back to the living room.

With less patience, she said, "I suppose, my darling, you have a reason for this unexpected early visit?" She looked pointedly at my foot, which was the only part of me I hadn't been able to keep in check. Chastened, I stilled its impatient tapping. Barbara often said the reason she sent me to ballet class was to give me an outlet for my nervous energy, and she thought dance would tame me. Melissa had been a placid child. I still couldn't sit still.

I had many good reasons for the visit. One of them was to make sure Barbara had disentangled herself from her potentially lethal relationship with Philip. That discussion would have to wait.

I pressed the ice to my forehead. "I called you last night. You didn't answer, and I was worried about you."

She was breezy in her answer but guarded in her expression. "Now you know you have nothing to worry about." She fixed me with the sort of expression she usually reserves for my father. "Nothing at all to concern you. We can talk later. Don't you have to be at work soon?"

"Yes. What about you? Aren't you working on a new book?" I turned to Philip. "And what about you? Are you a man of leisure?"

Philip smiled, baring his long white teeth. "For the moment, yes. Tonight, your mother and I are going to a preview of that new architectural exhibit at the Met. Some good friends of mine have underwritten it, and we've been invited to a private showing and reception."

I got up and slung my dance bag over my shoulder. "Isn't that the Franklin family endowment?"

He nodded agreeably. "Exactly. You, of course, are well acquainted with Jonathan. Have you met his brother, Laurence? Such a talented family."

In Bar Bleu, he'd referred to Laurence as a talentless hack. Barbara's apartment, however, was not the time or the place to discuss the contrast between what he told me and what I'd overheard him say to Jonathan, Savannah, and Austin. I hoped the next time he offered his opinion the conversation would take place at the Twentieth Precinct, and the police would be interrogating his relationship with the Franklin family.

With a start, I realized Philip was still talking to me. "I'm sure I can get an invitation for you as well if you're interested."

I looked at my mother, who refused to meet my eye. "Thanks, Philip, but I have plans. Maybe next time."

Barbara saw me to the door. I pulled her into the hallway, and in a furious whisper demanded, "What on earth are you doing with that guy? Don't you realize he might be a murderer? At the very least, he's a sleazy con man and fixer. Maybe a blackmailer. Get rid of him, before he decides to get rid of you!"

She patted my shoulder. "Leah, my darling, you're overreacting. I know what you think you overheard in that little adventure you and Gabi had. Trust me, you got it all wrong. I'll talk to you later and explain."

With more anger than I'd expressed to my mother since I was a teenager, I told her, "Make your excuses and get out of this date you have planned. Or I will change my mind and tag along."

She remained unfazed. "That would be lovely. Perhaps Zach can come as well?"

"If I bring anyone, it will be Jonah. Because if you continue to see Philip, you're going to need police protection."

I hailed a cab, in an unsuccessful effort to get to the studio in enough time to talk to Olivia before Madame began company class. Traffic on Broadway was a mess, and four blocks from the studio I got out of the car. Walking was faster.

I tossed my street clothes in the dressing room and texted Olivia, who didn't answer. She was already in her usual spot at the barre. Kerry stood next to her, in the place where I normally park myself. When I approached, both dancers looked up, but their body language prevented me from joining them. I didn't expect a warm welcome from Kerry. She'd as soon toss me into the orchestra pit as greet me politely. Olivia's attitude, however, was jarring. She looked at me with expressionless eyes, as if we barely knew each other.

Kerry giggled and pointed at my head. "Who'd you piss off this time?"

It took a moment before I realized she was referring to the bruise on my forehead. I shrugged. "You should see the other guy. The one who thought she could get away with murder by blaming it on an innocent person." It wasn't the most clever or prudent response, but it had the advantage of being the only one that came to mind. My misadventures with Olga, followed by a sleepless night, and capped by finding Philip practically in bed with my mother, had me on edge and mentally exhausted.

Kerry didn't follow up, not because she didn't want to, but because she's a rather dim bulb. Instead, she leaned closer to Olivia. I didn't hear what she said, but they both laughed like hyenas. The last time I saw Kerry and Olivia together, they practically came to blows. Seeing them chat together like best friends shocked and unnerved me. Olivia was my friend. Not Kerry's.

I settled myself behind Kerry and texted Olivia again. I was anxious to talk to her, and I didn't want Kerry to be part of the conversation. **Meet me after class. Need to talk to you!** Olivia glanced at her phone but ignored my message. A cloud of uneasiness descended upon me. When you don't know who to trust, you can't trust anyone. I tried to stay balanced, in my mind and in my body, but I wobbled on every relevé.

Madame entered the room, and I let the routine of my life take over and blank out the pressures of the outside world. When we finished the barre and took our places on the floor, I was surprised by my image in the mirror. Everyone else in the room saw the multicolored bump on my forehead. Only I noticed my skinnier body.

I never talk about dieting to nondancers. The sufferings inflicted by an extra five pounds on an already extremely slender dancer annoy normal people. They simply don't understand that five pounds is a significant percentage of my total weight. I feel it as acutely, if not more painfully, than a normal person would after gaining three times that amount.

More lightly than I had in weeks, I pirouetted and jumped with a joy I'd almost forgotten. Madame nodded and smiled. "Yes, Lelotchka, yes. Is looking very nice."

Buoyed by her praise, and the elevation of my *grand jeté en tournant*, I was ready to take on the world. It was a shame about Olivia, but I had more important things to do than worry about a little corps de ballet dancer on the make.

Much of the rest of the day was a blur of rehearsals. Learning new choreography is hard work and requires intense concentration. Austin's ballet was particularly challenging for me because it wasn't dependent on the music. Daniel was still recovering from his injury, and I was partnered with a new dancer, Joaquin Teixeira. He was taller than Daniel, and I'd never worked with him before. He seemed nervous, and I tried to put him at ease, but his hands were heavy on my waist. In the most difficult lift, the one that had injured Daniel, he grabbed me so tightly I could hardly breathe. It takes time to fall into a comfortable partnership, but we had very little of that left before opening night.

I was too absorbed by the demands of back-to-back rehearsals to register Olivia's absence. It wasn't until the end of the day that I realized she had yet to respond to my text.

I caught up with her on the way to the dressing room. "What's going on? We need to—we should talk. Let's have some coffee." I tried to lighten the mood. "Just to show you my heart's in the right place, I'm buying."

She didn't smile in return. "What is there to talk about? Anything you want to say, you can tell me now."

I stumbled a bit over my next words. Olivia had been more distant recently, but on that day, she seemed overtly hostile. There had to be a reason for the sea change. "I thought we were friends. Are you angry at me for something?"

She turned her back, putting one foot up on the bench to untie her pointe shoes. "I'm not angry, and I hope you'll always consider me your friend. But real friends don't keep secrets from each other. Unless they have something to hide, of course."

I dropped my dance bag and stared at her. "I honestly have no idea what you're talking about. I don't have any secrets from you."

Her tone was cold. "According to Kerry, you do."

I wanted to reason with her, but anger made me impatient. "If you believe Kerry, and not me, then you're as clueless as she is. That woman would stab her entire family and every 'friend' she's ever had to move up to principal dancer. You don't have to trust me. But it would be crazy to trust her." I softened my tone. "I'm worried about you. It could be dangerous to trust her."

Olivia's expression didn't change. "She told me you'd say that. I was such a naïve fool to think you were on my side, when the whole time you were trashing me to Austin, to Madame, and to who knows who else."

Stunned, I let her walk away. I'd been hurt by men. In matters of the heart, I was an expert in dealing with the loss of a romantic partner. But losing a girlfriend was a whole other kind of pain.

Chapter Twenty-Six

I'm dancing to the music of the madness inside me.
—George C. Wolfe

D eaf to the text messages that had poured in while I was talking to Olivia, I finally awoke to the demands of my phone and responded to the insistent buzzing. Barbara was anxious for me and Zach to join her and Philip at the Metropolitan Museum of Art, a desire she articulated in three texts and two voicemails. My father wanted to discuss my increasingly frosty relationship with Ann. She must have told him I rejected her offer to evaluate me quickly. Instead, I'd opted for the last appointment on her calendar. Gabi and Melissa clamored for updates on the murder investigation. If that were not enough, Madame and Olga were plotting an after-hours assault on the studio and wanted me to join them.

I answered the last request first, because Madame was still at the studio. We met in an empty rehearsal room. She was excited and fearful, but also pleased at the prospect of another adventure together. I put her off. "Before we do anything more, I need to talk to Detective Sobol. Olga had a close call last night. I don't care if she's connected to half of Brighton Beach's Russian mobsters. We need to figure out a way forward that doesn't put her, or any of us, in danger."

Madame agreed, with some reluctance. "I say yes to you, Lelotchka. But we meet tomorrow, yes? Only one week to opening night and we not have much time. Next week, we must every night be at theater."

I hugged her gently, mindful of her arthritis. "Excellent plan, Madame.

Tomorrow night we'll all get together. Why don't you call Gabi and Melissa? I'll let Barbara know."

We agreed to meet at her apartment, and, much comforted, she left. Madame's sympathetic kindness was still with me when Bobbie arrived to blow away, with cigarette-scented breath, any residual warmth.

She brandished the lock from her drawer in front of my face. "Did you do this?"

Relieved that the costume mistress had phrased her accusation as a question, and not as a statement, I said, "No. I don't even know what it is you're waving so rudely at me. What are you blaming me for this time?"

Bobbie nearly choked on her rage. "My desk! My drawer! My things! I can't work like this, with people sneaking around, and not respecting my privacy. I deserve better."

Ron emerged from the office, having watched the scene unfold from behind glass walls. He smirked at me, angling his head so Bobbie couldn't see him do it.

"Now, Ms. York, what seems to be the problem this time?" Ron's tone was insultingly phony. He stood by the open door, inviting her in. "Why don't you tell me all about it. Although most people have left for the day, I suggest a slightly lower volume. For your sake, not for mine."

Bobbie's contempt for him was plain. "Listen, you pretentious little brat. I was designing award-winning costumes while you were failing middle school pissing contests."

With an unhurried motion, Ron removed his glasses and polished them. When he put them back on, he inspected Bobbie with calm confidence. "I'm sure you're right about that, Ms. York. But you haven't won any awards for a very long time, and at the moment, you're the one getting pissed on. Not me." He waved her in. "Shall we?"

She stormed past him. He followed her, leaving the door open. She got up and slammed it shut. I took no pleasure in the pain of others, but if I had to pick someone to bear the brunt of Artistic Solutions' condescending treatment, Bobbie would have been at the top of my list. The aggressive and angry stance she presented to the world had grown so pronounced it was no wonder her head was on the chopping block. After many years with the company, Bobbie's days with ABC were surely numbered.

When I got home I decided to clear my brain with some Sherlock Holmes stories. A few pages into "A Scandal in Bohemia" my father called. He was uncharacteristically glum. "I want you and Ann to be friends, Leah. This job she has shouldn't put a barrier between you."

I was too tired for diplomacy. "There's always been a barrier between us. The only difference is that now you see it, too."

I heard creaking footsteps as he closed the door with a soft click, presumably to keep the rest of our conversation from Ann. "Leah, I want us to look at this situation as an opportunity for you and Ann to get to know each other better. Come see us tomorrow. We'll work it out. Let's not forget what Aristotle had to say about friendship."

I broke in before he could begin talking about necessary virtues, a lecture I'd listened to many times. "I really appreciate the invitation, but I have plans tomorrow. Opening night is in less than a week, and I'm very busy right now."

His voice was stern. "Too busy to see your parents?"

I looked longingly at my book, thinking that maybe some of Sherlock's acuity would rub off on me. "I love you, Dad, but Ann's feelings aren't at the top of my list, and mine have never weighed very heavily with her. Not even Aristotle can alter that fact."

He sighed. "You simply don't understand her as I do. If you took the time, I know you'd come to...maybe not love her, but to esteem her."

I didn't want to hurt his feelings, but I was seized by a cramp in my calf, and the pain made me less cautious and more impatient than usual. As I massaged the offending muscle, I said, "It's time for you to face facts. Ann doesn't want a relationship with me any more than I want one with her. Haven't you noticed how indifferent she is to me? And Melissa? And she has zero interest in Ariel and Benjamin. When was the last time she agreed to go with you to visit your grandchildren?"

While he fumbled for an answer I thought about our recent dinner together, when Philip had given us the slip to hook up with Ann.

I interrupted Dad's summary of the intellectual nature of perception "Let's put Schopenhauer aside for the moment and deal with the here and now." I took a deep breath. It's no easy task to tell your father you think his wife might be cheating on him.

Dad was as unfazed as Barbara when I told him of my suspicions.

"Don't worry about Ann and Philip. They do know each other, but the relationship is purely professional."

I was shocked. I thought there was no one more predictable than my father, other than Kant, who famously was so regular in his habits people set their clocks by him. Clearly, I had my work cut out for me if I wanted to achieve Sherlockian levels of observation. I didn't even know my own father.

I got Dad off the phone by agreeing to meet him for brunch at some time in the near future. By the time we met, I hoped to have more information on the extent to which Ann was involved with my mother's boyfriend. At best, both my parents had chosen lying, cheating partners. No, it was worse than that. Lying, cheating partners with an inexplicable connection to each other.

With those troubling thoughts swirling in the back of my mind, I finally answered Barbara, who had called three times while I'd been talking to my father. Without waiting for her to talk, I said, "I've decided I want to go to the Met opening. It's the only way I can think of to keep you safe."

Barbara laughed. "I don't want to be safe. For once in my life, I want to have fun. But if you do insist, in this dreary way, on keeping me safe, I hope you've arranged backup. Is Zach coming?"

I cut her short. "I can't imagine what you find so funny, because I'm not joking. And yes, I will be bringing someone with me. Hopefully, Jonah. If not him, then someone else up to the job of persuading you to give up Philip." I sighed with pretend regret. "I wasn't going to tell you this, because I know how much you value Dad's opinion, but he can't stand Philip. I just got off the phone with him. He said you can never trust a man who uses the same polish on his head as his shoes."

This observation cut short her laughter. "Your father would never say such a thing. The man doesn't have a mean bone in his body. That type of sarcasm is something I would say, and since you take after me more than you're willing to admit, I think you said it."

She was correct in her deduction, as she so often was. "We can debate this later. What's the dress code for the evening?"

"Black tie. Wear that nice pink gown I got you." As if I hadn't already told her I was inviting Jonah, she added, "Zach will love it. And hurry! I don't want to be more than fashionably late."

I hung up after ascertaining the exact hour and place we were meeting and called Jonah. Thanks to Sherlock Holmes, and my father's phone call, there wasn't nearly enough time for me to get to a black-tie-level of grooming, but I was going to give it my best shot. As a dancer, I'm an expert at quick changes.

"Jonah! It's me, Leah. This is an emergency. Do you have a tux? It doesn't have to be anything too fancy."

He sounded preoccupied. "I'm in the middle of a murder investigation, one that is intimately connected to you and your mother. How does formal dress count as an emergency?"

"I'll explain later. Get dressed in whatever you have. A suit is fine. Or a jacket and tie. I'll pick you up in an hour. Wait! Don't hang up. Meet me at the Met Museum. It takes longer to get into a gown than a suit. I'll meet you by the fountain on the left."

His tone was amused. "Is this finally a date with my favorite elusive ballerina?"

"No. This is business, not pleasure."

Chapter Twenty-Seven

Dancing is an art, because it is subject to rules.
—Francois-Marie Arouet

Banners, bright lights, and a procession of limousines marked the glamorous opening of the Franklin Foundation Exhibit on American Architecture at the Metropolitan Museum of Art. When I stepped out of the cab, the first person I saw was Jonah. I'd never seen him dressed in anything more formal than the nondescript jackets and ties he wore to work and was surprised and pleased he'd managed to come up with formal attire. Teasing, I asked him, "A rental?"

He laughed. "Nah. My parents bought it for me when I graduated college, hoping I'd someday lead a life a lot classier than the one I chose. They're still disappointed I became a cop." He examined me. "You are beautiful." He placed a gentle finger on my forehead. "Do you want to tell me who conked you on the head? I'll have him, or her, arrested. Or did you walk into a lamppost again?"

I was saved the trouble of answering when Barbara and Philip waved from the far end of the fountain. We joined the crush of people waiting to enter the museum. Jonah didn't enter with us. While my mother, Philip, and I went through security, he bypassed the line, showing his police ID to the guard. We entered The Great Hall, which was festooned with thousands of twinkly lights and hundreds of white roses tied in red, white, and blue ribbons. In the gallery above, a quintet of string players performed chamber music that was nearly inaudible over the chatter of the crowd.

It was even more elegant and exclusive than American Ballet Company's gala events. The rich, the powerful, and the well-connected mingled in a privileged throng of air-kissing amid one of the greatest collections of art on the planet. Philip led us to the entrance to the American Wing.

Mrs. Franklin, flanked by her sons Jonathan and Laurence, greeted us. She barely noticed Barbara, Jonah, or me, but smiled when she saw Philip, who kissed her lightly on both cheeks. She lifted the tip of one forefinger, and a waiter materialized with a tray of champagne flutes. Drinks in hand, we strolled around the perimeter of the room.

Jonah paused in front of a series of architectural drawings. "I'd like to come back when there aren't so many people. This is pretty impressive."

Philip agreed. "I've seen it already, as a work in progress. As Leah knows, I'm rather friendly with the Franklins. They're an accomplished family. American Ballet Company is lucky to be getting Jonathan as the acting director. He's got a very impressive background. Princeton University, followed by Yale Law School. Knows all the right people."

My fingers itched to toss the champagne in Philip's pretentious face. "He may know all the right people to invite to a gala opening at the museum, but he has no experience in the dance world. It takes more than money to run a ballet company."

Philip smiled, baring his large teeth that reminded me of a wolf's. "It's a global world now. ABC has to move with the times."

Barbara pinched my arm to keep me quiet. "Leah and I are going to freshen up. We'll meet you back here in a few minutes."

She hissed at me all the way to the bathroom. "Will you please relax? You're making everyone uncomfortable."

I was unrepentant. "As I think I've mentioned, your new boyfriend is one of the prime suspects in a murder case. Why are you pursuing a relationship with this lowlife? Or are you planning to offer up yourself as the next victim, in a crazed effort to prove his guilt?"

Barbara removed a lipstick from her bag and offered it to me. "You're pale as a ghost, except for that awful bruise on your forehead. At least put some lipstick on. And do try to powder over that horrid-looking lump on your head."

I looked in the mirror. She was right. I dabbed more makeup over the bruise and pressed vivid red lipstick onto my mouth. Still not satisfied, I blended a bit of color onto my cheeks for good measure.

Looking at her reflection I said, "It's nice to know that, as usual, you have your priorities in order. You're worried about my appearance and not about your own safety. Or mine. Murder aside, Philip is working with Savannah Collier, who has made it her mission to destroy us. Have you somehow forgotten there's a killer at American Ballet Company?"

Barbara took back the lipstick and with a steady hand applied a fresh coat. "Sarcasm is the lowest form of wit."

I was surprised she'd left herself open to so easy a comeback. "You omitted the most important part. The end of that quotation says that sarcasm is also the highest form of intelligence. Did you forget you're the one who made me study Oscar Wilde?"

Barbara laughed. "Good one, Leah. I always said you have as much talent in your head as your feet. My contention, however, is Wilde was being sarcastic when he said that!"

I couldn't share in her mirth. "Don't you understand—don't you see—that I'm worried about you?"

She grew serious. "Yes. I do see that. And I love you for it. But I'm not as dumb as I look." She smoothed the folds of her black silk dress. "You have to trust me."

Two women entered and we made room for them at the dressing table.

While they chattered loudly, I said in an undertone, "You want me to trust you, and yet you refuse to confide in me. Tell me what you're up to. Or I'm going to think you're having sex with Philip to get information from him, like some menopausal Mata Hari."

She rose from her chair and held open the door for me. "That's absurd. I finished menopause ages ago. Such a relief. So many horror stories, and in the end, it's a wonderful new lease on life. I never wanted to get old, but menopause almost makes the trip worthwhile."

We walked, arm in arm, back to where our partners were waiting. One glance at Jonah's face and I could see he and Philip had not bonded.

"Barbara, my dear, let me get you something to eat." Philip steered Barbara toward a long table, decorated with exotic fruits and flowers.

Jonah said, imitating Philip, "Leah, my dear, let me get you something to eat."

I laughed at his mincing manner. "I'm not hungry, but I would be happy to keep you company while you fill a plate for yourself."

He took my hand and caressed my palm with his fingers. "Are you ever hungry?"

I looked into his dark eyes. "All the time."

We found a corner of the room with two empty chairs and watched the social dance of New York society play before us, on one of the most glittering stages in the city. The mayor was there, as well as a constellation of A-list stars, each with a personal solar system of orbiting worshippers.

Jonah handed his plate to one of the many solicitous servers, who circled the room with an eagle eye. It was their job to make sure no one had to wait more than a nanosecond with a used plate or an empty glass. Jonah seemed completely at ease, as if he spent every night of his life at a gala and not in the grimy confines of a precinct on the Upper West Side of Manhattan.

Only one person caught his eye, a heavyset man in a suit that, despite expensive tailoring, could not mask its wearer's paunch. He looked familiar to me as well, although I couldn't quite place him. "Who is that?"

He grimaced. "I'm surprised you don't know him. That's Darius Kemble."

"We haven't met any of the executives at Artistic Solutions. I don't think we rate a visit from anyone higher up than an office boy."

Jonah had a sour look on his face. "Kemble has his finger in many pies. Real estate, gambling. He's also getting quite a name for himself in political circles, despite a nasty record of tax evasion. And worse."

I eyed Kemble's date. "Is that his daughter with him?" The young woman had auburn hair, green eyes, and a dazzling smile. "She's very beautiful."

Jonah snagged a thimbleful of soup from the buffet table. "That's his third wife. Kemble does have a daughter, who is probably also here, but they don't get along. The daughter is five years older than the wife, which has got to be awkward. I know you don't care for Ann but think how much worse things would be if she were younger than you."

I stood up to get a better look. "How do you know so much about them?"

Jonah helped himself to a few more hors d'oeuvres. "Kemble's been associated with some union-busting activities. And we suspect he has ties with the Russian mafia."

"She looks unhappy."

"Yes, she does." Jonah turned from watching the Kembles to gaze at me. "Nice dress."

I looked down at the pale pink satin with its lace overskirt. "Barbara bought it for me."

He fingered the fabric. "Your mother has good taste...in daughters." He got up abruptly. "Have you had enough of this?"

I took his outstretched hand. "I had enough of it before we got here. I don't enjoy these types of parties. I only came because I'm worried about Barbara."

He started for the exit. "I figured. I wondered why you invited me, instead of your doctor boyfriend, but as soon as I saw Philip, I understood my role in this dog and pony show. Now that I've done my job, I'd just as soon leave."

I waited while Jonah spoke with one of the security guards. When he was done, we searched the crowd to say goodbye to Barbara and Philip. He was deep in conversation with Kemble. Barbara was halfway across the room with two other women, including Mrs. Kemble. After saying goodbye we threaded our way past the still-growing crowd. A tall blonde woman, dressed in a low-cut, ivory satin gown, pushed past us, calling, "Zach! I'm over here!"

I turned to find Zach Mitchell coming in our direction. As awkward moments go, that was in the top ten of my entire life, and I'm including a flying leap onstage that ended with me in a heap on the floor, accompanied by gasps from the audience and a careful coverup from the dancers who'd had to avoid getting crushed by my flailing fall.

Zach and I couldn't pretend we hadn't seen each other. He bent over and kissed me lightly on the cheek. "Let me introduce you to Sloane, my ex-wife."

I swallowed. "And let me introduce to you to my, uh, to Jonah Sobol."

Zach drew his brows together. "Detective Jonah Sobol?"

Jonah tucked my arm under his. "That's right."

Sloane clearly had no idea who I was, or who Jonah was. She ignored us and spoke to Zach. "I've been waiting for ages. What took you so long?"

He gave her a twisted smile. "I'm a doctor, remember?"

She rolled her eyes, this time including us in her general disdain. "How could I forget, when you've reminded me of that fact for the last ten years?"

I was at a loss for words, but Jonah remained cool. "Nice to meet you, but we have another engagement."

Sloane laughed in supercilious astonishment. "What could possibly be more important or interesting than the party you're at right now? I assure you; half of New York City would give their eyeteeth to be here."

Zach answered for us. "Mr. Sobol is a cop. No doubt he too has a professional life that doesn't fit neatly into a nine-to-five schedule." He looked without friendliness at Jonah. "Speaking of which, I'm surprised to see you here. I'm disappointed, Detective, in how little progress you've made."

Sloane, who neither knew nor cared about the undercurrents of tension in the situation, pulled on Zach's arm. "Darling, we really must move on." She looked down at me. "Charming to have met you." She smiled at Jonah. "And lovely to have met you, too. I suppose you're here on professional business?"

Before Jonah could answer, a woman dressed in emerald silk, emerald necklace, and poisonous green fingernails, approached. "Sloane, dearest! Thank God you're here. Mrs. Franklin has been asking for you."

Preening with her own importance, Sloane finally made good on her promise to leave us. Zach lingered. He spoke to me as if Jonah weren't there. "I'm, uh, I didn't know you were going to be here. Can we maybe talk for a minute?"

Jonah looked at me. "I can wait for you outside."

"No, thanks." I turned back to Zach. "As Jonah has already explained, we have another engagement."

Zach edged between Jonah and me. "Leah. You don't understand. I promised Sloane I'd take her. I'm here only as an escort. Nothing more. And, just so you know, she calls everyone darling, because she can't remember anyone's name." His tone hardened. "I certainly didn't expect to see you here with the guy who's investigating a murder at your ballet company. Aren't there some kind of ethical rules governing that kind of behavior?"

Jonah reached into his pocket and pulled out his card. "Here's my contact information. Feel free to file a complaint."

And with that, we made our way back into the frosty night. Jonah was silent. I was slightly ashamed that I had used him as a means to intimidate Philip, and that he knew it. The episode with Zach, though, wasn't my fault. Jonah opened the door of a waiting car. His only words were to the driver.

I settled myself into the seat and looked at him out of the corner of my eye. "Are you angry?"

He snapped his seatbelt. "No. I'm hungry. All that tiny food was annoying. Feel like some diner food?"

"Sure."

Chapter Twenty-Eight

It's the heart afraid of breaking that never learns to dance.
—Bette Midler

J onah ordered eggs and pancakes. When he finished eating, and we were both on our second cups of coffee, he said, "Time to talk, Leah. No more solo turns for you in this murder investigation. Explain to me, right now, what tonight was all about. Philip and Barbara have been seeing each other for weeks. Why the mad rush to attend that party?"

I was nervous. "I've already told you what I overheard in Bar Bleu. Savannah, Austin, Jonathan, and Philip are all implicated in Pavel's murder. I thought my mother understood the danger and was going to get rid of Philip. Last night, I couldn't get her on the phone, so I went to her apartment this morning. Philip was there, walking around like he owned the place. I've never known Barbara to be so stupid."

"Your mother is anything but stupid, although, like all people, she has her blind spots. I can tell you one thing for sure: she doesn't harbor any tender feelings toward Philip. And he isn't in love with her, either. Whatever it is they have going on between them, it's a business arrangement. Not a love story."

I was bitter. "I agree with you, where Philip is concerned. I think he's using her, but to what end? I have no idea. As for Barbara, the last thing I expected, when I showed up at her apartment at eight o'clock in the morning, was to find him lounging around in his pajamas. Silk pajamas, to be exact. I thought I'd pass out."

Jonah laughed. "Rest assured, Philip is not going to forget the little talk we had this evening."

"What did you say to him?"

Jonah pushed aside his plate. "The details are unimportant. Like I say, I did my part. Now it's time for you to do yours. Something precipitated that call to Barbara and your rush to see her this morning. What was it?"

It occurred to me that a relationship with a homicide detective might be challenging. He was too good at reading people. Even without his perceptive comments, though, it was time to come clean. I told him about Olga, and with some embarrassment, about our disastrous attempt to search the offices of American Ballet Company. He listened carefully but did not comment. Without revealing the exact details of how I found the evidence, I also told him that Pavel was going to fire Savannah and that Bobbie was facing a humiliating demotion. Those facts were sufficient. He didn't also have to know I'd broken into Bobbie's desk or that Olga had rifled through the private papers of everyone who worked at ABC.

He was noncommittal. "Thanks for telling me. Too bad you didn't trust me enough to tell me earlier."

I was confused. "Aren't you interested? Surprised? Don't you want to investigate who threatened Olga last night? What's going on?"

He signaled for the bill. "You have your secrets. I have mine. I'm not at all convinced you've told me everything."

I waited until the waitress was gone before answering. "I'm getting sick of this. You're the third person in less than twenty-four hours to say that to me."

I withdrew a five-dollar bill from my tiny, jeweled evening bag and put it on the table.

He pushed it back in my direction. "I don't want your money. I want your confidence. Who, besides me, thinks you're keeping secrets from them?"

I blinked back tears. I don't cry easily, or often, but I was exhausted. "First, Olivia. Then, Barbara. And now, you."

He was neither surprised, nor, apparently, particularly moved. "I guess we're all trying to tell you something. Give me a call when you finally get the message."

The pace of rehearsals ramped up as we approached opening night. Daniel, who was slowly recovering from his injury, returned to company class, but he would not be able to perform until the midpoint of the spring season. I had to rely on Joaquin Teixeira to partner with me. After a slow start, we began that necessary process of learning to intuit each other's moves, and I found myself looking forward to dancing with him. Losing Daniel, after many years of dancing with him, was painful. Nonetheless, dancing with Tex, as everyone called him, was fun and exciting. As an added bonus, he appeared immune to gossip.

After dancing the strenuous pas de deux from *Don Quixote*, Tex massaged my feet with strong fingers. "What does Savannah Collier have against you?" he asked. "She told me to watch out for you, but as far as I can tell, you're about as cutthroat as a cupcake."

I tensed, despite the soothing massage. "I wish I knew. She seems to harbor a passionate grudge against me, but I've never figured out why or how. She did say that when she was in the company, I was mean to her." I laughed without pleasure. "I can barely remember her, let alone think of an occasion when I might have offended her."

Tex put his feet in my lap. "My turn." As I kneaded his instep, he said, "You have a reputation, for better or for worse, of picking talented dancers and choreographers to be friendly with. Everyone knows you're the one who picked Bryan Leister out of a bunch of choreographic wannabes, and now look at him. Every company in the world is begging him to choreograph for them." He grabbed my hand. "You also have the reputation of ignoring everyone who doesn't meet your standards."

I teased him. "You must be pretty special, then, for me to spend so much time hanging out with you."

He smiled. "I am. I've also just massaged your horribly misshapen toes. I'm not sure if it's the talent in my hands or my feet that you admire." He jumped lightly to a standing position and struck a pose. "Or perhaps it's my manly beauty."

"You're not that good looking!" I protested, even though he was.

He extended a hand to me. "Did you know Austin's sad little ballet finally has a name?"

"Yes, I do. Let's hope the title isn't a prediction."

And, with that, Tex and I took our places as the tuneless opening bars of Austin's plodding dance, *Desperate Measures*, began.

I didn't think much about my conversation with Tex until later that afternoon, at the rehearsal for *Precious Metals*. Nothing about the rehearsal went well. Everyone was bone-tired, and even Madame was out of sorts. She forced the weary girls in the corps de ballet to repeat their first variation over and over again, and when she finally dismissed them, it was to tell them to find an empty room and continue to practice on their own.

Madame's exacting methods and approach were deeply rooted in her very Russian sensibility, as well as her training. All three of us, Mavis, Olivia, and I, understood the historical importance of these sessions. We were responsible, not only to ourselves, but also to future generations of dancers. One day, we would coach a few lucky kids, and we owed it to them to memorize every scrap of what Madame told us. We would be the living link that connects dancers from one generation to the next.

As the plaintive strains of a clarinet filled the room, we gracefully picked up our props. Mavis held a curved golden pitcher, Olivia held a fan of bronzed leaves, and I had the silver sculpture, which I'd privately dubbed the Death Spiral. At the end of our dance together, we laid our burdens in front of the room.

We curtseyed to Madame. Sweat was pouring down my face, and with nothing else handy, I wiped the droplets with my hand.

Olivia's eyes opened wide, Mavis shrieked, and Madame turned a whole new shade of pale. I whirled around to face the mirror and was shocked to see a dark streak of red across my face. My fingers were the same shade of crimson.

Mavis circled me from a safe distance, as if afraid I was about to turn into a ballerina-eating zombie. Olivia backed away, looking as if she was about to throw up.

Madame inspected the metal sculpture without touching it. She pointed to the tip of the handle, which had a powdery scarlet residue on it. She withdrew a clean towel from her bag and gently wrapped the prop. "I give to that nice detective, Lelotchka. Please to not worry. We figure out who play this mean trick." As calmly as if every rehearsal ended in this fashion, she sat and waited for a police officer to retrieve my ballet prop.

I swallowed my fear and said, "Yes, Madame. It's probably just a prank. Some of the new guys have a really sick sense of humor."

Olivia said, "I'll watch your dance bag, if you want, so you can wash up."

Mavis walked with me. She opened the door of the studio and the bathroom and waited until my hands were relatively clean.

"You're lucky it didn't happen onstage," she said. "That would have been rather more awkward. The audience might have thought you had blood on your hands."

My stomach did a double somersault. Getting powder-bombed in a rehearsal was bad. Having it happen on stage would indeed have been worse. Mavis admired her beautiful face while I digested the implications of what she said. I didn't expect a heart-to-heart chat with her, and I didn't get one. But she came quite close to treating me kindly, and for that, I was grateful.

The dancers at American Ballet Company had endured murder, attempted murder, and all manner of freak injuries. Perhaps because I was already physically depleted by the rehearsal schedule, this cruel joke exacted a terrible emotional toll.

Opening night was in less than one week. If we could make it until then.

Chapter Twenty-Nine

You can dance anywhere, even if only in your heart.
—Source unknown

I didn't take company class with Madame on the first day of dress rehearsals. Instead, I went to Studio Dance, a large school not far from the theater. Their teachers were first-rate, and I often went there in the off season, or when I needed a change of pace. On that morning, however, I had a very different mission. I was determined to outwit and unmask the killer.

My first thought had been to enlist the help of Ruth, Miriam, and Eileen. I met these elderly ladies on a bus to Atlantic City, at a time of great peril, and they proved themselves both brave and loyal. But the Gambling Girls, as they called themselves, knew nothing about ballet, and my plan required an insider's knowledge of dance.

With that thought in mind, I entered Studio Dance well before class started. Amid professional dancers and talented amateurs, three women stood out from the rest of the students in the class. Their bodies were slim and strong, but their faces were wrinkled with age. I mentally dubbed them the Weird Sisters. Their knowledge of ballet was encyclopedic, and their intense love for the art of dance ruled their lives. They existed in their own bubble, not simply by virtue of their age, but because they were, in fact, a bit weird. Most people at Studio Dance avoided them, put off by their occasional tendency to talk to themselves. But who could blame my beloved Weird Sisters? Very few people cared to acknowledge their existence.

We were friends. Over the years I'd taken Abigail, Audrey, and Izzy to lunch many times. Delighted to have a real ballerina as a willing listener, they regaled me with stories of performances they'd attended, going back to when Rudolf Nureyev electrified audiences. And when I was most in need of a friend, they proved themselves fiercely loyal. The Weird Sisters were formidable allies.

Abigail, Audrey, and Izzy needed very little explanation. To their great delight, I handed them three passes to the dress rehearsal, along with a printout of the backstage area.

"I want you to sit in the last row of assigned seats. If anyone gets up, especially if that person heads backstage, I need you to text me." I hesitated. "I'm asking you to look out for me, because I don't know who to trust."

They nodded solemnly. "We won't let you down," Abigail assured me.

Izzy was worried. "What if someone tries to stop us?"

Abigail gave her a twisted smile. "We're crazy, remember? Just a bunch of nutty old ladies. The worst that will happen is we'll get thrown out."

Audrey looked stricken. "I don't know what I would do if I couldn't go to the ballet. It's our life!"

Abigail put her hands on her hips. "Leah needs us. Nothing else matters."

I hugged her. "I promise you won't suffer any blowback. And I'll get all of you free seats to any performance that hasn't sold out."

Izzy was overcome. "Seats? That would be fantastic! We hardly ever get to sit."

Like other balletomanes living on a limited income, the Weird Sisters usually bought same-day standing room tickets. First, they stood on line, sometimes for hours, to get a ticket. Then they stood for the entire performance, which would test the endurance of people half their age. Abigail, Audrey, and Izzy were, however, adept as sneaking into empty seats during the intermission.

As soon as the class ended, I rushed to the theater. An hour later, the ushers let the first people inside the auditorium. Other than my elderly friends, the audience at the dress rehearsal was made up of paid subscribers. For the sum of one hundred dollars, people can become "Friends" of the company and earn one ticket to a dress rehearsal. Even that relatively modest sum, however, was beyond the reach of the Weird Sisters.

Desperate Measures was first on the schedule. The set designer fussed and fretted as three stagehands pushed large white plastic blobs from behind the wings. This was not a three-person job. The blobs looked heavy but were hollow. I could have moved them myself.

Austin retreated to his seat at the back of the theater. Five minutes into the first section, his anxiety propelled him out of his seat and into the aisle. Heedless of the passionate interest his frantic demeanor evoked in the audience of well-bred, well-heeled audience members, he charged the stage. I looked for Abigail, Audrey, and Izzy, but they had disappeared.

Waving his arms wildly, and shouting over the music, Austin didn't direct his comments to anyone in particular. "I can't see your thumbs! There is absolutely no difference between the one-inch distance and the two-inch distance. You are ruining my ballet!"

One by one, we stopped dancing. Madame emerged from the wings. She was kind but firm. "I watch the dance with close attention. All thumbs most definitely in place. No thumb unturned." Her expression was serious, but the twinkle in her eye was unmistakable.

Austin sputtered. "When the dancers were walking around each other I could not see the difference between thumbs out, thumbs in, and thumbs halfway. And I was watching very closely."

Daniel, who had been watching from the wings, said what everyone in the theater knew, including the dance fans in the audience. "There is no way a tiny difference like that could possibly read from the back of the house. You're the only one who ever thought it would work. Give it up, Austin, and concentrate on getting the rest of this dance ready for opening night."

There was a general agreement from the circle of dancers. Austin was near tears, but his drama held little interest to me. While the others debated the angles and poses that would magnify the effect of our thumb positions, I checked the dark corners of the stage and tried to keep track of everyone at the rehearsal. The drop from the stage to the orchestra pit below wasn't high enough to kill anyone, but it was plenty tall enough to put any dancer, no matter how fit, out of commission for a good long time. I edged upstage, away from any possible "accident."

Tex nudged me. "What's the matter? Apart from this train wreck of a ballet, of course."

I shivered. "I have this awful feeling someone is watching me. Watching us."

He pointed to the occupied seats in the orchestra. "News flash, Leah: Fifty people are following your every move, so that the second you finish they can crowd the stage door to get your autograph. You, of all people, should be used to that by now."

I tried to quell a rising tide of fear. "Good point. Except that ABC hasn't had the best safety record recently. Aside from several relatively minor injuries, we have had a murder. And an attempted murder. The police still don't know who did it."

He immediately got serious. "I know. That scares me too. Everyone has a different idea about who did it. But what can we do?"

Daniel, who had been listening to our conversation while everyone else was following the Great Thumb Drama, said, "We can be careful. Very careful. No one is safe until we know who the killer is." He grinned at me. "Unless you plan to unmask him in some dramatic fashion?"

I tried to answer his smile. "I do like the element of surprise. The killer won't know what hit him." After a moment, I added, "Or her."

Ron, who was taking notes for Jonathan, called out from the shadows. "My suggestion is to paint everyone's thumbs. If you paint them with something reflective, they'll really stick out. Most effective, I think. Especially because the lighting for this ballet is so muted."

Austin turned to Bobbie. "Can you arrange this?"

Bobbie smiled, pleased to have the opportunity to turn him down. "Tempting, but *no*. Tell makeup. They'll take care of it."

Madame stepped forward. "This is a most creative and brilliant idea, but perhaps not so easy in the execution. Many dancers already must do the quick change. Very difficult, I think, to remove all traces of paint. Perhaps put a sock on thumb instead. Or use a glove."

Austin ignored Madame's suggestion. He was too entranced with the idea of painting our thumbs to consider the practical consequences. "That is brilliant! Simply brilliant! Everyone, back onstage. I'll get some paint samples here and we can try it out."

The audience's response to Austin's ballet was not enthusiastic, but they applauded until their hands were raw for the rest of the program. *Precious Metals* got a standing ovation, which was gratifying, even though the standees numbered in the dozens and not the thousands.

At the end of the rehearsal, I lingered onstage with Daniel and Tex. We still had a few sections to iron out. After we finished, the men headed to their dressing area, and I headed to mine. As I turned the corner, a slight scratch caught my attention. I was afraid it was a mouse, or worse. I stomped my feet, to scare away any rodent with the temerity to invade our sacred space.

I was halfway down the corridor when the feeling of being watched returned. A movement from behind a long rack of tutus could have been the wind, except there was no air in that windowless passage. I darted into the adjacent prop room and grabbed a dagger we used in *Romeo and Juliet*. It was made of lightweight plastic, but it looked real. Another jiggle from behind the rack of tutus startled me, and I screamed as loudly as if a legion of rampaging Roman warriors was headed my way.

"Stop! Leah, it's us!"

No rampaging Romans. Just three very nervous ladies, wielding bright knitting needles.

Abigail chided me, "I told you we'd keep you safe. Now, don't you be so scared. We got your back."

Audrey regarded the plastic dagger I still had in my grasp. "That isn't very good protection, dear. Don't you knit?"

I laughed hysterically. "I think I'll take it up again."

In unison, they turned down the passage and exited the theater through a side door. They must have been a lot better at reading maps than I was. Few people had the ability to navigate the maze of backstage corridors without plenty of practice. Even I occasionally took a wrong turn.

Tex and Daniel were waiting outside to escort me to the studio. They didn't want to leave me to the mercy of the balletomanes who swarmed the stage door. As Tex predicted, every audience member was there. Along with the other dancers, we signed photographs and old programs before heading back to the studio for a last-minute costume fitting and thumb painting. Circling the crowd with as much subtlety as a brass band at a parade, the Weird Sisters stood guard. My phone buzzed with a text: **We're still undercover! Pretend you don't know us!**

In a rare moment of unity, most of the dancers walked together back to the studio. It was the first warm day of the year, and the unexpected mild temperatures and bright sunshine seemed to melt away petty grudges. We stopped for coffee, which we brought to the open tables across from Lincoln Center. The men bought big salty pretzels, which they wolfed down with an abandon I would never know. We lingered over our drinks and then walked slowly, in a deliberate effort to prolong the unexpectedly peaceful interlude. When we got to the studio, we even joked about the clanking noises the elevator made. I almost forgot how scared I'd been. By the time we got to the top floor, I persuaded myself that the sensation of being watched was the product of an overactive imagination.

Olga was in the costume room, sweeping up scraps of fabric. She had a blank expression on her face and didn't look at me. She said, in a singsong rhythm very different from her usual staccato delivery, "Hello, Ladies. Hello, Gentlemans. I am Olga. Will not disturb you, no?"

Austin pointed to his chest. "Me Austin." As if she hadn't already introduced herself, he said, "You speak English?"

Olga nodded with enthusiasm and said, as if not sure of the words, "Yes. Olga know a little of the English. But very little, Mister Aus-tin."

Austin, having demonstrated how welcoming and inclusive he was, lost interest in Olga. He turned fretful. "Where is Bobbie? Where is Savannah?" he asked us, as if we were somehow to blame for their absence. He tapped impatiently at his phone. Cursing, he slammed open the door and tore down the stairs. None of us followed him. We were in no rush to break the calm mood of the last hour. We lingered, talking and joking, until the sickening blare of an ambulance siren interrupted us.

This time it was Savannah who was taken to the hospital. She was the latest victim of what the newspapers were now calling the ABC Killer.

Chapter Thirty

You get obsessed by dancing, because there seems to be no choice.
—Lisa Rinehart

Savannah did not die. She was released from the hospital twelve hours and sixty-seven social media posts after she was poisoned. Most of what I knew came from Daniel, who had escorted her home from the hospital. Because he was still injured, Daniel was the only dancer who didn't have to report to the theater.

Seated across from me at a table at Café Figaro, Gabi argued that Savannah should be removed from the list of suspects.

Melissa didn't agree. "She could have poisoned herself. There's no better way to establish your innocence than to make yourself a victim, and Savannah is an expert in that area."

I too was far from ready to exonerate her. "She could have googled 'poisonous house plants' the same way I did after the first news reports came out. It wouldn't have been difficult to figure out which one of Ron's potted monstrosities would do the trick. I also wouldn't put it past Savannah to exaggerate her symptoms. The average hospital stay for oleander poisoning is one to three days. She was in the hospital for twelve hours. She got nowhere near a fatal dose."

Gabi still wasn't convinced. "You're assuming she knew she was a prime suspect. But unless she thought she was in imminent danger of getting arrested, she had no motive to take that big a risk."

Melissa was thoughtful. "Perhaps the opposite was true. People had started to lose interest in her, and this was the perfect way to get back in the limelight."

My sister's words startled me. "You think she's the kind of killer who needs everyone to know how smart she is?"

Her words came slowly. "Paradoxically, some criminals seek a close relationship with the police who are investigating their crimes. That fits well with what you've told me, especially as it relates to her behavior toward Jonah."

Gabi hooted. "Jonah is hot. She wants him to bonk her, not cuff her. Unless the cuffs are chained to a bedpost in Jonah's apartment. Then all bets are off."

We were at my favorite table, in the rear of the café, which gave me room to stand up and stretch. "Is there some reason we're not discussing Ron? The oleander plant was in his office."

My sister, who does not share my need for physical movement, stayed seated. "I think it's more likely Ron was the intended target. The killer is, a little too obviously, trying to implicate him."

Gabi tapped her long, thin fingers on the table. "Who has a motive to kill Ron?"

I sat down and looked over my notes. "Everyone, including Savannah. Ron was Pavel's right-hand man. No one else had his confidential access to information. Maybe Ron was blackmailing the killer, who tried to turn to turn the tables on him by fingering him for the attack on Savannah."

Melissa scrolled through the latest headlines. "I'm not buying this serial killer story the press is peddling. I don't think the police are, either. The attacks aren't random. They all link back to Pavel."

Mrs. Pizzuto came to our table and deposited four biscotti, which was two more than we'd ordered. "Just in case that nice detective comes by," she explained. "And you, Leah, no more dieting! Too skinny, even for you."

Mrs. Pizzuto, for once, had not overstated how thin I was. I'd finally lost those five pounds, along with another few I wasn't trying to shed. Not a moment too soon, either, since in a few hours I would be dancing at the opening night of the season, clad only in a white leotard, thumb paint, and a look of pained concentration.

"Thanks, Mrs. Pizzuto, but Jonah isn't coming. It's just us today."

She pushed the plate closer to me. "Then eat two cookies."

I didn't argue with her. It was like arguing with my mother, whose stubbornness was encoded in her DNA.

Gabi took a biscotti. "Feel free to leave them all for me. The only place I'll be dancing is at the after-party."

Pre-performance nervousness coursed through my body. "Speaking of dancing, I have to be at the theater soon. Let's plan out our next line of investigation, preferably one that ends without anyone getting hurt. Or dead."

Gabi signaled to Mrs. Pizzuto to bring more coffee. "I'm glad we didn't invite Madame or Barbara to meet us today. We have to protect them."

Melissa was grim. "Barbara is still involved with Philip. And that's a dangerous place to be."

I was quick to agree. "Right. That's why it's your job to take care of her today. As soon as we leave the café, I want you to go to her place. Have David pick you up there, so between the two of you, you can keep her safe."

She said as she texted Barbara, "I haven't given up on convincing her to dump Philip. I don't know what's taking her so long. She's usually lost interest by now."

I hugged her. "Try hard. She respects your opinion. Maybe you can succeed where I've failed."

My sister grabbed the remaining biscotti ahead of Gabi. "I need sustenance. Dealing with Barbara is a sweat job. But I'm also worried about Madame." She looked at me. "And you. You're the one I'm most worried about. I'd rather stick with you and let David guard Barbara. Our nanny is spending the night, so we're both free."

I drained the rest of my coffee in three quick gulps. "Madame is busy with last minute details. I've arranged for Olga to be with her all day, so she'll be well protected."

Gabi stirred a spoonful of sugar into her second latte. "Did you ever find out who that mysterious cleaning lady was, on the night you and Olga were in the studio?"

My heart beat faster, thinking of the pistol-packing woman who'd threatened Olga. "No. I told Jonah about her, and he said he'd take care of it, but he was angrier with me than he was worried about an armed and dangerous intruder."

Melissa shut her eyes. My sister is a genius, so when she's deep in thought we don't bother her. After a moment or two, she opened her eyes. "I can think of only one reason Jonah wasn't interested in what you told him."

As soon as the words were out of her mouth, I knew where she was going. I felt like an idiot for not figuring it out earlier. "He already knew about the woman in the studio. And that cleaning lady was no lady. She was a cop."

Melissa patted my arm in approval. "Exactly. Didn't he say he was going to station someone at the studio?"

I stood up again. Squeezed against the back wall, I had no room to pace, so I shifted my weight from one foot to the other. "Yes. He had Diaz there every day. In uniform. But he must have had someone undercover as well. The police aren't dumb. They probably had the same thought we did—that no one pays much attention to the cleaning staff."

Melissa nervously picked at the crumbs on her plate. "Let's get back to the investigation. The biggest takeaway for me, from a psychological standpoint, was that Savannah couldn't walk away from the ballet world. If she didn't make it as a dancer, and then couldn't even hack it as an administrator, she would have been devastated."

I sighed. "Now you're making me feel sorry for her."

Melissa patted my arm. "Let's leave our emotions out of it. We need a plan. Neither the police presence at the studio nor anything we've done has worked. We don't have much time. Let's figure out what we need to do next. At this point, especially for you, Leah, doing nothing might be more dangerous than taking action."

Gabi was eager. "Let's start today. It has to be you and me, Melissa, since Leah needs to all her energy to dance."

The last thing I wanted was for any of them to take immediate action, which might interfere with the plans I'd made. "I don't think there's much we can do before the performance. But everyone will be at the theater tonight. That's when we make our move. There's no better time to entrap our killer than when every suspect is enjoying an open bar and sitting in the same place at the same time."

Melissa studied her empty coffee cup. "Leah is right. If we keep poking, something will emerge. And let's not forget that the lies people tell can be as revealing as the truth. We already know a lot about these people, and they don't know we know it."

I was anxious to get on with the rest of my day. "When we get to the gala, let's agree to divide and conquer. Gabi, you concentrate on Jonathan. Make sure you wear something super sexy. Then corner him and grill him until there's nothing left of him but a pile of ashes. And when you're done with him, nail Bobbie to the wall. Melissa, you take Philip and Ann. Preferably not together. I'll have Madame question Savannah tomorrow, although I think she's going to be recovered enough to come to the party, if not the performance."

I paused to drink some water and organize my thoughts. "I'll take Ron and Austin. One of them might know enough to provide the key that unlocks the whole puzzle. I'll corner Ron this afternoon and Austin after the performance. Austin may not have been directly involved, but like Savannah, he's the kind of person who's too dumb to know he's being used. I can threaten him by telling him if he doesn't spill his guts, I won't keep my thumbs in place during his dreadful ballet."

Gabi laughed. "Forget serial killers. What kind of issues does someone have to have to be so fixated on thumbs?"

Melissa wiggled her fingers. "Are you kidding? Freud would have had a field day analyzing Austin's brand of envy."

We laughed hard enough to blow away our fear and worry. I handed them each a list of questions. "Look these over and add whatever you think is good."

Melissa studied the pink sticky notes I'd appended to my original summaries. "This is going to make for some awkward conversations."

I put the notebook back in my bag. "We're still missing something. Some thread that ties all these people together. The police have their methods. And they're good. But they don't know ballet. We do."

Melissa protested. "The only thing I know about ballet is that I was terrible at it. Our ballet teachers couldn't believe we came from the same parents."

I tried to sound confident. "Please, trust me on this. We have nothing to lose. We'll be surrounded by people, not to mention plenty of security and undercover police officers. We're not going to do anything before the gala, so there's nothing to worry about."

I wrung a reluctant assent from Gabi and Melissa. Relieved they would be safe for at least the next few hours, I proceeded with my plan to nail the ABC Killer.

Chapter Thirty-One

A dancer, more than any other human being, dies two deaths.
—Martha Graham

With only a few hours until curtain call, I had very little time. Confident that Melissa, Gabi, Barbara, and Madame were safely out of the way, I headed to the studio. On the way, I called Jonah. His phone went immediately to voicemail. I didn't bother leaving a message.

I hoped to find Ron at the studio, but the place was empty. Everyone was at the theater, preparing for the opening night gala performance. Disappointed in my desire to talk to Ron, I decided to take advantage of the deserted building. Everything I needed was already at the theater, and for once I was free of my heavy dance bag.

The door to the main office stood wide open, as did most of the doors to the individual rooms inside. Pavel's cubicle, which now belonged to Jonathan, had been completely remade in its new owner's image. Jonathan's degrees from Princeton and Yale hung in gilt frames, alongside photographs from his famous and accomplished family. Shoved into a corner of the room, Pavel's desk waited to be taken away. The police, of course, had already thoroughly searched it, but perhaps it still held a clue to Pavel's tragic death. I opened every drawer and inspected the underside, but if there had been anything of value in the desk, it was no longer there. Every drawer in Jonathan's desk, which looked like a piece of modernist sculpture, was locked. Terrified of damaging a piece of furniture that probably cost more than a car, I didn't dare jam the locks, as I had with Bobbie's desk.

Next, I checked Ron's office. It was the only one with the door still closed, to protect his fragile flowers. I had no idea what I was looking for, but the empty office provided too tempting an opportunity to turn down. As always, the heat inside was made even more unpleasant by the cloying scent of his potted plants. It occurred to me that those plants provided Ron with a good excuse to wall himself off from the rest of the office staff.

I froze as the soft sound of footsteps got louder and closer. With no place else to hide, I ducked under his desk. It was nowhere near as spacious as Jonathan's, and I banged my head on the underside as I pretzeled myself in the small space.

The footsteps stopped. My heart was pounding hard enough to crash through my chest. An exasperated voice echoed through the room. "Ms. Siderova. Get out right now."

A tall woman, with dark hair and a stern expression, regarded me with resigned patience. "What the hell are you doing this time?"

The last time I'd seen her, she was wearing the uniform of the New York City Police Department. This time, she was wearing gray overalls and carrying a mop.

I untangled myself and stood up. With a friendly smile, I said, "Officer Morelli. I-I can explain."

She didn't return my smile. "Do I need to arrest you to keep you out of the way?"

When I checked my watch, her tone grew even more sarcastic. "I'm sorry. Am I keeping you from an important appointment?"

I leaned against the wall for support. "I swear, this is all a misunderstanding. But if you do arrest me, can you do it after tonight's performance? If I don't get going soon, I'm going to miss my cue, and Austin will have a nervous breakdown. And it will be on your head."

Officer Morelli didn't find me funny. She escorted me out of the studio and slammed the door. As I made my way to the theater, I tallied my failures. Thanks to my ineptitude, all of my suspects knew I was on the hunt. The least I could do was protect anyone else from future peril.

I entered the theater through the stage door. Raoul, who had been guarding the back entrance to the theater since the Pleistocene Epoch, shook his head at me. I was late, and he was as much a stickler as Madame when it came to arriving on time. I raced to my dressing room and plastered my face with makeup. My fingers trembled so violently; it took three tries to affix my false eyelashes. I washed my hands carefully so that no trace of makeup remained on them and skinned into the white leotard. I tied the ribbons on my pointe shoes, ran a few stitches through the knot to keep them secure, and sprinted to the stage to take my place in the wings.

Olivia grabbed me. "Where have you been? I was worried sick about you." Her face was filled with a warmth that had been missing for many days. Her words were like a balm.

"I'll explain later. Right now, I need some of that silver paint for my thumbs."

Ron, who had been lurking noiselessly in the background, appeared with a pot of paint. "You're late." He wore plastic, disposable gloves to protect his fingers from the fluorescent paint. When he finished anointing my thumbs, he patted me with unwelcome intimacy along the small of my back. I felt a chilly dampness where he touched me, but I couldn't touch myself until the paint dried.

He nodded reassuringly at me. "Don't worry. I'll cover for you. Just take your place onstage."

I didn't answer, because I wasn't going to return the favor by covering for him. There wasn't much I could do, though, as the sound of the music's dissonant opening bars filtered through the still-closed curtain. Onstage, Tex was warming up. Behind the mask that covered the top half of his face, his eyes were anxious. I looked up at him. "Don't worry. I won't let you down. Wait here."

The dressing room closest to the stage was reserved for our guest stars. I banged the door open. Mavis was seated at her dressing table, applying the finishing touches to her makeup. She was starring in the second ballet. I rifled through her costumes as she yelped in protest.

I ripped off my white leotard and grabbed a black one, pulling it up over my chest as I ran back onstage.

Janelle, who was understudying my part, ran in from the opposite direction. With sincere sympathy, I told her, "Not this time." Janelle would have to wait for her *42nd Street* moment.

I took my place in front of one of the hollow white blobs that dotted the stage. She smiled in understanding and whispered, *merde*.

Dancing on one of the greatest stages in the world was exciting and inspiring, and the extra thrill of a sold-out audience brought out the best in us. *Desperate Measures* was not destined for immortality, but the dancers moved through the awkward passages with fluid ease. We bowed and curtseyed to loud cheers. Austin, dressed in the same black pants and turtleneck shirt the male dancers wore, strode onto the stage to applause that doubled in volume when the conductor and the pianist joined him. I smiled and gestured to the audience, who kept clapping. One of the young dance students at ABC's school brought me a large bouquet of flowers. I came forward to accept it and pulled a pre-loosened red rose to give to Tex. He bowed his head in tribute, took my hand, and kissed it.

Although some people grumble over the tackiness of this ritual, the audience loves it and would feel cheated without it. As a side bonus, it usually means even more applause. For once, though, I wanted the clapping to end. I was in an agony of impatience to get back to my dressing room to call Jonah. Finally, the curtain closed. Ron had disappeared.

Austin tried to stop me. "What the hell happened to your costume? You were the only woman in black. You ruined my vision!"

I pushed him aside. "Sorry about that. Technical difficulties." I was halfway down the passage when I called him back. "Have you seen Ron? He was helping out backstage."

Austin sniffed. "Ron is not welcome backstage. He took it upon himself to help with the thumb painting, and he did a terrible job."

Perhaps Ron was in a reserved seat in the audience. Or maybe, he was still lurking in the wings. I had exactly twenty-five minutes to find him before the stage call for *Precious Metals*.

I brushed past fellow dancers, who generously complimented me on my performance. Mavis was less kind. "Personally, I've never needed a costume to help me stand out from the crowd."

I ignored her spiteful comment. "Watch out, Mavis. Be careful out there. And *merde.*"

Expecting equal cattiness from me, she was nonplussed. "When did you turn into such a little ray of sunshine?"

With so much on the line, her petty digs lost their ability to hurt me. I smiled and said, "Like it or not, we're all in this together."

I got to my dressing room. Stuck onto the mirror a sticky note warned me, as if I needed the reminder: *TRUST NO ONE*

My heart was pounding. A haze of worry and fear fogged my brain as I searched for my phone. It wasn't in its usual charging spot. I grabbed my dance bag, which was unusually heavy, and dumped the entire contents on the table. No phone. But the prop I needed for the next ballet, the scrolled, metallic piece of sculpture used to kill Pavel, landed with a crash at my feet. Was that another warning? Or was it a threat?

Chapter Thirty-Two

I had to join three times in a magical dance, for rhythm was the wheel of Eternity.
—W.B. Yeats

The fifteen-minute warning bell rang. A dresser arrived, out of breath, in time to dust my hair and arms with silver glitter. She secured a silver circlet set with rhinestones on my head and hooked me into my tutu. She tugged at the bodice, stepped back to examine me, and frowned. "Too loose. Give me a minute to fix this." She withdrew a needle, already threaded, and tried to stitch the fabric so that it fitted more closely to my waist.

I pulled away. "Thank you, Rosie, but I have to go."

She looked at her watch. "It will take me two minutes," she insisted. "Ms. York will be very angry with me if she sees I've let you go onstage like this."

Rosie's concern regarding Bobbie's temper was well-founded. I was on fire to leave, but with so little time before the final ballet of the night began, there was little I could do until the final curtain. "Okay, Rosie, but you have to do me a big favor. Let me borrow your cell phone."

I was halfway through the recorded message when the stage manager grabbed me. "On stage! Now!"

I tried to tell her what to do as we rushed down the winding hallway to the stage, but I wasn't sure she understood it was an emergency.

The stage was filled with a blue light that cast a ghostly glow upon me, Mavis, and Olivia. The scenery consisted of a shimmery forest of metallic trees and a starry backdrop with a crescent moon. Mavis held a golden pitcher, Olivia a fan of bronze leaves, and I, of course, clenched a copy of the silver murder weapon. The Death Spiral.

In the week that led to this moment, Mavis had been catty. Olivia had been cool. I had been consumed with the fallout from Pavel's death. As soon as we began dancing, though, the outside world slipped away. Mavis became the Golden Lady, I, the Silver Maiden, and Olivia, the Bronze Girl. In the dark corners of the theater, danger lurked. But onstage, everything was beautiful and serene.

René Vernier, the artistic director of ABC when I joined the company, used to stand in the wings until the very last minute when he would rush to his seat to view the ballet from the house. His instructions were always the same: "Be great."

That night, I was.

In the last seconds of the ballet, first Mavis, and then Olivia, struck their final poses atop the stairs. I stepped into an arabesque on pointe. Time slowed and then stopped. The conductor had the orchestra draw out the last note. And still, I balanced on two inches of pointe shoe. A slow roar built in the audience, and when, with exquisite care, I sank to the floor with my arms outstretched, the cheering and stomping crashed through the theater.

Precious Metals earned a standing ovation. When Madame came onstage, the cheers echoed through the theater. The older fans had probably seen her perform in this iconic ballet, on this legendary stage. Those who didn't were clearly aware of the seminal role she'd played. We were prepared for many curtain calls, which we'd rehearsed with the same care we'd devoted to the ballet itself. In a gracious sequence, we stepped forward and curtseyed with the entire group. Next, the three of us curtseyed together, followed by individual bows to the audience. We then sank in deep curtseys to acknowledge Madame. Mavis led the conductor of the orchestra onstage, and we joined the audience in applauding him as well. Last, Jonathan Franklin Llewellyn IV came onstage and took his turn in the limelight.

When the curtain came down, a crowd of well-wishers swarmed the stage.

In a daze after the exertions of the performance, I forgot to replace my silver prop on the table. One of the prop runners approached me. "I almost went crazy getting a replacement. The one we had disappeared. I ran back to the studio to get another one, and when I got back you already had a different one. What's going on?"

In the excitement of the dance, I'd forgotten about the mysterious appearance of the silver sculpture in my dance bag. I told him the truth. "It just appeared in my dressing room. Maybe someone was playing a prank."

He was bitter. "That joke could have cost me my job." He eyed me suspiciously. "Are you sure you don't know who did it?"

This time I lied. "I have no idea who could do such a thing. I promise I will look into it and report it."

Mollified, he picked up Mavis's golden pitcher and Olivia's fan of bronze leaves. Another prop runner, under the eagle eye of the prop master, gathered the gold, silver, and bronze stars the corps de ballet carried in the last act of the ballet.

I squirmed through the crowd. Every few steps, someone hugged and congratulated me. My success onstage appeared to have obliterated the cloud of suspicion that had clung to me in the aftermath of Pavel's death and Savannah's vicious attacks. As far as I could tell, Savannah wasn't there.

The assurance I felt onstage stayed with me. The crowd began to thin out, as people made their way to the elegantly set tables for the post-performance dinner dance. All dancers were required to attend, for these events provided a significant source of income for the company. I wished for the safety and connection of my phone but had to continue without it.

The otherworldly feeling that comes after a performance, when you're not quite ready to return to reality, diminished. The link that connected Pavel's death, and the attacks on Ms. Crandall and Savannah, led to only one person. I didn't know all the details or possess sufficient evidence. But I knew enough. I didn't have a revelation, as much as I finally recognized what some part of me already knew.

I wound a shawl around my shoulders and returned to the props table, where I nicked my silver sculpture, hiding it under voluminous folds of fabric. Armed with the same weapon that had sent Pavel to his grave, I hurried back to my dressing room to change out of my tutu and pointe shoes. This was no time for delicate maidens. I needed a much tougher role model if I was going to outwit the ABC Killer. Perhaps the merciless Von Rothbart of *Swan Lake* would be my inspiration.

The door to my dressing room was closed. It wasn't instinct, or intuition, or an innate sense of danger that made me pause. It was the trace of powder beneath the door that tipped me off. It was the same powder that had been in Ron's office when I'd slipped and nearly injured my fragile knees. The same powder that marred my white leotard before the curtain went up on Austin's ballet and that had forced my last-minute costume change.

Without a phone, I couldn't call for help. And if I left, I would lose my chance to prove Ron's guilt. Slowly, with the silver weapon in my right hand, I turned the doorknob with my left.

I should have remembered, when plotting the outcome of a scene, it's best to anticipate the possibility that another choreographer has set the stage for a very different ending.

Chapter Thirty-Three

Everything is beautiful at the ballet.
—A Chorus Line

I flung open the door of the dressing room, silver weapon in hand, ready to do battle. Except there was no one to fight. Olivia lay on the floor, unconscious. A river of bright red blood dripped from a gash on the side of her head.

I dropped the silver ballet prop and screamed for help. Half-dressed, Mavis was the first to arrive. With her trademark economy of movement, she sped back to her dressing room, returned with her phone, and called nine-one-one.

Shaking so hard I could barely get the words out, I told Mavis, "Keep an eye on her for me."

She yelled, "Where are you going?"

I didn't answer her. I didn't have time. If I hesitated, Ron would once again remove the evidence and elude the police.

By this time, a crowd had begun to gather in the corridor. I grabbed Tex. "Give me your phone."

Without arguing, he handed me his phone. I called my number, hoping to hear the opening notes of the Chopin waltz I'd chosen for my ringtone. Nothing. Either it had been silenced, or Ron was no longer in earshot. Next, I called the Twentieth Precinct. The officer who answered told me Jonah was already in the theater. I explained the situation and then left the dressing room, taking my prop with me. The Death Spiral had killed Pavel. I hoped it would save me.

The stagehands, unaware of the drama backstage, had loud music playing as they struck the set. I rushed past them and entered the backstage maze of corridors. I flew past boxes, scaffolds, and rows of garment racks, toward the exit door. I was nearly there when an arm shot out from behind a large crate and knocked the Death Spiral out of my hand. Before I could fully process what happened, my attacker pulled me into a dark corner, threw me on the floor, and jammed his knee against my back. The point of a knife pressed into the side of my neck.

"Nice try, Leah." Despite the hoarse whisper, I recognized his voice.

I gasped for air, my face pressed against the floor. "Let me go. I promise—I-I won't tell anyone. I'm on your side. I can...I can help you." I dug my toes into the floor, trying to gain control, but I couldn't move.

Ron sounded amused. "You're not nearly as good an actress as you think you are. You are going to do what I say. Or I will kill you."

I was too terrified to move. The point of the knife pressed hard enough into the flesh in my neck that drops of blood began trickling from the wound. I knew, thanks to Barbara's research for her latest murder mystery, I would not survive a deeper push into the artery.

Tears choked me. "I'll do whatever you say. Please don't kill me."

Ron spoke softly. "I have your phone. You will call Jonah Sobol and tell him that Austin Dworkin attacked Olivia."

My mind was racing. If I followed Ron's orders, he would surely kill me as soon as I ended the call. If I didn't do as he said, he would kill me anyway.

I forced myself to take a deep lungful of air. Terror had made me breathless. "I'll do whatever you want. But I really am on your side. I don't care about anything or anyone except ballet." Tears ran down my face, mixing with the blood. "You saw tonight what I can do. Take care of me, and I'll take care of you. I'll—I swear, I'll tell everyone you're the reason for the renaissance in my career. That you're the only one who believed in me. The press will love it. There's nothing they love more than a comeback story. We can be a team."

I sensed, for the first time, he was listening to me. I kept going. "You think

I care about Pavel? He was going to push me out. You think I care about Ms. Crandall? Or, for God's sake, Savannah? And I would gladly throw that rat, Jonathan, to the wolves. You don't have to threaten me. I would have done it anyway."

He drew the point of the knife across my throat, caressing my neck with the blade. He sounded almost regretful. "I tried to get rid of you without killing you. I never thought you'd make it this far. What tipped you off? Was it the gel I smeared on your costume?"

My voice trembled. "Yes. It helped me understand the purpose behind giving me all those difficult roles. You thought I'd fail. Or get injured and have to sit out the season. You powder bombed your office and the place where I stand at the barre." I steadied my voice. "But it all worked out, for both of us. I'll tell everyone you were the inspiration for my success."

"Make the call, and then we'll talk."

I sniffled. "Give me a minute. If Jonah hears me crying, he, uh, he'll come running. And we don't want that."

The pressure on my throat eased, as Ron pulled back the knife. Not much. But enough so I was more than a hair from a mortal wound.

I flexed my feet, still encased in pointe shoes, and tensed my body. Gasping, as if I needed more air, I lifted the center of my back and pressed my shoulders against the floor. When Ron withdrew my phone from his pocket, I was ready. If he'd possessed a dancer's disciplined body, he would have been able to anticipate what happened next.

I coughed, as if I were choking. Ron, who had to keep his knee pressed against my back, the knife pressed against my throat, and the phone pressed to my ear, lost the tension he needed to keep me imprisoned on the floor. I collapsed my back and feet and shot my arm against his face, aiming for his glasses.

He cursed as I tried to wrench myself out of his grasp. I nearly got free, but he grabbed at my tutu and tried to slash me with the knife. I screamed, but the stagehands were too far away to hear.

With a final, desperate move, I gambled on the only thing I knew I could count on. I swerved and executed a perfectly placed *grand battement*. When I kicked him, the edge of the hard pointe shoe hit his hand, and he dropped the knife. That basic ballet move gave me the few seconds I needed to escape.

Chapter Thirty-Four

Get my swan costume ready.
—Anna Pavlova

I staggered through the exit, into the pitch-dark, frigid night. The guy on the other side of the door didn't know a pirouette from a *piqué* turn. But he did know his way around a crime scene.

I clutched Jonah's arm as my legs dissolved beneath me. "It's Ron. He's the killer. He—he hurt Olivia." Pent-up tears rained down my face. "And he tried to kill me." Deep, shuddering tremors shook me. "You have to get him, before he goes after anyone else."

Jonah pulled me back into the theater. "What did he do to you?" He strained to see my face. "It's too dark here. Come into the light."

I forced my body to stillness. "I'm fine. But you should go. Get him before he ditches the evidence. I have to find Olivia. She's hurt. Badly hurt."

In the shadows, he drew me to him. "I know. Security and EMT are already with her. I'm not leaving you."

I drew a deep, shaky, breath. With a confidence I was far from feeling, I assured him, "I'm fine. A little the worse for wear, but that's nothing new. You don't have to worry about me."

Jonah wrapped his arm around my waist. "I'll take you back to your dressing room." He squinted in the darkness. "I'll get a medic to check you out. Diaz and Morelli are right behind me."

The words were barely out of his mouth before both police officers charged through the open door. The stagehands turned on all the lights, and in a matter of moments, the entire theater, front and back, was overrun with cops. Some dancers were already at the gala, but those who danced in the last ballet were still backstage.

Farrow joined us. "We're securing the building. No one is going anywhere."

I was bewildered by the sudden presence of so many police officers. "How did you get here so fast?"

Farrow was terse and tense. "Some of us have been here all night. The rest were on high alert. Then we got the call some kid was hurt." Seeing my stricken face, he said, "She's gonna be okay."

Olivia. She was alive. I tried to get to her, but my legs wouldn't hold me up. Tex came to the rescue. He carried me to a seat in the wings and held me steady as I bent over my legs, hoping the dizzy, sick feeling would stop. My hair, which had come undone, stuck to the still-bleeding gash in the side of my neck.

After a few deep breaths, I was able to sit up. "Thanks, Tex. I think I'll be okay. But do me a favor. Find out how Olivia is doing."

Tex pointed to the blood, which was slowly dripping down the side of my neck. Now, he was the one who looked faint. "Let me get someone for that."

I put my hand to the wound. "I'm okay. I'm scared about Olivia."

He whistled softly. "Girlfriend, you are a pistol. Olivia's fine. Dazed and bruised, but she's like you. She doesn't want to go to the hospital."

I swallowed. "Make her go."

Tex disappeared into the wings and returned bearing a box of tissues. The bleeding from my neck slowed, but blood continued to pour from a cut on my ear.

I examined my costume, which was badly torn. I trembled at the sight of it. The dense layers of tulle and metallic inserts had saved my life. Tex bent down and helped me remove my shoes. My legs were still shaking, as if they had a life of their own.

Jonah brought Ron back into the theater. I shrank from the sight of him.

Ron had a bewildered look on his face. "I'm sorry, Detective, I don't know what this is about. I just heard about poor Olivia. And apparently, Leah was hurt as well?" He tsked like a librarian three times his age. "This isn't going to look good for the company."

I broke in. "He tried to kill me! And Olivia! Don't listen to him."

Ron maintained his pleasant expression. "Leah, this is awful. I don't blame you one bit for being so upset." He shrugged, as if baffled. "Where, and when, am I supposed to have attacked you?"

I looked into his maddeningly smug face. "You're not going to get away with this." I turned to the police officers. "He tried to kill me." I pointed to the hall behind us. "Right there. Five minutes ago." I showed them my torn costume. "And here's the evidence."

Ron moved his head from side to side, as he pretended to examine the shadowy area beyond the wings. He smiled forgivingly. "It's so dark back there, it's no surprise you got confused. I feel terrible about this. Though you seem to be fine, thank God." He continued, in a stern voice, "Officers, please let the others know to be on the lookout for a man of my height and weight." He squinted and pointed to Austin, who was standing with a group of dancers on the other side of the stage. "Someone like that, perhaps."

Diaz and Morelli exchanged glances. Was it possible they were going to let him go?

Evidence. He had to have left evidence. I looked at his face. Something about him was different. "Where are your glasses?"

He stayed cool. "Contact lenses. So much more comfortable. If you're looking for a man with glasses…" He pointed again to Austin. "He's right there."

I got up too quickly and had to sit down again. "I broke Ron's glasses, fighting him off. They'll be here somewhere."

Ron laughed. "Someone's glasses may be here, but not mine."

Jonah returned. Under the bright working lights, he saw, for the first time, the bloody mess of tissues. "What the—" He paused, a sick look on his face. More sharply than I'd ever heard him speak, he commanded Morelli, "What did I tell you? Get one of those medics here. Immediately. Didn't any of you see she was hurt?"

He called another of the police officers. "Search the immediate area. No one moves until we find the weapon. And those missing glasses."

Ron still wasn't rattled. Leaning against the wall, his hands in his pockets, he said, "Good idea, Detective. We must find the person who committed this heinous crime."

Jonah was brief. "We need your statement. At the station house. Officer Diaz will escort you there."

Ron was pleasant but firm. "I am needed here. What happened tonight is terrible, and it's up to me to do damage control. I will be happy to meet you tomorrow morning. Shall we say, ten o'clock?"

Farrow answered, with a sour look on his face. "You can say whatever you want. We will escort you to the precinct tonight. Now, in fact."

I turned to Jonah. "Don't let him get away with this."

Jonah's mouth was set in a grim line. "We have your testimony. That should be enough."

His words were more sanguine than his expression.

A cold wind blew in from the open door, as Diaz and Ron exited. With only a strapless tutu to protect me, I shivered violently, from the cold and from the stress. Farrow retreated to give Jonah and me a few minutes to talk.

Jonah spoke with soft urgency. "Leah, my darling. Give me something. Anything."

I wracked my brains. I already guessed there would be no fingerprints. Ron had been wearing gloves when he smeared paint on my thumbs and gel on the back of my white leotard.

When I accused him, Ron had been so casual, leaning against the wall, hands in his pockets, as if he hadn't a care in the world. And then, it hit me. "His wrist. Check his wrist. I kicked the knife out of his hand. If his wrist isn't broken, it wasn't for lack of trying."

For the first time, Jonah smiled. "That's my girl."

I knew he was trying to make me feel better. "That won't be enough to convict him, will it?"

Jonah helped me to my feet. "No. But it's a start."

Chapter Thirty-Five

Dance is your pulse, your heartbeat, your breathing...
—Jacques d'Amboise

Many hours passed before I was able to leave the theater. As soon as I was free, I went to the hospital where Olivia was treated for a concussion and an angry-looking wound to her head. I waited impatiently while the police took her statement. Her parents arrived, and it was another half hour before I could see her.

I called Zach. It was his weekend to be with his daughter. Although he couldn't come to the hospital, he arranged for a top plastic surgeon to care for Olivia. The gash in my neck, while scary, needed only a bandage. Much of the blood had come from a tiny cut on my ear.

The surgeon was cheerful. After he finished with Olivia, he examined me and said, "You got lucky. Missed the carotid artery by a few millimeters."

I didn't feel lucky. After he left, I embraced Olivia. "What happened? What were you doing in my dressing room?"

Her eyes closed. "I tried to warn you. Left you the weapon. For protection. Thought Jonathan was killer."

I was shocked. "Is that why you dated him?"

Her voice slurred. "Left you those notes. In your bag, and in your dressing room." She tried to open her eyes. "I was worried about you. I wanted to help catch the killer. Why didn't you trust me?"

Her mother peered at us from the doorway, anxious to be with her daughter. I kissed Olivia goodbye and left.

It was past three in the morning, but there was plenty of work left to do. Barbara, Madame, Gabi, and Melissa were all waiting for me.

Despite the hour, all of my co-conspirators were wide awake. They swarmed me the moment I walked in.

Melissa was the most direct. "What happened? We were at the gala and had no idea what was going on backstage. All we knew was the police kept anyone from leaving, because someone was attacked. When you didn't answer your phone, we were frantic with worry."

Barbara held her stomach. She looked as if she were going to throw up. "We thought you were…"

I didn't tell them any details of how Ron attacked me. I didn't even tell them I'd gone to the hospital to see Olivia. It was still too raw to talk about. Instead, I told them about the aftermath. They were silent, as they digested the implications of Ron's denial.

Gabi said, uncertainly, "But the police have your statement. You're an eyewitness."

I took a deep breath. "I know that, and you know that. And yes, the police know that. But he denied everything. It was creepy how nonchalant he was. He acted as if I were some hysterical female and claimed it was too dark for me to identify him."

Barbara was indignant. "That's absurd. I don't care how dark it was. Couldn't you identify him by his voice?"

I slid off the chair and onto the rug to stretch my aching legs. "Of course, I could. The police believe me. The question is, can they put together a strong enough case to convict him? To be honest, I didn't see his face. I know without a shadow of a doubt that it was Ron, but I'm not going to lie about what happened."

Melissa, as always, was logical and precise. "What about fingerprints? He must have left some trace on you or on the knife."

The warmth from the fire could not soothe the cold chills that coursed down my back. "He was wearing gloves. That's the first thing I noticed when I saw him backstage before the performance. He was helping the makeup people paint our thumbs. I already suspected him, and when he smeared my back with some of the greasy stuff he's been leaving in his wake, I knew for sure. If Tex had tried to turn me upside down during our lift, he would have ended up dropping me on my head."

Madame picked up her wineglass with shaky fingers. "Very clever, this Ron. He tell me it was your fault Daniel get hurt. If you fell onstage, he would make it seem *you* are problem. Two partners. Two falls. Same ballerina."

Gabi exclaimed, "I was wondering why you were wearing a black leotard, especially after you were so upset about wearing a white one. It totally worked, by the way. You looked fabulous. Very skinny and beautiful."

I gave myself a moment to enjoy the praise. "Thanks, Gabi. Unfortunately, that change of costume also almost killed me. When Ron saw me run off the stage and return in a different leotard, he knew for sure I was on to him."

Melissa said, "You danced beautifully, as if you hadn't a care in the world."

I clutched my head. "Right now, we have nothing but problems. We have to do something. The first thing should be to find out if Savannah was a willing partner or a witless one. And no one yet knows Ron's motive. If we can't find enough evidence against him, we have to figure out a way to entrap him."

The doorbell rang. It was a welcome break from our tense speculations.

Olga charged in, nearly upsetting a gold-rimmed, crystal vase sitting on a delicate table. I scrambled to my feet to greet her and tensed for her usual bear hug. But she was very gentle. "I hear of your so terrible time you had. Very worried about you, Lelotchka."

The cool, rational façade I'd cultivated to keep everyone from worrying, crumbled. I brushed annoying tears from my cheeks. "I'm fine, Olga. I'm proud of you for keeping Madame safe."

She was grim. "But I let you be hurt. Never again. I not stay long. Have much work to do." She looked sternly at all of us. "Leave everything to me."

With that, she left. Madame tried to get her to stay for breakfast, but she refused.

Madame said, "Olga say she close to finding evidence against Ron. Must be patient. In the meantime, first plan is to eat. I get breakfast for us. We

216

talk. Then, Lelotchka, she must rest. Can you dance," she checked her watch, "tonight?"

When performers say the show must go on, it sounds like a cliché, but it became a cliché because it's eternally true. When the curtain went up, I, and all the other dancers, musicians, stagehands, and support staff would be in place. It's what we do.

The doorbell rang again, and Madame and Barbara bickered over the bill. Barbara was bested at the skirmish, but if I knew my mother, she'd figure out a way to win the war, probably by sending Madame a case of her favorite champagne.

I was surprised at Madame's choice of food for our meal. Bagels, cream cheese, lox, and dense, cinnamony rugelach were not often on her menu. Only the large platter of fruit and the mound of sliced vegetables fit in with her rigorous approach to nutrition. In response to my questioning look, she patted my arm.

"Must not let you get too skinny, Lelotchka. While we dine at gala, you get attacked. Is okay to enjoy for once."

She had ordered one of my favorite meals, but I could barely eat it, let alone enjoy it. To please Madame, I chewed on a small section of a bagel, but my body had endured too much stress. I yawned, in spite of myself.

Madame pushed some fruit on my plate. "Eat. Will do you good."

I could barely lift a fork. "Madame, if I'm going to get back onstage tonight, I have to go home and rest."

She was immediately remorseful. "But yes, of course. I make bed in spare room for you. Very nice. And we will be very quiet."

It was tempting to simply fall into the closest bed, but I knew I'd be more comfortable at home, even if it meant climbing all those stairs. Madame agreed and had me wait while she filled a bag with enough food to feed the entire corps de ballet.

Barbara shared a cab with me. "You do realize, don't you, that you are still in danger."

I opened the window a crack. Without some fresh air, I feared I'd faint, if only from exhaustion. "We know our enemy now, which we didn't know before. But I have a plan."

"The last one didn't work out. You almost got yourself killed." She took the sting out of her words by hugging me close. "I don't mean to sound harsh, but I'm terrified. You should come home with me. I'll take care of you. And I'll go with you to the theater."

Barbara's bluntness deserved no less in return. "You can't even take care of yourself. What on earth are you doing, hanging around with Philip? He may not be a murderer, but he is a sleaze. I don't know what you see in him."

Barbara pulled her arm away. "You have no idea what you're talking about. Philip is a perfectly nice, interesting, and cultured man."

I opened the window a little wider, partly to annoy Barbara. "He's a perfectly nice, interesting, cultured con man. Probably a blackmailer as well."

Barbara flushed. "If that's what you think of me, then there's nothing I can do to change your mind."

I didn't give up. "Don't try that with me. It's not what I think of you, and you know it. It's what I think of Philip. I've told you more than once what he said in Bar Bleu. He wasn't nearly as cultured then as you seem to believe." My brain was as tired as my body, but I forced myself to stay alert. "What I still don't know is what Philip does for a living."

Barbara was evasive. "I've already explained to you he's a consultant."

I breathed in the fresh morning air. "What's the name of the company? And what's his role?"

She leaned over to close the window. "I'm freezing."

I opened it. "And I'm out of patience."

With an exasperated sigh, she said, "He has his own consulting company. He gets people together. He does high-end referrals and references. That's how he was able to get Jonathan the post as artistic director."

This sounded too innocent to be true. "He didn't sound like a guy who's in HR. He sounded like a gangster, shaking down someone he was blackmailing."

The cab pulled up in front of my apartment building. "As always, darling, you can be so dramatic."

I felt real regret at hurting her feelings, but it was something I should have done days earlier. "I think he's cheating on you. With Ann."

Barbara is nothing, if not full of surprises. "I know. As does your father. We're not as dumb as we look."

Chapter Thirty-Six

I use dance to embellish, extend, or enlarge upon an existing emotion.
—Gower Champion

The five-flight journey up the stairs to my apartment was slow and painful. When I finally made it to my tiny railroad flat, I headed for bed. Dozens of texts, voicemails, and messages begged for attention, but I spoke only to my father. I downplayed the evening's events as much as I could. On the day I signed my first contract with ABC, ending his dream of sending me to college, he had a heart attack. While I didn't think I was completely responsible for the state of his arteries, I wanted to spare him as much stress as the circumstances allowed.

I donned a well-worn pair of sweatpants and a T-shirt and settled under the covers. The minute I closed my eyes, I had nightmarish visions of Ron, Olivia, Pavel, and Ms. Crandall. Moments after I fell asleep, the alarm went off. I did a quick inventory of my body and decided company class was not going to help.

I fell back into a restless slumber. Jonah's phone call woke me three hours later.

"Listen, ballerina girl, we have to talk."

I struggled to a seated position. "I'm so tired, I don't think I can make much sense right now. How about after tonight's performance?"

He didn't hesitate. "No. I don't want to wait that long. But then again, I never want to wait to see you."

I laughed, and the tension in my neck eased. "I bet you say that to all the witnesses."

His voice turned serious. "You sound exhausted. I'm coming over anyway."

"Sounds good. I've already got breakfast ready."

Twenty minutes later, he was in my kitchen, wolfing down some of the finest bagels in New York City. Dark circles shadowed his eyes. "Thank Madame for me. This is my favorite breakfast." He smiled, despite his obvious weariness. "Nice place, if you don't mind the hike."

He looked so much at home, I forgot that he'd never been there before. I picked at a slice of lox. "Give me the rundown. Is Ron in custody?"

He put down the bagel. "No. The DA isn't ready to file charges. Ron got himself a high-powered lawyer. We'll get the job done. But it isn't going to be easy. We've been watching him for the last two weeks."

I felt sick. "Why didn't you tell me you suspected him?"

Jonah hitched his chair closer to me. "The last thing I wanted was for you to go after him yourself. A lot of good that did me."

I nervously poked the food on my plate. "I don't understand why the DA is hesitating. He doesn't have to take my word for what happened. Didn't Olivia give a statement?"

Jonah tipped more coffee into his cup. "Yes. She told us she walked into your dressing room, and someone hit her on the head. She never saw who did it. Olivia is one lucky girl. She's your height, your build, with your dark hair. I think Ron was after you, and simply hit the first person to walk in. He could have killed her after he knocked her out, but he didn't. I doubt it was because he was being kind. She wasn't his target. You were."

I rarely cry in front of people. In private, I've been known to weep at sentimental commercials for washing machines and dryers, but in public, I pride myself on my stoicism. But I was at the breaking point. I told Jonah I needed a sweater and went into the bedroom and pressed my eyes, willing the tears to stop. He sat next to me and held me until my shoulders stopped shaking.

I pushed him away and hid my face. "Don't look at me. My face is a mess."

He brushed aside my hair and kissed me, with lips that burned against mine. His grip tightened and we fell back into the tangle of blankets. It was as if my skin had been starved of food and didn't know it until that moment.

And then, it was over. He pushed me away and got off the bed. In a strangled voice, he said, "Not now. This is—I'm on a case." He stopped and seemed to struggle for words. "However, I reserve the right to continue where we left off, as soon as this is all over. I'm sorry."

My body was on fire from his touch. "I know. I'm sorry, too."

He swallowed. "Let's go back to the kitchen. It's safer there."

We sat at the postage-stamp-sized table, wedged next to the fire escape, and looked out on a patch of brown grass in the back of the building. It was easier than looking at each other. I got up and ground more coffee. It was going to be a very long day.

I needed some outlet for the energy that thrummed through me. I could barely stand still as I waited for the water to boil. "I didn't have Ron at the top of my list of suspects until a few hours before he tried to kill me. After I changed my costume, of course, he knew I was onto him. He must have already had a plan in place to frame Austin. They both have blonde hair and glasses and they do look a lot alike."

Jonah rubbed his forehead. "He was a person of interest for us, which is why I had Morelli go undercover at the studio. She kept a close watch on the office." He shook his head. "I guess great minds think alike, since you had Olga there."

I was indignant. "Why didn't you tell me about Morelli? Olga and I were terrified. And she felt awful, as if she had let me down."

I poured boiling water over the coffee grounds and waited. He shrugged. "I didn't tell you, because the police don't tell the public when they place someone undercover. Don't try to change the subject. What did you do before you got to the theater?"

I searched my memory. "Nothing that should have motivated him to murder me. I went to the studio, looking for him. But he didn't know that. He wasn't there."

Jonah circled my wrist with two fingers. "Did you think he would be intimidated by your ninety-pound self?" I turned my hand and opened my palm. He snatched his fingers away.

I withdrew to finish making the coffee. "Yesterday, I met with Melissa and Gabi at Café Figaro. While we were talking, I realized only one person benefited from all three attacks. At first, I thought the attack on Ms. Crandall occurred because the killer feared she knew something about Pavel's murder. I wasn't sure about Savannah. I thought she might be the killer, or that she was in league with the killer. Melissa thought the poison was self-administered."

I sat down and sipped the hot coffee. "Then, I thought, what if the connection between the three episodes wasn't sequential? From the start, I assumed Pavel was the primary target, and Ms. Crandall and Savannah in some way posed a threat after the fact. But what if the killer planned all along to murder all three? In that case, the killer had to be someone who would benefit separately from all three deaths. If Ron had gotten the same termination letter Savannah and Bobbie got, he would benefit from Pavel's death. Ms. Crandall was the office manager, so she probably knew about it even before Ron did. She never stood a chance. As for Savannah, I think he used her to further his own ends. When she reached the end of her usefulness, he poisoned her and gambled that no one would believe he'd so directly implicate himself. Weeks ago, when I complained to him about Savannah's attacks on my character, he seemed as pleased as if he'd done it himself. Which I think he did. Savannah did what he told her to do. And that made her very dangerous to him. I'm surprised it took so long for him to go after her."

Jonah took out his notebook and jotted a few items. He spoke slowly and calmly. "I've got every available person working on this. He won't get away with it."

I paced the length of the kitchen, which allowed only three steps in any direction. "Did you examine his wrist? What's his explanation for that? I'm sure it must be bruised."

"He has a witness who will swear he hurt it when he slipped in the men's room."

I would have gotten more nervous, if it were humanly possible to get more nervous than I already was. "How is that possible? Hardly any time passed in between the point that I kicked him and when the police brought him backstage."

Jonah was bitter. "He's a quick thinker, I'll give him that. He must have gone directly to the men's room, where he pretended to slip and bang his wrist against the sink. A guy who was in one of the stalls heard him curse, and Ron showed him his wrist."

I was horrified. "What does that mean? Will he be at the studio? At the theater? Who's going to protect us from him?"

His tone was soothing. "Jonathan put him on forced leave."

I was terrified. "Is that the best you can do? What's to prevent him from stalking me?"

Jonah was patient. "I've got a twenty-four-seven detail watching him, and I'm assigning Morelli to keep an eye on you for the next forty-eight hours. We should have enough to charge him long before then. As for the other dancers, the place will be crawling with cops, uniformed and plainclothes, plus the usual security detail." He paused. "I'll be at the theater no later than six-thirty. I promise I won't let you out of my sight. And Morelli will keep you safe between now and then. She's on her way here now."

"Will she be in uniform?"

"Yes. I'm not looking to use you as bait. No one will come near you with Morelli by your side. She's smart and she's tough."

Thanks to Olga's experiences with Morelli, I knew exactly how tough and quick she was. "Good choice. But tell her not to come here." I gave him an address near the Brooklyn courthouse.

After taking a few moments to jot down the address, he asked, "What's there?"

I didn't know whether to laugh or cry. "That's my uncle, Morty. I can't believe I'm saying this, but I'm putting him on the case."

Jonah was angry. "First of all, you're not on the case. Second, I've met your uncle. I wouldn't put him on the case of a missing newspaper. Did last night teach you nothing?"

I spoke in a reassuring tone. "I'm kidding about putting him on the case. But I really am going to meet with him today, before I go to ballet class. I'm going to talk to him about getting a restraining order against Ron."

Jonah hesitated. "I'm not sure that will work. Maybe a temporary restraining order? Doubtful, but worth a try. Other than that, steer clear of Morty. You don't need his lowlife buddies hanging around."

I nodded, as if I agreed with him. "I have to get to ballet class."

He bent down, almost like he was going to kiss me but stopped himself. "I'll see you later. Wait for Morelli."

After he left I filled a dance bag with everything I'd need for a day at the lawyer, the ballet studio, and the theater. And the murder investigation.

Uncle Morty was not the most obvious choice for a partner in crime. Unlike my father, who earned degrees in philosophy from Brown and Harvard, Morty barely scraped through the Southern Texas School of Law. How he ever passed the bar, none of us has been able to figure out. Knowing Morty, though, it was not beyond the realm of possibility that after failing three times he paid someone to take it for him. Morty's specialty was landlord-tenant relations, where he dealt with people he cheerfully called "the scum of the earth."

I dialed his number. His voice sounded resigned. "I thought I'd hear from you. Have you been arrested again?"

I laughed. "Thanks for the vote of confidence, Uncle Morty, but so far, there's no all-points bulletin out for me. I do need your help, though. I want to take out a restraining order against the guy who tried to kill me. I also may need your help in committing a crime."

He coughed noisily into the phone. Humor is not his strong suit. "I don't commit crimes before lunch. Meet me at my office, and we'll talk over some pastrami sandwiches." After a slight pause, he said, in a burst of uncharacteristic generosity, "I'm buying."

I was touched. Pastrami sandwiches were expensive, and Uncle Morty was not a big spender. The last time we met for lunch, it was at a hot dog stand in front of his office.

"I have a better idea. I'll buy the sandwiches. Extra mustard, right?"

Sounding much cheered, he said, "You're on."

Chapter Thirty-Seven

If art is to nourish the roots of our culture, society must set the artist free...
—John F. Kennedy

Officer Morelli called. "I'm on my way to your apartment. Don't move until I get there."

I paused at the entrance to the subway. "I told Jonah I had to make a quick pit stop at my uncle's place. I'll call you when I'm back on the Upper West Side."

She wasn't pleased. "You shouldn't be going anywhere alone. You know that. I've got your address. I won't be long."

Now I was the one who wasn't happy. "I'm on my way to Brooklyn. I don't want to make you schlep all that way. I'll call you."

She was quick. "Don't you hang up on me. I'm in Brooklyn right now. Text me the address."

I sent her the address on Schermerhorn Street and hoped for the best as I crammed into the crowded subway car of the A train. It was a painful trip. The sudden jolts and screeching stops felt like an all-out assault on my joints and my nerves. I was panicked over Ron's success in avoiding arrest. My ability to dance also worried me. To outsiders, it probably sounded trivial to focus on dancing in the face of far more profound troubles. So be it. Once again, ABC would be performing in front of a sold-out crowd. Those ticket holders deserved the best I could give them, even if voyeuristic interest, and not artistic passion, motivated them to come. I also owed it to myself. I drank most of a bottle of water mixed with some orange juice and hoped it

226

would get me through the next ten hours.

At a deli halfway between Morty's office and the subway stop, I bought a pastrami sandwich and added a couple of sour pickles, as well as two Dr. Brown Cel-Ray sodas, one regular and one sugar-free.

Morty's office was dusty and dark. The wood furniture was upholstered in nubby brown fabric, the floor was covered in brown carpeting, and the walls, which twenty years ago might have been a cream color, had darkened with age. I wondered if the color scheme had been inspired by the owners of the firm, Brown & Brown. The two brothers who founded the company specialized in ambulance chasing. Morty handled real estate.

Mrs. Brown greeted me, with more excitement than was her wont. "I heard what happened at the ballet last night! Are you okay? They said on the radio you ballerinas are under a lotta pressure. It's no wonder people are getting killed." She searched my face for signs of incipient homicidal rage.

I didn't take offense and assured her, "We're no more violent than lawyers."

She seemed satisfied with that answer. "Well, you take care of yourself. You can go right in. Morty is waiting." As I passed, she sniffed loudly. "My, that smells good."

I promised to bring her a pastrami sandwich on my next visit. After my last performance of the season, I would treat myself, too. But not before.

Morty looked approvingly at the grease spots on the bag. "Love Dorfman's Deli. Great sandwiches. You know what makes a great pastrami sandwich?"

I was patient. "Uncle Morty, I'm not here to debate the quality of rye bread. I'm here to talk about the deaths at American Ballet Company."

He took a huge bite and talked around the food. "Shoot. I'll do whatever I can. And don't worry about paying me." He laughed unconvincingly. "Family discount. Plus, you're a repeat customer."

I gave him a quick overview of the more lurid events. Morty was thoughtful, though not in the way I hoped he'd be. After listening carefully, he homed in on the part he deemed most compelling. "This is high profile. You think the press will put my name in the papers?"

I didn't take offense. Morty is family, as my father liked to remind me, but that didn't make him any different from the other lawyers at Brown and Brown. I forced the conversation back to what was important to me, and he gave his expert legal opinion. Disappointingly, he didn't think I'd be successful in getting a restraining order, and as the minutes ticked by, I became increasingly anxious. Officer Morelli texted me from the street, and I told her to come up to the office.

"Thanks anyway, Uncle Morty. I'm more interested in nailing Ron than I am in getting a restraining order against him. It was worth a try."

He immediately became wary. "Don't do anything foolish, Leah. I won't be part of one of your harebrained schemes. I'm a lawyer, and I have a reputation to uphold."

I stood up. "I appreciate that, which is why I don't want to involve you directly. But I do need help of the non-legal variety. Get me one of your guys. Is Solly still kicking around?"

Morty grinned. "Solly? Yeah. He's still in the old neighborhood. His sons are now part of the family business, if you know what I mean."

I slung my bag over my shoulder. "Give me his number. If you talk to him first, tell him to get a few of his buddies together to meet me at the theater tonight. Tell him I'll make it worth his while."

My trip back to the city was considerably more comfortable than the ride on the A train had been. Morelli drove me in a patrol car, and I had the luxury of a chauffeured ride back to the city that didn't cost me a dime.

I settled in. "Do you want me to keep calling you Officer Morelli? What's your first name?"

She kept her eyes on the road. "Francie."

I closed my eyes. "And you grew up in Brooklyn? Were your parents fans of *A Tree Grows in Brooklyn*? That's still one of my favorite books."

Francie sighed. "Yeah. It's like I can never live it down."

I couldn't believe it. "You should be proud. Francie was my hero growing up. Who was yours?"

She smiled for the first time. "Harriet, from *Harriet the Spy*."

"I loved Harriet!"

Francie gave me a baleful look. "That's nice. But don't think I'm gonna let *you* be a spy. I'm here to protect you. From Ron and from yourself."

I gave her the address of Studio Dance and let myself fall into a deep, and thankfully dreamless, sleep.

I woke with a start. Summoning every ounce of willpower I possessed, I entered the dance studio and forced my throbbing limbs into a leotard, tights, and raggedy leg warmers. Officer Francie Morelli was none too happy to have to sit among the rapacious ballet mothers and chattering, catty girls, who found her height and uniform hilarious. She muttered, "I hated ballet. My mother forced me to go for two of the most miserable years of my life."

I was sympathetic. "My parents signed me up for basketball. And volleyball. It was humiliating."

She smiled. "Then you know how I feel."

Francie had given me the perfect opening. "There's no reason for you to have to hang out here. Get yourself a cup of coffee or something to eat. The class is only ninety minutes long, and I probably won't stay till the end."

She was torn. "I'm not supposed to let you out of my sight."

"I'm not out of your sight. The windows of the studio look out on the street. You can watch me from the café on the corner. Why don't you grab me a cup of coffee, too?"

To my great relief, she finally agreed to get coffee. I didn't want her around while I plotted with the Weird Sisters. I was afraid she, or Jonah, would stop me.

Thankfully, no one from the company was in the class. I greeted the teacher, whom I knew slightly from a brief guest appearance at the Houston Ballet. He pulled me aside, hoping for inside information on the violent events of the previous evening. I told him only the information that had already been released.

I had two goals. First, I had to work out the kinks in my muscles to prepare for the evening's performance. Second, and more importantly, I once again needed the help of the Weird Sisters. I knew they'd be there. They never missed a class.

Abigail was tearful. "We were so worried about you. But we couldn't get backstage. The guards wouldn't let us see you."

I patted her on the back. "Trust me. If you're up for a challenge, I'll make sure you get backstage tonight."

I was about to grant them their dearest wish.

Chapter Thirty-Eight

It has taken me years of struggle...to learn to make one simple gesture.
—Isadora Duncan

I needed one more person for my plan to work. With some reluctance, I texted Bobbie York: **Emergency-call me.**

She didn't text back, so I phoned her. While I waited for her to pick up the call, I was treated to a recording from *The Magic Flute* called "Hell's Vengeance Boils in My Heart." Even her ringtone was designed to intimidate.

Bobbie answered in character. "What the hell do you want? I'm busy."

I was brief. "Ron killed Pavel. I need your help to make sure he doesn't get away with it."

Her tone was cautious. "Are you sure about Ron? The police let him go."

If I could have reached through the ether to strangle her, I would have. "The police need more evidence. That's where you come in."

Bobbie's hoarse, two-pack-a-day growl deepened. "Not interested. I'm in charge of costumes. Not murder investigations. I'm not going to put myself in danger to help you."

I ignored her selfishness and didn't give in to anger. "There are two reasons you should act. The first one is simple: no one in that theater is safe with a killer on the loose. A killer who will be backstage."

Her tone was cool. "I presume the cops have that covered. Why should I risk myself? I direct the wardrobe department, not the police department."

I did a few deep pliés, using the calm movements to cool my temper. "The

231

second reason is if you don't help put Ron behind bars, I am fairly certain you will be the next target."

She nearly choked with anger. "You've got some nerve, threatening me! I'm filing a complaint against you, and then—"

I broke in. "I'm not threatening you. I'm warning you. The police have cops all over the place. They're protecting the dancers. Officer Morelli is with me right now. Who's watching out for you? Nobody. Nobody except me."

She muttered, "I still don't trust you."

I gripped the phone so hard my fingers hurt. "Tell me something I don't know. And then I'll tell you something you don't know. Ron Wieder has systematically gotten rid of every single person in a position of authority. That includes everyone who's had the courage to speak out against him. Pavel Baron is dead. Ms. Crandall was brutally attacked. Savannah was poisoned. And I nearly died last night, after he attacked me."

Unable to resist the pleasure of insulting me, she said, "If what you say is true, it makes no sense for him to attack you. You're not that important."

If I hadn't been desperate, I would have given up. "Put aside your personal feelings about me, and for once in your life, listen to reason."

Her simmering resentment didn't abate. "I will never forgive, or forget, your behavior toward Peter."

Explaining to Bobbie that her husband was as appealing to me as Uncle Morty would not have helped matters. "Let me be clear. Your tenure in the costume department will end after this season. You know it, and I know it. Now are you willing to help?"

She stammered a bit before responding. "Th-th-that's not true."

I spoke quickly. "Quit wasting my time. Not only do I know your days are numbered, I also know who your replacement is." While everything else I'd told Bobbie was true, this last statement was not. But the situation was dire. "Ron isn't the only one at Artistic Solution who thinks you're a dinosaur. You will be replaced by a younger, cheaper, and, if you'll forgive me, much better-looking woman. Someone who won't get into a rage every time someone walks into her office. A nonsmoker, of course."

Her voice was weak. "Jonathan is the acting director. He won't allow that to happen."

I laughed. "I hope you're not serious. Jonathan is acting director in name only. And that's all he wanted. His name on the program and the chance to make a heartfelt speech once a year. Ron's been in the background the whole time. He's calling the shots. If you had half a brain, you would have seen that coming from a mile away." I sharpened my tone. "Your call. I need you. And you need me. If you're serious about your own career, not to mention your own safety, you'll do as I say."

The double appeal, to her vanity and her self-interest, did the trick.

Her breath came fast. "Tell me what you want me to do."

She listened without interruption. "It will never work. It's a stupid plan."

"Will you do it, anyway?"

Bobbie, who knew she had nothing to lose, answered without hesitation. "Yes."

Once again, the theater was filled to capacity. We were accustomed to enthusiastic audiences, but that night, there was an extra buzz. The only role I had before the intermission was in the crowd-pleasing pas de deux from *Don Quixote*. Once again, I was paired with Tex. His brilliant, buoyant jumps and precise pirouettes had the crowd roaring their approval. Many in the audience knew the steps almost as well as we did, and they anticipated each bravura moment.

Despite my weariness before the curtain went up, I experienced that magical combination of weightlessness and strength that makes for memorable performances. I hopped on pointe, as easily and surely as if this were my only means of ambulation. Moments later, my left foot stayed nailed to the floor, as I used my right leg to whip around in multiple *fouetté* turns. It was one of the best performances of my life. I knew it, my fellow dancers knew it, and the audience certainly knew it. Dancers tend to milk the audience for extra curtain calls, but even after we left the stage, the shouting and stamping continued, and we had to return for two more unscripted bows. It was exciting, but not as thrilling as I hoped the end of the evening would be.

The second we exited the stagehands began setting up for Austin's ballet. They dragged the large, white plastic blobs onstage, cracking jokes about how they looked like interstellar poop. If any of them noticed the holes I'd poked into the plastic, no one said anything.

I pointed to one of the smaller blobs. "Mack, can you take a look at this? It seems to be broken. Austin will have a major meltdown if anything happens to these monstrosities."

Mack was not happy. The stagehands earn at least twice the salary of the highest-paid dancer, and they take their job seriously. He whistled to the other stagehands, and they joined him in examining a crack in the plastic surface, which I'd made backstage in the moments before the pas de deux. While the stagehands pulled the offending blob backstage to fix it, I texted Bobbie. She ushered a trio of black-clad women onto the stage and inside three of the remaining blobs.

Bobbie was grim. "Where did you dig them up? This is never going to work."

She wasn't the only one who was worried. Thanks to daily ballet classes, the Weird Sisters were fit and strong, but the next twenty-five minutes would tax the endurance of a trained athlete.

I ignored Bobbie and told the women, "Keep your phones on silent. Wait until I come get you. If you see anything amiss, text the number I gave you. It's a direct line to Detective Sobol."

None of them answered me. Panicked, I peered inside the blobs. They hadn't passed out or suffered a coronary occlusion. They were fine. The Weird Sisters were simply following the rules of the theater and, more particularly, the rules of ballet. They were already immersed in their roles.

Bobbie shook her head and left to oversee the costumes for *Desperate Measures*. The title had never before seemed so apt.

Chapter Thirty-Nine

If I can't dance, I don't want to be in your revolution.
—Emma Goldman

All three movements of *Desperate Measures* passed as if in a dream. Despite extreme anxiety, my body, as it always did, took over during the performance. The logical part of my brain stayed quiet and went along for the ride. I think the performance went well. Or as well as it could have gone. *Desperate Measures,* despite the dramatic title, was still a snooze of a ballet. I surreptitiously checked the wings, but if anything was amiss, it was hidden in the shadows.

I was anxious for the curtain to fall, but over and over again, we bowed, curtseyed, acknowledged each other, the pianist, and the conductor. Austin stepped onstage and extracted from the audience at least three more bows than was warranted. I was supposed to hand him a bouquet of flowers, but at my signal, Solly, Morty's friend, brought the ritual tribute to him. Austin was so excited he failed to notice that a squat, middle-aged man in a too-tight tuxedo was doing the honors, instead of a sylph-like ballerina.

When the curtain came down, Solly grabbed Austin. With a heavy Brooklyn accent, he said, "Hey, buddy, right dis way." Austin struggled, but Solly held him in a steely grip.

I didn't find out until later the exact form of persuasion Solly used, but Austin followed him with more docility, if less enthusiasm, than Mary's eponymous lamb. I waited in the shadows for the crowd onstage to leave, worried about the Weird Sisters.

Breathless and dehydrated, I was grateful for the water bottle one of the dancers handed me. I unscrewed the top of the bottle with sweaty hands.

I needn't have worried about my three ladies. In a perfectly choreographed move, the Weird Sisters ladies emerged, a bit stiffly, from the blobs where they'd been hiding. Shouting at the top of their lungs, they yelled, "Stop! Leah! Drop it!"

I stared open-mouthed as Abigail threw herself at me, knocking the water bottle out of my hand. Audrey and Izzy tried to grab the black-clad dancer who'd given me the water bottle, but with a swift and brutal gesture, he knocked them aside.

Jonah, Farrow, and three other police officers surged toward them. The ladies directed the police as effectively as their Shakespearean namesakes. "There's your man! The ABC Killer!"

They swarmed around the dancer. In the dim backstage light, dressed in a black costume and mask, Ron was indistinguishable from the group of male performers onstage. Hiding, as he had for months, in plain sight.

Ron looked around, as if bemused. "What's happening? Who are these women?"

Abigail crossed her arms and looked at him with triumphant satisfaction. "Your worst nightmare."

Even after Officer Diaz handcuffed him, Ron kept up the pretense of innocent bystander. He looked at Jonah. "Detective, I assure you, this is all some terrible misunderstanding. I don't know who these women are, but believe me, they do not belong here. They are trespassing. I suggest you take them in for questioning."

Audrey nodded her head so vigorously she looked like a bobblehead doll. "We saw him. In the wings. He put something in Leah's water bottle."

Izzy added, with a proud smile, "We had him pegged from the start."

Detective Farrow, unnerved by the odd trio, was understandably skeptical. The stagehands, Austin, and the male dancers were all dressed in black. The dancers had removed their masks for the bows. "How did you identify him?"

Ron brightened. "Yes! These old ladies are mistaken." With a sigh of pretend frustration, he said, "Once again, Austin Dworkin has fooled you."

Right on cue, Solly led Austin, red-faced and fuming, back onstage. Solly said to Ron, "Nice try, ya little piece of—" Solly broke off and tried again. "Uh, like I say, nice try, buddy boy, but I had the kid in hand the whole time." He poked Austin, who nearly toppled over. "Tell him, sonny."

Austin shouted, "Arrest this man. He threatened me! Said he'd break my knees if I opened my mouth."

Solly looked hurt. "It was for your own good. Listen, kiddo, ya gotta calm down. It ain't healthy to be so nervous." Solly shook his head and addressed the cops. "He's a very emotional guy. Reminds me of my ex-wife. Always with the drama. But aside from that, the kid's clean. He didn't do nothing." He pointed at Ron. "It was that guy that was sneaking around."

Abigail looked admiringly at Solly. "This gentleman is telling the truth. Austin is innocent, and Ron is lying. With or without a mask, we knew right away he wasn't one of the dancers. You can't fool us. Did you see his legs and feet?" With a pitying look, she added, "Zero turnout." She posed in second position, her feet at a hundred and eighty-degree angle. "I always had good turnout. Just lucky, I guess."

Solly was impressed. "That's amazing. How long did it take for you to learn to do that?"

It was an interesting question, given Abigail's age. She looked quite happy, and with her flushed cheeks and defiant attitude, very pretty.

I wanted to hug her, but I was frozen in place, protecting the tiny puddle of water. There was very little left in the bottle, and I worried there wouldn't be enough for the police to analyze. With the tips of two fingers, I retrieved the bottle, hoping I hadn't obliterated any usable fingerprints. With gloved hands, one of the police officers took the bottle and screwed the cap on. He smiled at me. "Don't worry, Ms. Siderova. We should have enough here to analyze and to put that Ron Wieder in jail for a good, long while."

Tex, who had been waiting anxiously on the sidelines, was close enough to catch me when my legs gave out. I leaned on him. "I—I need to sit down for a minute."

One of the stagehands obligingly brought a folding chair, and Tex placed me gently on it. His eyes were dark with concern. "I can take you to your dressing room. Or someplace more comfortable."

Jonah interrupted. "Thanks, but I'll take it from here."

In an undertone, he said, "I can't leave you alone for a minute. Is this what life is going to be like with you? One crisis—not to mention one man—after another?"

Abigail, who made no attempt to camouflage her interest, said, "You better keep an eye on her."

I twisted away from them, ashamed of the tears that refused to stay at bay. "If Detective Sobol falls down on the job, I know I'll have you ladies to watch out for me."

Audrey agreed. "We'll always have your back."

Izzy added, "If you guys are done with your love fest, does anyone want to talk about the fact that after all these years, we were onstage at Lincoln Center?"

Abigail was complacent. "And the stars of the show."

Chapter Forty

Art is not what you see, but what you make others see.
—Edgar Degas

Ron's murderous rampage as the ABC Killer made headlines for a mere five days. It might not have lasted even that long had there not been a spate of accidents concerning roof jumping, or as the YouTube stars call it, free jumping. This was how Ron evaded police surveillance on the night when, for at least the second time, he tried to kill me. With plainclothes officers guarding the front door and back entrance of his apartment building, Ron escaped by leaping from his rooftop to the neighboring one. It wasn't much of a leap. The rooftops on his block were separated by no more than a foot. It was more like roof stepping.

A few days after Ron's arrest, I met my parents at a local diner. I instructed them not to bring their partners and was relieved neither of them argued the point. It was a Monday, which meant the theater was dark, and I had a full twenty-four hours to rest.

Dad had an egg white omelet. After his heart attack, he adopted a healthier diet and began exercising. I suspected his physical trauma was part of the reason he'd married Ann, the queen of health, wellness, and studied calm.

Barbara and I ordered coffee with a side of water. I wasn't hungry, because I'd finished off the leftovers from Madame's breakfast before we met. If Barbara knew the number of calories I'd already consumed, she would have ordered a martini on the side.

She helped herself to a corner of Dad's rye toast. "Leah, I am starved for information. Did you ever find out the reason behind that mysterious trail of powder?"

I clenched my hands to keep them from shaking. "It was ordinary foot powder, mixed with a bit of scented oil. Ron left anonymous gifts for several dancers, including me. Even a few grains of it made the floor extremely slippery, which explained why so many dancers wiped out in the weeks before Pavel died."

Dad put down his fork. "What was the point? What did Ron have to gain by doing that?"

I wanted to get up and stretch, but we were in a booth. "The police don't think he had any specific targets in mind. It was a diversionary tactic. A distraction. And it worked. I was sure that Mavis was powder-bombing the competition. I'll have to apologize to her."

Barbara put down her morsel of bread. "In a twisted way, I guess that makes sense. If he could create a sense of mystery around those bottles of powder, and the trails they left around the studio, that misdirection would complicate the investigation."

I slipped off my shoes and flexed my aching feet. While the rest of my body was still skinny, my bunions had grown considerably larger. "I think there was more to it than that. From the start, it was clear to me that Ron enjoyed hurting people, emotionally and physically. He was like a kid pulling wings off a butterfly."

Over Barbara's protest, Dad signaled to the waitress to bring more toast. "The papers said he's pleading insanity. Tough to do, but that might be his only option."

I smiled. "That's yesterday's news. In between then and now, Olga hacked Ron's account, copied everything she found, and sent it to the police. Anonymously, of course. Turns out, Pavel wasn't simply going to fire Ron. He was going to press charges over financial misconduct. Ron left his previous job under a similar cloud. He was desperate."

Dad looked stern. "Olga's behavior sounds highly unethical. What kind of person is she?"

I hoped my father would overcome his disapproval. "Olga is what they call a spear phisher. But don't worry. She only works for good guys. Most of the time. You'll meet her later. And when you do, I think you'll love her."

Barbara rapped him on the knuckles. "Don't be such a stiff, Jeremy. She didn't give the police anything they wouldn't have gotten without her. But now, Ron won't get bail. Olga did us all a great service."

My parents were understandably focused on the murder, but I had other items on my agenda. "It's time to come clean about Philip. Spill. Both of you."

Barbara rested her cheek in one hand, as if deep in thought. "Let's see. If you must know, soon after Philip and I started seeing each other, I lost interest in him. He was not, as you so often told me, my type. But he was a reputation defender, and you needed help. He did a pretty good job of squelching Savannah." In response to my bewildered look, she said, "He helps people, and companies fix their online reputation. It's really quite interesting. For instance, when you overheard him say he would take care of things for Jonathan, he was simply offering his services. Jonathan wanted the prestige of being named the director of American Ballet Company but had a most unsavory reputation. Philip was in a position to help him."

This still sounded dodgy to me. "His so-called services sounded more like blackmail, or a shakedown, than a legit consulting company. And I distinctly heard him tell Savannah she could keep harassing me Was that part of his business plan? To create a need for his services?"

Barbara turned down the corners of her mouth. "I'm not saying he's a candidate for sainthood, though he did have his uses. In spite of what he told Savannah, she didn't follow through, did she?"

Her explanation did little to allay my concern over their relationship. "In my book, if he threatened exposure in exchange for services, that's still blackmail." I turned to my father, who was quite uncomfortable with the turn the conversation had taken. "What is Philip's connection with Ann? Did he 'fix' things for her as well?"

He sighed. "Yes. As I think you know, things were not going well with her private practice. There were some very bad, very unfair reviews, as well as a malpractice suit. She was really struggling. She contacted Philip.

He helped her mend her online profile, and he introduced her to Darius Kemble. American Ballet Company had just signed a contract with Artistic Solutions, and Philip helped get her on board. I thought, at first, it was a bizarre coincidence that your mother was dating the same person who had helped Ann get her job, but now I'm not so sure. I think he was very deliberate in which women he pursued."

Barbara, annoyed at Dad's implication that it was her money and not her charm that interested Philip, tossed a piece of rye toast at him.

I couldn't resist. "What would Kant have to say about Ann's lack of transparency? Or yours?"

He put down his fork. "Kant would most certainly not approve, which you already know, or you wouldn't have asked." He heaved another, deeper, sigh. "Ann and I are taking a little break from each other. She's got a six-month gig in LA, with a ballet company there."

Despite two cups of coffee, and a conversation full of surprises, I was bone tired. Dad put his hand on mine. "No more coffee. You go home and rest. We can talk again later." He hugged me. "I love you."

Tears sprang to my eyes. With some disgust, I said, "I'm turning into a weepy female. I've cried more in the last few days than I have in my entire life."

Dad smiled. "You don't have to be strong in front of us."

He returned to the university, and Barbara walked me home.

I was still unhappy that Barbara hadn't confided in me. "Why didn't you tell me earlier about Philip?"

She paused to light a cigarette. "Why didn't you tell me earlier about your plans to catch Ron?"

I stopped short. "Those two things are not at all alike. I was trying to keep you safe from a killer."

Barbara wrinkled her nose. "And I was trying to keep you safe from Savannah. You're always so dramatic. I guess that's what happens after a life spent onstage."

The sun was warm, and people up and down the block were sitting out on their stoops, enjoying the mild weather. Barbara, after a brief argument, sat down with me, after putting a section of newspaper under her.

She cautiously lowered herself onto the step. "You're wearing cheap blue jeans. The pants I'm wearing cost two hundred fifty dollars." She hastened to add, "They were marked down to fifty dollars. But they're worth five times that much."

I admired her stylish pants and her willingness to sacrifice them for me. Barbara took out the latest edition of *The New York Review of Books* and turned to the Personals column. "There are so many interesting men this week! What do you think about this one: *Widowed Romeo seeks his Juliet, 55-65, for long walks in the park, jazz at Lincoln Center, and maybe more.*"

I was not nearly as charmed. "I know hope springs eternal in the human breast, but Romeo and Juliet both died."

Barbara smoothed my forehead. "You worry too much. You're going to get wrinkles."

I was philosophical. "Sooner or later, it happens to the best of us."

She got up and tossed her ground out cigarette butt into a garbage can. "I've got to get going. I'm working on a new book, *The Macbeth Murders*. Professor Romanova is going to travel to Scotland to solve the mysterious deaths of three academics. It's going to be a hoot. Lots of Shakespearean references. It was your aging ballerinas that made me think of it."

I kissed her goodbye. "Sounds hilarious. I'm sure all your English teacher fans will be thrilled, but don't tell Abigail, Audrey, or Izzy I refer to them as the Weird Sisters."

"I promise, although I'd love to tell them how much they inspired me. I got a whole new lease on life once I switched from Chaucer to Shakespeare." She shaded her eyes and peered down the street. "Are you expecting anyone?"

I stayed seated. "Yes."

She smiled knowingly. "In that case, I'll say a quick hello and goodbye." She stood up and handed me her newspaper. "This is for you. There's a great article in the local news about the Weird Sisters and a rave review of you in the Arts section. I have seven more copies at home."

Jonah greeted Barbara. She surprised all three of us by embracing him.

"It's good to see you again. I can't thank you enough for all you did."

He regarded her somberly. "Thank you, Ms. Siderova. I appreciate that. Leah was very brave."

Barbara was complacent. "Yes. She takes after me." She brushed invisible specks of dirt from her expensive pants. "I suppose you two have a lot to talk about. Will I be seeing you at Madame's party tonight?"

He looked at me. "I'm not sure."

Barbara left, and he took her place on the stoop. I showed him the article on Abigail, Audrey, and Izzy. "My Weird Sisters are heroes."

He seemed tense. Angry. "You put the lives of three civilians in danger. Three elderly ladies. Did it ever cross your mind we could have had trained police officers do the job?"

"You did have trained police officers there. We couldn't have done it without you. Trust me, I wouldn't have risked placing the ladies onstage if your people weren't stationed in the wings to protect us. But Austin's ballet had constant entrances and exits. No way they could get within ten feet of the stage without getting run over by at least a dozen dancers. If it were possible, I would have been happy to have had police officers inside those awful blobs. But how many of them would have been able to fit? With all due respect to the NYPD, I needed people who were tiny, flexible, and knew ballet. The second my ladies saw Ron they knew he wasn't a dancer."

His lips twitched. "Yeah. I heard all about it. No turnout." His expression darkened. "You should have told me what you were planning. You trusted three old ladies to guard you and that two-bit Brooklyn mobster Solly Greenfield to guard Austin. But you didn't trust me."

I clasped my hands together to keep them from trembling. "When we—when you were in my apartment. In my bed. You left. Pushed me away. Why?"

He turned to look at me. "You know why."

"Yes, I do. And it's the same reason I didn't confide in you. I didn't want to ask you to do anything that might conflict with your job. What would Detective Farrow have said, if you told him you had tapped the Weird Sisters and a mobster to help with the murder investigation?"

He didn't answer.

I contemplated his dark brown eyes and grave expression. "Don't look so stricken."

He said, in a tight voice, "Don't you understand? I was crazed with worry about you."

I edged closer. "Get used to it."

Acknowledgements

I want to thank my editor, Shawn Reilly Simmons, for her patience, time, and talent, as well as those other wonderful Dames of Detection, Verena Rose and Harriette Sackler.

I am indebted to my kids. And there are a lot of them. Luke, whose sharp and witty edits made this a better book than it would have been without him, and daughter-in-law Emily, who generously shared her medical expertise regarding knife wounds and head injuries. Jacob, who applied his logic and his ironic sense of humor to the more improbable clues I came up with. Geoffrey, for always believing in me, a sentiment he never failed to repeat during countless late-night phone conversations. Gregory, for his artistic sensibility and pragmatic point of view. Jesse, for the long hours he worked on my website, and daughter-in-law Kris for her patience. Becky, who for many years was the only other female in the house, and whose support is as dependable as it is unstinting. And I'm endlessly inspired by the newest generation: Sophie, Viola, and Ava. Like me, they love a good story.

I owe a lot to my sisters, who are many and various. First, in every way, is the sister I was lucky enough to grow up with, Karyn Boyar. Next are my sisters-in-law: Lisa, Barbara, Jane, Gail, and Lolly. Last, but not least, I want to thank my talented Sisters in Crime.

To my brother Richard: I wish you were here to see the publication of this book.

Much gratitude is due to the many people who provided their expert advice. Chief among these: My critique partner, Corey LaBranche, editor Lourdes Venard, and agent Dawn Dowdle. And to Claudia Guimaraes Cutler and the many dancer friends who have supported me, your kindness, patience, and talent knows no bounds. Thank you, from the bottom of my heart.

To Vladimir (The Duke) Dokoudovsky (1919-1998) His brilliance still shines for generations of dancers who were lucky enough to earn a place at his barre.

This book is dedicated to Glenn, who still thinks—after all these years—that he's the one who got lucky.

About the Author

Brooklyn-born Lori Robbins began dancing at age 16 and launched her professional career three years later. She studied modern dance at the Martha Graham School and ballet at the New York Conservatory of Dance. Robbins performed with a number of modern and ballet companies, including Ballet Hispanico, the Des Moines Ballet, and the St. Louis Concert Ballet. After ten very lean years as a dancer she attended Hunter College, graduating summa cum laude with a major in British Literature and a minor in Classics. Her first On Pointe Mystery, *Murder in First Position*, won first place in the Indie Book Awards for Best Mystery, was a finalist for a Silver Falchion, and is on the short list for a Mystery and Mayhem Book Award. Her debut novel, *Lesson Plan for Murder*, won the Silver Falchion Award and was a finalist in the Readers' Choice and Indie Book Awards. It will be re-released by Level Best Books in June, 2022. Short stories include "Accidents Happen" in the anthology *Murder Most Diabolical* and "Leading Ladies" in *Justice for All*. She is an expert in the homicidal impulses everyday life inspires.

https://linktr.ee/lorirobbinsmysteries

https://www.lorirobbins.com

https://www.instagram.com/lorirobbinsmysteries/

https://twitter.com/lorirobbins99

https://www.facebook.com/LoriRobbinsMysteries/?fref=ts

https://www.pinterest.com/lorirobbinsmysteries/_created/